# Canvas of Lies

RACHEL FITZJAMES

Copyright © 2025 by Rachel Fitzjames

All rights reserved.

No part of this publication may be reproduced, distributed, or transmitted in any form or by any means, including photocopying, recording, or other electronic or mechanical methods, without the prior written permission of the publisher, except as permitted by U.S. copyright law. For permission requests, contact the author.

ISBN: 978-1-967700-05-9 (Paperback)
ISBN: 978-1-967700-04-2 (Ebook)

Library of Congress Control Number: 2025914482

The story, all names, characters, and incidents portrayed in this production are fictitious. No identification with actual persons (living or deceased), places, buildings, and products is intended or should be inferred.

Book Cover by Maldo Designs

Editing by Melissa Rotert – Wordplay Copy & Line Edits

# A note to readers

Each book in the Spruce Hill series features on-page, open-door steamy scenes, along with swearing and some degree of suspense. There may be a limited amount of on-page physical violence as well as the threat of peril facing one or more characters. Specific content in this story that might be of concern to readers includes marital infidelity (not the main characters), death of a parent, and an on-page car accident. As a general reassurance, no animals or children are ever harmed in my books.

For more details, please visit my website at or use the QR code below.

*To those who believe
in the power of
friendship.*

# Contents

| | | |
|---|---|---|
| | Prologue | 1 |
| 1. | Chapter One | 9 |
| 2. | Chapter Two | 19 |
| 3. | Chapter Three | 35 |
| 4. | Chapter Four | 48 |
| 5. | Chapter Five | 56 |
| 6. | Chapter Six | 69 |
| 7. | Chapter Seven | 78 |
| 8. | Chapter Eight | 89 |
| 9. | Chapter Nine | 98 |
| 10. | Chapter Ten | 110 |
| 11. | Chapter Eleven | 121 |

| | | |
|---|---|---|
| 12. | Chapter Twelve | 133 |
| 13. | Chapter Thirteen | 141 |
| 14. | Chapter Fourteen | 148 |
| 15. | Chapter Fifteen | 158 |
| 16. | Chapter Sixteen | 172 |
| 17. | Chapter Seventeen | 180 |
| 18. | Chapter Eighteen | 187 |
| 19. | Chapter Nineteen | 199 |
| 20. | Chapter Twenty | 211 |
| 21. | Chapter Twenty-One | 218 |
| 22. | Chapter Twenty-Two | 226 |
| 23. | Chapter Twenty-Three | 237 |
| 24. | Chapter Twenty-Four | 247 |
| 25. | Chapter Twenty-Five | 255 |
| 26. | Chapter Twenty-Six | 264 |
| 27. | Chapter Twenty-Seven | 270 |
| 28. | Chapter Twenty-Eight | 279 |
| 29. | Chapter Twenty-Nine | 290 |
| 30. | Chapter Thirty | 299 |
| 31. | Chapter Thirty-One | 307 |
| 32. | Chapter Thirty-Two | 311 |
| 33. | Chapter Thirty-Three | 317 |

| | | |
|---|---|---|
| 34. | Chapter Thirty-Four | 326 |
| 35. | Chapter Thirty-Five | 335 |
| Epilogue | | 347 |
| Also by | | 354 |
| Acknowledgements | | 355 |
| About the author | | 357 |

# Prologue

## KAT: THEN

I KNEW, AS EARNESTLY as any ten year old girl could, that I was destined to fall in love with Nicolas Beaumont.

At thirteen and more than a head taller than me, he was already handsome in his long-limbed, adolescent way, with curling black hair and soulful brown eyes. Nico's father, Pierre Beaumont, was a famous French chef who'd come to Spruce Hill, New York, to work for my family when I was still in diapers. Nico and I became fast friends not long after.

Though I kept my infatuation with Nico firmly under wraps, knowing he'd either tease me for it or look at me with that pitying smile I'd seen on some of his friends, I could never resist a chance to be around him.

Nico avoided the main house whenever possible, but to me, the Beaumont cottage was practically my second home. We spent our free time together, whether we were exploring the woods at the back of the property, inventing games to play, or sitting quietly in a hidden section of the house—Nico with a book, me with my tools and whatever electronics I'd decided to take apart and put back together.

On the night that changed everything, not long after my tenth birthday, my parents threw a party for a bunch of their rich friends, the kind of party children were never welcome at.

I knew that my father was a hotshot lawyer with rich, powerful clients, and my mother had told me very sternly that the children were to stay away from the party. Some of the guests had deposited their own kids in the playroom where a handful of nannies were chatting about celebrity gossip, but the oldest of us had snuck out an hour earlier to entertain ourselves.

The other kids wanted to play pirates, but I refused. I was forever forced to be the princess captured for a hefty ransom, never a pirate myself. Nico assured me it was because they were afraid of my swashbuckling skills and convinced them hide and seek would be more fun anyway.

It was my fault we'd ventured into the most dangerous territory in the house. Nico wanted to hide in the library, but I'd grabbed hold of his hand and bolted down the hall. It wasn't the first time we held hands, but creeping through the dark and breaking all the rules gave the brief trek an air of danger that made everything feel sharper, more important somehow.

He and I were curled up into tight little balls under the massive desk in my father's office, our legs pressed together from knee to shin.

"Do you think they'll find us, Nico?" I whispered.

He gave me a stern look and held a finger over his lips. "If you keep talking, they will. Hush, Kitten."

We were *never* allowed in my father's office. In reality, we weren't even allowed in this part of the house. Though no one had come right out and said it, not yet anyway, I was almost certain that my father didn't want Nico anywhere near me. Even if Nico had wanted to obey that unspoken directive, I made it impossible, because I couldn't imagine life without him. I followed him everywhere, dogged his every step, inserted myself into every game and adventure that he and his friends arranged.

In the end, he had to either take me under his wing and keep me safe or leave me to storm off and get myself into even worse trouble on my own. I was plenty capable of that, and he knew that perfectly well.

No one got into trouble quite like I did, and somehow, Nico always ended up getting busted right along with me.

Only another minute or two passed before we heard footsteps from the hall outside, then a hushed giggle that had Nico's eyes gleaming at me in the dark. The party tonight was way on the other side of the house—it was the only reason the two of us had dared to sneak into this wing during our game. If we were caught by a grownup instead of the seeker, we were in for a world of trouble.

When the office door opened and light spilled across the room, Nico clasped my hand and squeezed, shaking his head to remind me to stay silent. We couldn't see anything but the wall of windows behind my father's desk chair. The glass reflected a flash of light from the hallway before darkening again when the door closed.

For a second, the room was silent and I prayed that whoever had opened the door had simply turned around and left.

"Are you sure no one will come this way?" asked a breathless woman.

"No one would dare," the man answered smoothly, then the woman giggled again.

Though I didn't recognize her voice, the one who responded was clearly my father. I jerked in surprise and Nico squeezed my hand again.

"At least we don't have to worry about my husband. What exactly did you do to him?"

My father's voice was a low growl when he responded, "Nothing you need to know about."

"You are *so* bad."

I frowned at Nico in the dark, wondering why she said it like it was a good thing, but he just shook his head at me. His expression shifted as I tried to identify the sounds coming from the other side of the desk—like sloppy, wet kisses, interrupted by an occasional grunt.

When the giggles turned to moans and the whispered words grew increasingly explicit, Nico clapped his hands over my ears.

It wasn't enough to muffle the sounds completely, though, and he dropped his forehead against mine, squeezing his eyes shut until I did the same.

Suddenly, loud voices echoed in the hall outside the office and the door flew open, sending another flare of light across the room.

"And this, ladies and gentlemen, is where the magic happens," my mother announced.

Everything went silent, then someone smothered a laugh and said, "Apparently so."

My mom's shrieks pierced the air. There was no way *not* to hear her, even through Nico's palms. Though I wished he'd kept them pressed over my ears for protection from it, my mouth dropped open and he let go to cover it before I could make a sound that might draw attention to us.

The adults were all talking at once: screaming outrage from my mother, deep-voiced protests from my father, the fascinated chatter of the audience just outside the door.

It felt like hours, huddled there together under the desk, but eventually the sounds faded and the intruders left amidst a good deal of shouting about alimony and prenups. We waited until the footsteps faded, then waited some more, just to be sure, before Nico took my hand to draw me out after him.

We shook out our legs, weak and quivering from holding still for so long, slipped carefully out of the office, and sprinted for the stairs at the far end of the hallway.

Over the years that followed, I tried hard to forget about that night. My mother, thanks to her own high-priced lawyer, walked away with enough money to move to St. Croix—with said lawyer in tow—and left full custody of me to my father, which boiled down to being left mostly to my own devices. It didn't matter that she'd had affair after affair throughout my childhood, only that he got caught doing the same.

Publicly. *Very* publicly.

Since their prenup was ironclad, he didn't bother to fight her on anything, not even to push her to keep me in her life. On one of the rare occasions he actually answered instead of brushing me off when I asked why, he uttered the only words of wisdom he ever gave me.

*"You can't fight fair with someone who has no sense of fairness."*

It seemed rich, coming from a man who fought with strangers for a living, but it never quite left my memory bank.

My friendship with Nico seemed as altered by that one segment of time as my relationship with my father, though in the opposite way. I could barely look my dad in the eye after that night, not that he ever seemed to notice. My continued existence was a mild annoyance to him, at best, a serious inconvenience at worst.

It stung, realizing how disposable I really was to both my parents, but Nico was there to cushion the blow.

We were bound together even tighter afterward, well beyond the friendship that had existed between us beforehand, beyond even my childish crush. Something akin to adulation filled me when I thought about how he'd cupped his hands over my ears, rested his face against mine, and held my hand for the rest of the night. Even after one of the other boys made a kissy face at us and teased Nico about it, he didn't let go.

That hopeless devotion lasted right up until the day Nico left for college, bidding me farewell with a jaunty grin and a quick, "See you later, Kitten," that forced me to accept he'd probably only ever viewed me as a friend, or maybe—even worse—as a tag-along little sister.

I swallowed my humiliation and tried my best to move on.

Life without Nico around lost a bit of its shine, but high school swooped in to fill the gaps left by his departure. I did see him a few times over those years, usually from a distance, but gradually the infatuation faded, even if the old affection lingered.

Once, when I'd hacked my long, honey-blonde hair into a short pixie cut and gone running down the front walk to hop onto my boyfriend Zeke's motorcycle, I caught a glimpse of Nico standing around the side of the house with his dad, staring after me with a forbidding expression that rivaled my father's.

*Read it and weep,* I thought, pulling a helmet over my cropped curls.

As we pulled away from the house, a sharp twinge of regret stabbed through my chest, but I forced it down—forced myself to ignore the hurt that built up during those years.

If I'd known what was to come, I wondered if I might've turned back, let Zeke ride away without me, and taken the time to run to Nico as I always had when I was younger instead of fleeing from him.

Hindsight was, in fact, a bitch.

# Chapter One

## Kat

"Earth to Willoughby, come in, Katherine Willoughby."

I jerked to attention, blinking stupidly at my assistant, Erin, who'd voiced a question I hadn't heard and now arched a perfectly shaped brow at me.

"Sorry, what did you say?"

Erin rolled her pretty green eyes toward the ceiling as though searching for strength to deal with her daydreaming boss and said, "That history professor you went out with last week. Are you going to see him again? He was cute, in a geeky sort of way."

"The professor's name is Alan, and I don't know if I'll see him again," I said, rubbing my temples with both hands. "How do you know he's cute?"

"I might've stalked his social media for you. He seems like the type to have studied the female orgasm extensively. I can tell these things, you know. It's a gift."

"Right, how could I forget about your amazing gift?"

Erin's off-color commentary didn't faze me at this point, though I wasn't in agreement about Alan's study habits—I wasn't even convinced he knew what a female orgasm was. Our non-relationship hadn't yet progressed to that point, but there didn't seem to be much chemistry between us.

"Look, I'm just about done here, if you want to head out to ship those packages. Thanks for your help today."

"Anything for you, boss," Erin chirped. "And text that poor guy back! You need some fun in your life, Kat. It'd be good for you to go out, have a drink, maybe get laid once in a while. Let him dazzle you with his nerdy charm. You might be pleasantly surprised, you know."

I snorted and waved her away. As Erin left the office, silence descended, cloaking me in peaceful solitude. I leaned back in my chair and closed my eyes, ignoring the internal organs of the Teddy Ruxpin that lay spread across my desk.

Breathing new life into old things was my drug of choice. I couldn't recall a time when I *didn't* take things apart just to put them back together again. Inspecting their inner workings, surrounded by gears and gadgets, I could drift into my own little world, like entering a daydream, while I returned an object to its former glory.

If only my life outside of work were so easy to fix.

Business was booming at Kat's Keepers, the vintage toy resale shop I'd started when I was still in college. With Erin to assist in managing inventory and scouting for items, we made enough to maintain a small warehouse at the edge of Spruce Hill, New York, where rent was cheap. The only other business nearby was a car garage called Saucy Wrench, owned and operated by a handful of female mechanics. I'd only been there a couple times for oil changes, but I felt like we were kindred spirits inhabiting this side of town.

The property wasn't smack dab in the middle of Main Street where all the shops were located, but casual foot traffic wasn't really my market. We fixed up antiques and collectibles, things that most people didn't see the value of aside from a hit of nostalgia.

Running my little business was about as far from my father's glamorous lifestyle as I could get. I still recalled with perfect clarity the look of utter disdain on his face the time I'd asked him to stop at a yard sale when I was six years old. Though I doubted there'd been anything worthwhile to find—or that my childhood self would have recognized it back then—the spread of old toys and dolls across that wide driveway had looked like heaven to my young imagination.

So many things I could've fixed, even if only to give them a destination that wasn't the trash.

I couldn't deny that I now found a great deal of satisfaction in making a good living in a way that disgusted my father. It was a win-win situation all around. And now that I had Erin to help out, everything was easier.

After I reassembled Teddy, I placed him back on the shelf and finished loading up a box of unsold toys to drop off for donation the next day.

Some of my resale items went for a decent amount of money, but anything that didn't sell, no matter how long I'd spent fixing it up, I donated to a local charity called Path of Hope that helped refugee families establish homes in the area. I'd started volunteering with the organization in college and stayed involved through every stage of building Kat's Keepers from the ground up.

No matter how long it'd been since we moved into the warehouse, there was something eerie about being on my own after Erin left. The two of us were practically complete opposites, but we worked well together. I hadn't realized how lonely I was before she joined me, and I often didn't notice just how lively she made things until she was gone.

Still, in the silence, Erin's advice haunted me. *Have fun, get laid.*

I scoffed. The business had simply taken up most of my free time as I got it off the ground, that was all. I had plenty of fun, but I didn't want to waste time on a meaningless fling that was more likely to hurt a sweet guy like Alan than to give me any kind of fulfillment before I ended things.

"I have plenty of fun," I mumbled aloud.

When the obnoxious cuckoo clock on the wall chimed the hour, I drew on the butter-soft leather jacket I'd picked up at a thrift store the previous month, shut down my computer, and made my way to the back door of the warehouse. In the dark winter months, Erin and I took care to leave together—it wasn't a bad area of town, if Spruce Hill even had such a thing, but the deserted parking lot behind the warehouse could be unsettling in the dark and I felt responsible for Erin's safety.

We even took a self-defense class together one summer, and while we'd spent more time laughing than trying to take one another down, I always figured the two of us could tag-team an assailant in the event we needed to actually defend ourselves.

In September, though, the sun didn't set until after seven, so I had no qualms about sending her home when I lingered until the clock struck five. I hummed a jingle from some old gum commercial while I locked up and activated the alarm system. As I rifled through my purse, looking for my trusty lip gloss, an engine growled and I spun toward the sound.

A white van was parked at the side of the building, blocking the driveway into the parking lot—the kind of van with no windows in the back.

The kind I always imagined a kidnapper would drive.

For a second, I froze, then a familiar grin flashed at me through the passenger's side window before the door opened and a blast from my childhood hit me like a cannonball to the stomach.

"No freaking way," I breathed. "What the hell are you doing here, Nico?"

Memories galloped through my head, both good and bad. Sweet moments shared with my first and best friend melted into the hurt of him turning away, keeping his distance from me, leaving me alone *again*, and bitterness crept in.

Nico closed the door of the van and leaned back against it, crossing one foot over the opposite ankle like he had all the time in the world to stand there staring at me. Fuck, he looked good. He'd grown into those long limbs and his hair was as unruly as ever, falling nearly into the dark eyes that surveyed me from head to toe in a warm, leisurely way that threw my pulse into overdrive.

I scowled at him. "Nice van. Did you go into kidnapping after college? Become a pirate, after all?"

God, that smile. It'd been ten years since I last saw him and it still had the same power to hurl me right back to the height of my adolescent crush.

"No, Kitten," he said quietly, "but we need to talk."

Anger bubbled up into my throat. Back in high school, I would've given my right arm for Nico to talk to me. His unexpected appearance tonight filled me with a riotous mixture of fury and hope.

It made me want to scream.

"We *need* to, do we? At twilight, behind my business, while your creeper van is blocking the driveway? Who's driving, anyway?"

He pushed away from the van in question, grinning as he strolled over to me. "That's Gumby. He's a friend. Would you believe me if I told you that was all coincidence?"

"No."

At my sharp response, Nico laughed. "I'm not here to kidnap you, just to talk."

Why that annoyed me so much, I didn't know, but it was enough that I poked an angry finger into his chest. He barely flinched, while I was left wondering when the hell he'd developed muscles hard enough to jam my finger on.

"What do we have to talk about that couldn't have been said in a phone call, Nico? My number can't be that hard to find."

"Kitten," he murmured, the old nickname so soft and so sweet that my temper built in direct opposition to his intent. He wrapped his long fingers around mine, holding my hand to his ridiculous pecs. "Please. I promise it'll only take a few minutes and if you still want me to leave after that, I'll go."

My temper often got the best of me—I was too impulsive, too quick to react. I knew that about myself and had worked hard to control those urges, but staring at my childhood crush, at the man he'd become, I lost it.

Nico's eyes flared when I jammed our joined hands into his chest, using them to push him back an inch or two before his fingers tightened.

"You waltz back into my life after ten years, chauffeured in a creepy van, for a conversation that will only take a few minutes? What the hell are you up to, Nicolas Beaumont?"

He cocked his head and shifted toward me, using his grip on my hand to keep me close against his chest. So close I could barely catch my breath as his warm, soothing scent—tones of vanilla and bergamot—surrounded me.

"I need your help, Kat."

*Too many years.* I spent too many years wishing things were different between us, waiting for him to come back to me, wondering where my friend and protector had gone.

With a sound of frustrated rage, I shoved against his shoulder, hoping to free myself from his grasp.

Unfortunately, the curb was just behind him when he stumbled backward. Not even Nico's usual grace could stop him from tripping over it. As we went down, his body curved protectively around mine, but our momentum swung us both into the wooden pallets stacked beside the dumpster. The sound of splintering wood accompanied a flash of sharp pain as my shoulder and the side of my head collided with the wall of the building.

Dimly, I heard Nico calling my name. I blinked at him, wondering why my arm stung so badly, but when my eyes finally focused on his face, Nico's visible relief distracted me from the pain.

"Jesus, Kat," he muttered, brushing a loose strand of hair from my face. "Are you okay? Did you hit your head?"

"I'm fine." The words were harsh, but his gentle concern grated on me.

I forced my gaze away from him to see my purse had spilled and my phone shattered into pieces on the asphalt beside us, shards of glass glittering in the setting sunlight. Nico's friend—the chauffeur or accomplice, whatever he was—opened his door and froze halfway out of the van, like he couldn't decide if he should interfere.

"You broke my phone," I grumbled.

"I'll replace it. Are you hurt?" He looked closely into my eyes like he'd be able to spot an injury through force of will alone.

"No, but I *am* pissed about my damn phone. I need that for work."

Nico reached over and lifted it, frowning down at the remnants of the screen and inner mechanics spilling out where the entire back had broken loose. "I think it's a lost cause. I'll get you a new one as soon as I can."

I sighed. "Fine, but it better be an upgrade."

"I think we should get your head looked at, Kitten, just to be safe." He rose to his knees beside me and brushed a finger along my temple. "Gumby can drop us at the clinic."

"Not a chance," I shot back.

"Nothing is ever easy with you, is it?"

My scowl only intensified. "Guess not."

He grinned and tossed the phone into the dumpster beside us before I could protest that I might be able to fix it—or at least get the SIM card out of it. I wasn't as good with modern electronics as with vintage mechanics, but I could've given it a try. Feeling a little too woozy to articulate all that, I simply glared until he spoke again.

"Look, I'm here to ask you to come out to my cabin with me, okay? I'll explain everything there and we'll get you sorted out. If you want to go home after that, I'll bring you back right away."

With him crouching over me, brow furrowed and mouth tight with worry, I couldn't remember why I'd tried to make him go away in the first place. This felt like every teenage fantasy come true, aside from the ominous van and the broken phone—like Nico was a white knight riding to my rescue instead of the reason I was on the cold, hard ground in the first place.

I stared up at him as the strength of our childhood bond flared in my chest. The boy who'd meant the world to me was now a man asking for my help.

Maybe an adventure was just what we needed to rekindle that friendship.

"Okay," I said with another sigh, but as Nico took my arm to help me to my feet, a wave of dizziness almost sent me tumbling back to the asphalt. Before I realized what was happening, he swept me into his arms and carried me toward the van.

Maybe he wasn't so bad at playing white knight, after all.

## Chapter Two

### NICO

GUMBY SHOT ME AN accusatory look as I buckled in, but he said nothing. His only role in this mess had been to drive—maybe I was paranoid, but I didn't want to risk my car being spotted anywhere near Kat's place of work. I especially didn't want anyone reporting to her father that they saw us chatting.

While I might not be big news in Spruce Hill myself, anything pertaining to Aidan Willoughby, including his beautiful, slightly eccentric daughter, would definitely make waves.

Now that she was safely ensconced in the back seat of the van, my tension should've lessened, but it raged inside me still. I'd tried to sit back there with her, but she insisted she wanted room to put her feet up and that my "stupidly long legs" were in her way. Sometime during the forty minutes it took to reach the cabin, she dozed off.

Anxiety churned in my gut at seeing her so still, especially after the tumble she'd taken, but she'd developed a vehement distaste for doctors when she was seven years old and bit through her bottom lip after falling off some monkey bars. I couldn't even count the number of times she'd hidden childhood injuries from both her father and mine. Eventually, when I was old enough to recognize the severity and insist on telling an adult, she started hiding them from me, too.

Convincing her to do anything she didn't want to do was virtually impossible. Hauling her ass to a doctor when she insisted she was fine? Not the hill I wanted to die on, not now.

Literally, maybe. I would put nothing past her when she was truly pissed.

"Your girlfriend doesn't seem too happy to be here," Gumby muttered.

"Not my girlfriend," I reminded him, "and I think your van made a bad first impression."

"Chicks dig the Gumby-mobile, my friend. The bad impression was all you. Are you sure this is the right move?"

"This is my only move."

He snorted. "My plan was better and you know it. Besides, then you could've swept the lady off her feet in style, instead of creeping her out with my van."

Gumby's view of the law was a bit more flexible than most. When I told him about the painting Kat's father had stolen from my family, Gumby offered to simply steal it back. Given that he had a criminal record and I couldn't let my only friend go to prison because of me, I'd turned him down.

He still didn't agree with my methods, but he'd let it slide—until now.

The artwork had hung in our little cottage on the Willoughby property for as long as I could remember. I grew up hearing stories about the woman depicted in it, Céleste Bicardeau, my father's grandmother several generations over.

Céleste had been barely eighteen when Hugo Clément, a famous Impressionist who traveled in the same circles as Renoir and Monet, arrived in Avignon in the 1870s and asked her to pose for his work. The man had given Céleste the finished product, Woman in Lavender, as a gift, a tribute to her beauty. She was barely identifiable in the Impressionist oil painting—just the back of a lovely, lonely figure against the fields of lavender—but the family breathed the tale like oxygen, soaked up every textured brush stroke like part of our very bloodline.

All my life, my father told me the painting would be mine one day. Only those close to our family knew of its emotional significance, but my father warned me time and again that the piece would be worth a great deal of money if anyone discovered the artist's identity. That kind of monetary value would glow like a beacon to those who wanted to profit from the art instead of appreciating it for its history.

It didn't have Clément's usual signature on it, but he'd scrawled a note of appreciation across the back of the canvas, invisible to anyone looking at the painting from the front.

That wasn't the only thing hidden, though.

When I was in my final year of college, I'd come home after midnight once to find my father carefully smoothing his finger over the back of the frame.

"What are you doing?"

His expression shifted, though I couldn't quite read it back then. "Listen to me, Nicolas. If anything ever happens to me, anything strange, you take this painting and disappear."

"Disappear?"

"Leave Spruce Hill. Go back to France, if you like. Anywhere. Just take it and get far away from this place, from the Willoughby family."

At first, all I could process was the painful thought of leaving Kat behind, but I'd already been doing that, ever since the day her father threatened to throw us out on the street if he caught me sniffing around her.

"What did you put in there?" I moved closer to the table and watched his finger moving over the wood grain.

"Right here," he said, landing his fingertip on a spot near the bottom right corner. "There's a micro SD card in here. Remove the painting and break the frame if you must, but all the information you need is there."

"What information? What's going on?"

He stayed silent for a moment, then stood, hung the painting back on the wall, and clapped his hands on my shoulders. "Leverage. Proof that things are not as they seem. You can use it to protect yourself."

That had been the end of the discussion.

After my father's death two years ago, I rushed home for the funeral, and in the painting's place hung a different piece of artwork entirely.

With nothing more to lose once the risk to my father's career was gone, I confronted Aidan Willoughby. The man, as coldly calculating as ever, denied ever noticing the artwork. I remember lunging at him, shouting a number of heated expletives, and then I was promptly dragged from the premises by Willoughby's burly security guards.

The old, familiar fury burned in my gut. There was no certificate of authenticity, no insurance, not even a will describing the artwork and leaving it to me. There was some money set aside for me and for that I'd been immensely grateful, but it couldn't make up for the loss of the painting.

The one tangible reminder that even with my father dead, I wasn't alone, that I had roots, history—it was long gone, and so was whatever proof my father had hidden within.

I was no David, ready to take on a Goliath like Aidan Willoughby with all the resources the man had at his disposal. Walking away empty-handed had been, without a doubt, the hardest thing I'd ever done. Only the raw determination that I would someday best Willoughby at his own game had given me the strength to proceed.

With every passing day, the chances of him finding what was hidden inside the frame increased. My father was gone, but I had a feeling it would point a neon sign straight to me.

Whatever that leverage was, I needed it. *Before* he uncovered it.

"I wouldn't get caught. Hell, your girlfriend would probably help us."

With a sharp glare, I ignored the way calling Kat my *girlfriend* made me feel and said, "Neither one of you is setting foot on the property, Gumby. This is my problem and I'll solve it without risking either of you."

"I'm feeling a little slighted, Nico, that you think I'd get caught by some sleazy attorney."

"He has security," I reminded him. "And a reputation, which you know damn well."

He rolled his eyes. "Yeah, yeah. Frightened witnesses, greased palms? That's child's play, my friend."

"Two of his mistresses had husbands turn up dead, Gumby. Beat to shit, bodies left in the woods. He has ties to at least one major crime family in the city. Rivals gone missing, slam dunk cases falling apart in his favor. You're not getting anywhere near him, and neither is Kat."

After my dad died, I was certain Willoughby had me followed for weeks, waiting for me to make a move. Even months later, there were times when I caught sight of someone tailing me out of the corner of my eye. At first, I thought for sure he'd found the hidden evidence, but as time went on, I realized he must have just been covering his bases.

Still, it wasn't child's play, not even close—Aidan Willoughby was dangerous.

"Whatever you say, boss."

Gumby had staunchly supported only the most direct route at retrieving the painting, fancying himself some kind of elite cat burglar. When I told him it was out of the question, he'd devoted himself to becoming my sidekick. There had been a dozen other plans, possibilities I'd investigated, researched, and ultimately discarded.

Then, as if by a stroke of pure luck, I was sitting in a cafe one morning six months ago and happened upon a headline describing the lost Hugo Clément painting discovered in the collection of none other than Aidan Willoughby. The piece was worth somewhere in the realm of twelve million dollars, though the man in question had modestly protested, insisting he had no intention of selling a piece he'd so long admired for its beauty.

My first impulse was to throw my laptop across the cafe, my second to run to the bathroom and vomit up my breakfast, but those urges were followed swiftly by the tiniest seeds of a plan.

If Willoughby knew I was behind any of this, it would all be over before it started. I knew I'd have to tread very carefully, make sure I covered all the bases, so Willoughby had no reason to suspect I was involved in any part of it.

I'd spent these last several months working out the details, acquiring the necessary skills, and waiting for the right opportunity. A museum in Rochester, barely an hour away from Spruce Hill, was hosting a traveling exhibit featuring Hugo Clément's work. The buzz surrounding the exhibit inevitably led to a handful of news stories on Willoughby and his undiscovered painting.

This new publicity served as the perfect cover. Anyone with half a brain could put two and two together, recognize the monetary value of the artwork, and take advantage of what should be Willoughby's weakness—his only daughter.

"This will work," I said, my voice low in case Kat was awake. "It has to."

"Then it will."

Gumby was nothing if not loyal. I appreciated it more than I could say.

Every few minutes, I glanced back to check on Kat, each time wondering why I'd waited so long to make contact. Had I really let her father scare me away, or had my own regrets held me back?

She was the biggest variable in this plan, the only thing I couldn't be sure of. There was once a time I never would've questioned her cooperation—the two of us had understood each other as surely as if we'd been connected by some kind of inner wiring. Partners in crime, us against the world.

Now? She was practically a stranger.

Katherine Willoughby might be predictable as clockwork in some aspects, but her mind worked in mysterious ways. I wouldn't make any assumptions when it came to her reaction to this situation, especially after the burst of temper back there in the parking lot.

Any chance of the quiet conversation I hoped to have in her office was gone now, so I'd have to make the best of this turn of events.

As a child, Kat was smart—scary smart, able to take apart toys and electronics, then piece them unerringly back together—but she'd lived a charmed life there in the house I'd dubbed "The Castle" so many years ago. Here in Spruce Hill, the Willoughby family was as close to royalty as anyone could get, even if her father spent more time in the city than in town.

We'd been friends, once. The best of friends.

I settled back in my seat and closed my eyes, allowing my mind to present a slideshow of images from our youth: Kat, at two or three years old, held by a nanny in the huge kitchens at the Willoughby home as my father prepared dinner; at age eight, chasing after me and my friends; at ten, that fateful night under her father's desk.

Things had changed after that night. Our bond had strengthened even further.

That was where childhood blurred into adolescence in my memories, where things between us shifted. I'd always known she had a harmless crush on me, especially after that day, but as the years passed and my own feelings toward her started to change, the situation became dangerous.

There was no way I would endanger my father's position with the family. Mr. Willoughby had always looked at me with a sneering contempt that made it clear my presence was barely tolerated—if not for my father's absolute refusal to leave me behind in France with my uncle, I would never have ended up a member of the Willoughby household.

The night she tried to kiss me, just after the start of my senior year in high school, when she was a freshman, I knew I needed to force a wedge between us.

Her father hadn't caught us, thank fuck, but he must've seen the way she looked at me—or the way I looked at her, when I thought no one was looking—because he cornered me only days later to issue his first and final warning.

Keeping my distance became necessary, as much for Kat's protection as my own.

She'd been a cute little girl, with bouncing blonde curls and those blue eyes too big for her elfin features, but she'd blossomed into far more. Her hair had grown long again since the last time we saw each other. It was pulled back in a fancy braid today, with curling wisps that had come loose to frame her face. That blonde shone bright as sunshine when we were children, but over the years, it darkened to a burnished gold.

Those blue eyes were sharper than I remembered, no longer able to hide either the intelligence or the temper underneath her sparkling exterior. She wasn't the golden child she'd once been, that much was clear. These days, Kat Willoughby was unapologetically herself.

And man, I liked it.

With that worn leather jacket on, she'd looked edgy and hot as fuck when she walked out of her warehouse. The turquoise tank top underneath made her eyes pop and revealed strong shoulders framing the delicate bones of her collar. Those fitted black jeans tempted me to run my palms all the way from her hips down to the ankles encased in combat boots with rainbow laces.

Luscious and curvy—she'd gone from a gawky little girl to a full-figured goddess.

I hadn't anticipated the sizzle of attraction that rocketed through me, which was stupid when I thought about it now. Had there ever been a time when I *didn't* want her? Not since we both hit puberty, at least.

Rehashing the past definitely wasn't part of my plans for the weekend; what good would it do? After this was over, I might never see her again.

When we'd tumbled to the ground outside Kat's Keepers, my senses had been cloaked in panic, but the memory of her body against mine came rushing back now with perfect clarity. Those curves, the supple limbs, then of course that spark in her eyes—I gave myself a solid minute to remember, to imagine what could've been, and then I shut it down.

I couldn't afford to slip up now, no matter how Kat tempted me to forget myself.

When Gumby parked outside of the cabin, Kat didn't stir. I wondered whether it might be a trap, but she'd always been impatient, full of fire. If she planned to knock my teeth out, she'd probably have done it already. I unbuckled and hopped down from the seat of the van, opening the back doors to reach in toward Kat.

I set my hands on her shoulders to give her a gentle shake, hoping to rouse her. When she let out a sharp cry of pain, however, I released her quickly and looked down at my right palm. It was streaked with her blood, a sight that threatened to choke me with a swirl of guilt and regret.

"What the hell?" I whispered.

She blinked up at me, those big blue eyes dazed, then her long lashes swept slowly down as she closed her eyes. The setting sun behind me cast a golden glow over her, giving her an almost angelic aura. When she didn't snap at me, didn't bother to bite out some sarcastic remark about my carelessness, the guilt settled into a cold, hard knot in my stomach.

"Okay," I said softly. "It's okay, let's get you inside. I'll take care of everything, I promise."

Gumby turned in his seat. "Shit, man, you need help?"

"If you could grab her purse and open the door, I'll take care of the rest. Thanks, Gumby."

"No problem. Let me know if there's anything else I can do. And good luck with this one. I have a feeling you're going to need it."

I rolled my eyes as he ran to throw open the cabin door. Though Kat flinched when I lifted her into my arms, she didn't struggle. Her body was limp and warm, her dark lashes still against the curve of her cheek. After I carried her inside, Gumby gave a nod, set her purse on a side table, and closed the door behind him. A minute later, the van pulled back out along the narrow road in front of the cabin.

I laid Kat on the dining table behind the couch. Under the bright light of a rustic chandelier over the table, it was clear something had sliced through the upper sleeve of her jacket and into the soft flesh beneath it. I muttered a curse under my breath.

"I'm just going to grab the first aid kit and some scissors from the silverware drawer. I'll have to cut the sleeve off."

"Like hell you will," Kat growled, forcing her heavy eyelids upward. "This jacket is worth more than your life, Nicolas Beaumont."

"There she is," I murmured.

The rush of relief nearly made me giddy as I reached out to cup her cheek. I let my thumb brush lightly over her skin, then drew it away before she could turn her head to bite me—she'd done it once years before, an injury which I remembered all too well. Though she glared, I winked before jogging into the kitchen for supplies to get her cleaned up.

"Let's get this precious jacket off in one piece, then," I said when I returned to her side, sliding my arm under her shoulders to help her sit up. "You're sure your head is okay?"

"For Christ's sake, Nico, I said it's fine and it's fine. You're the one giving me a headache."

I lifted my hands in surrender, but her expression stayed belligerent as she glared back at me.

Slowly, I reached for the jacket, watching her for any sign of pain. Kat closed her eyes on a sigh, but she forced them open again as I carefully tugged her right sleeve off, then made my way around to the left side and paused.

"Just do it," she hissed.

I winced in sympathy as I peeled the left sleeve down, set the jacket aside, and scrubbed a hand over my jaw. Streaks of red coated her arm, painting the skin from her bicep almost to her wrist, though the gash near her shoulder had stopped bleeding.

*Small miracles,* I thought, but shit, it looked like a lot of blood. When she swayed slightly, I wrapped my arm around her to ease her back down.

"I never took you for the kidnapping type," she said weakly, watching my face as I gently bathed her forearm with warm water, working upward toward her elbow.

"I didn't kidnap you. You agreed to come with me."

"So do little kids when a stranger offers candy or puppies." Her tone still lacked its usual ferocity, but the sass hadn't diminished.

"Why couldn't you just talk to me?" I replied, lifting my eyes to meet hers.

For a moment, she looked as disoriented as she had when I opened the door of the van. She stared up at me, then I turned my attention back to her arm and soaked a fresh gauze pad with antiseptic.

"You could've just picked up the phone," she ground out between clenched teeth, "instead of bringing along Pokey and his creeper van for the ambiance."

I choked on a laugh. "His name is Gumby, but I might have to call him Pokey from now until the end of time."

"Whatever," Kat grumbled, but she gasped when I swabbed the wound.

"Give it a second, the sting will fade," I murmured, keeping my voice low and soothing.

It definitely did *not* soothe her; she looked ready to stab me. I could've sworn I heard her teeth grinding together as I smeared ointment along the thin cut before wrapping her upper arm in gauze. When that was done, I surveyed my handiwork.

"At least you don't need stitches. If I had to guess, I'd say your beloved jacket snagged on a nail from one of the pallets. When was your last tetanus shot?"

"Oh, for fuck's sake, Nico," she snapped. "You just took me from my place of business, dragged me out to the middle of who knows where, and tetanus is what you're worried about? When I get through with you, believe me, tetanus will be the last thing on your mind."

I sat back to gather up the bloody towels. "I'm worried about you, yes. You're important to me. Of course your safety concerns me."

"You scared the hell out of me, showing up like that," she said slowly, her eyes narrowed to angry slits. "That's not enough to concern yourself with?"

"I'm sorry you were scared, but I was trying to be discreet."

"What the *hell* is going on?"

Her temper had always pricked at my own like nothing else in the world. I threw the towels aside and leaned down, bracing my arms on either side of her and lowering my face until it was only a few inches from hers.

She lifted her chin in a glorious picture of defiance. There was no way to win this kind of battle with Katherine Willoughby, but it promised to be the fight of a lifetime.

"I'll explain everything when I'm good and fucking ready. Until then, I guess you can consider yourself my hostage."

# Chapter Three

## Kat

When Nico swung away from me, I eased myself into a sitting position, letting my legs dangle off the edge of the table. I watched him stomp around the kitchen, slinging the towels into a tiny washing machine stacked in the corner, and wondered if I should be afraid instead of furious.

After the briefest consideration, I tossed that thought aside. No, I was pissed, and being pissed always trumped being scared.

Still glaring in his direction, I cursed my treacherous heart for speeding up at his proximity, cursed my body for reacting to him with such longing when the rest of me was so frustrated I could scream. Especially after watching that same slow, sweet smile that had always gutted me spread across his stupid, handsome face.

Since he was currently paying no attention to me, I let my gaze drift over the interior of the cabin. It was small, rustic in a cozy sort of way. I had no idea where we were or how long I'd been in the back of that van, though I guessed we hadn't gone too far based on the setting sun that framed Nico's body when he opened the van door.

His long, lean, beautiful body.

Casting that observation into the depths of my brain—where I'd locked away every bit of my attraction to Nico so long ago—I took in the rest of my surroundings. The kitchen, dining area, and living room were all sections of a single large room. The bathroom door stood open across from where I sat, and I assumed the other door along that wall led to a bedroom.

Nico's expression while tending to my injury had been apologetic, but I recognized the stubborn set of his jaw. It made me wonder, in the midst of this bizarre situation, whether I could even claim to know him anymore.

The boy I'd adored had grown up, and I had yet to learn the man he'd become.

But no, Nico wouldn't hurt me—no matter what changes the years had brought, I knew him well enough to be certain of that. And shit, I couldn't deny the little thrill that had trembled through me when he growled the word "hostage" in my ear.

Still, we'd come a long way since the day I left on the back of a motorcycle my senior year of high school.

That was the last time I saw Nico, standing there with his father. I left for college two months later and hadn't looked back, taking myself as far away from home as I could get. Nico's father died during those years, I knew that much, but I hadn't even known about the funeral. My father was too self-centered to think to inform me, and Nico . . . well, when I learned about it later on, I couldn't quell the hurt that he hadn't seen fit to tell me about it himself.

Pierre Beaumont had been one of the only adults I'd ever truly trusted, one of the only ones to care about me in return during a time when I felt the hollow ache of abandonment most acutely. Now, looking back with the benefit of adulthood, I was able to view our past a little more objectively.

I was far from the only one here who'd lost something essential with Pierre's death. Regret flooded my chest.

"I'm sorry about your dad, Nico," I said quietly.

He froze in the middle of drying his hands on a clean towel in the kitchen. I felt steadier now, but I stayed where I was, afraid my legs might not support me if I hopped down, as tempted as I was to go to him.

"I didn't find out until months after the funeral. I would've come. I would've been there for you."

All the air left his lungs in an audible whoosh.

"I know." He paused, as though about to say more, then simply repeated, "I know."

With that, the tension eased and the anger faded. We locked eyes for a minute, the weight of all the intervening years falling away, until Nico turned back to what he was doing. He kept busy for another few minutes in the small kitchen, set the oven to preheat, and then walked over to the table to stand in front of me.

As if by mutual agreement, we paused to look one another over.

I had only the skinny college boy and gangly adolescent he'd once been to compare to the man before me. He'd filled out, broadened in the shoulders, sharpened in the jaw. The same black curls fell across his forehead and brushed at the collar of his t-shirt, but he was no boy, not anymore.

He looked a little scruffy, a whole lot sexy, and more enticing than ever.

"Your hair got darker," he said, reaching out to brush his fingertips over the wisps escaping my braid. "How's your arm feeling? And your head?"

It was a close call, but I managed to avoid leaning into the caress. "I'll survive."

"I'll get you some painkillers. I mean it, I had no intention of putting you in any danger." His dark eyes filled with concern as he lowered his hand.

I shrugged like this was an everyday occurrence. "Why am I here, Nico?"

This was it. The moment of truth. A muscle in his jaw ticked as he stared at me, tension vibrating from him anew. I gazed back, trying to hold onto some semblance of patience when I wanted to reach out and shake him until he spit it out.

"Your father has something of mine. I need to get it back. I'd like you to be my insurance policy."

I drew back and blinked at him in confusion. "Insurance policy? Were you really going to kidnap me?"

"Of course not," he barked. "I hoped you would trust me enough to come with me. I wouldn't involve you in this against your will. I didn't want to involve you at all, but I need leverage."

"So you're planning to trade me for whatever this thing is?"

Nico hesitated almost imperceptibly, then nodded, and I exploded—even though he looked like he was expecting it, he still flinched as the words flew from my lips.

"Are you out of your goddamn mind? He hasn't given a shit about me in decades, Nicolas, if *ever*. What the hell makes you think he would actually value my life enough to barter with it? And for fuck's sake, you think he'll believe you'd hurt me if he doesn't do what you want? I thought you were smart, Beaumont, but apparently I was wrong."

He lifted his eyes to the ceiling like he was trying to stay calm, then speared me with a thunderous expression.

"I might not be as brilliant as you, but I'm not a complete idiot. If it comes down to it, he's not going to know I'm the one holding you hostage. As for whether he values your life, I'm not touching that topic with a ten foot pole, but he sure as hell values his pristine reputation. You really think he'll want his refusal to save his daughter's life plastered all over the news? Last I heard, he had his eye on the Attorney General's office."

That gave me a moment of pause as I considered it. My father cared for very little in this life—not his daughter, certainly not his ex-wife.

Money, power, and prestige? Those were everything to him.

Then again, the man had an army of publicists out there to stamp out negative rumors and rumblings. If he could figure out how to spin this to his advantage, Nico was going to be sorely disappointed.

"Even if he falls for this, did you ever stop and think that I might take issue with being shoved back into his loving arms? I don't want to see him, Nico. I am not a bargaining chip," I hissed.

"Don't you think I know that?" He thrust a hand through his hair before glaring at me. "Forgive me for thinking you might tolerate a brief exposure to the man for my sake."

When we were kids, I'd have put up with practically anything for Nico's sake. Now? It would take something life-changing to convince me this whole endeavor was worth the hassle of dealing with my family.

"What is it you want to trade me for?"

He flinched again, like the words were shards of glass striking him. "I can't tell you, not yet. Kitten . . . I need you to trust me, just for a little while. Please. You know I would never hurt you or put you at risk, but this is important and I'm desperate."

I stared at him intently, wondering just what the hell he was up to. With a sigh, I said, "Fine. Where exactly are we?"

"I can't tell you that either," he said, then raised a placating hand when I scowled. "Not because I don't trust you. I don't want you to be complicit in any of this, Kat. The less you know, the better."

"Right. Okay." I fell silent for a moment. "So what happens tomorrow when my assistant shows up at work and I'm nowhere to be found?"

Nico grinned a little, revealing a dimple I hadn't seen in more than a decade. It captured me, melted my resistance, until I had to force my eyes away.

"If you agreed to help me, I intended to ask you to text her to say you were sick and taking some time off to rest up, but since your phone died a tragic death, you can use my burner."

I rolled my eyes. "Burner. How very spy thriller of you. Why are we in a cabin? I thought you lived in town?"

"I own this cabin and we're a safe distance from town, that's all I can say for now. I didn't want anyone seeing us together, not if this plan is going to work."

My gaze jerked back to his face. "There are security cameras out back at the warehouse."

"Not a problem. They were remotely disabled this morning."

"What exactly have you been doing all these years?" I asked, frowning at him. The careless shrug he offered was not altogether reassuring, so I heaved a sigh. "Fine. Forget I asked. So I'm your hostage now. Am I a prisoner here, too?"

"I'd like you to stay while I work through the plan, but I hadn't intended to tie you up."

When I arched a brow, that slow smile of his took on a different light. Fire streaked along my veins, though I tried to hide it. My cheeks burned in direct response to the tempting array of images he'd summoned from the depths of my imagination.

"Unless requested, of course," he added, his voice soft and dangerously seductive.

"I'm sure that won't be necessary."

His low chuckle resonated deep within my belly, but after another slow perusal from the top of my head to the boots on my feet, he took a deliberate step backward. The sudden distance both calmed and irritated me as he winked and handed me his phone.

"Here, text your assistant. I'll put dinner in the oven."

As children, Nico had never done more than hold my hand, and even that had been infrequent, aside from the night of the incident. I thought back, but even when I'd practically thrown myself at him my freshman year—clumsy though it had been—Nicolas Beaumont had been the perfect gentleman.

He'd certainly never smiled at me like *that* before, never run his eyes over me in a nearly tangible caress.

As I forced myself to ignore the way my blood sang inside my veins, I slipped down from the table and sat in one of the chairs, facing the kitchen. I took a few deep breaths as I fired off the text, telling Erin I was using a neighbor's phone since mine was dead. She responded immediately, asking what I needed her to do in my absence, and some of my anxiety about being away from work faded under her assurance that she could handle it all.

Standing in front of the stove, Nico opened a cardboard box, cut through a layer of plastic wrap, and slid the pale circle into the oven.

"Is that a frozen pizza?" I asked incredulously.

Nico laughed. "My dear Papa is rolling over in his grave right now, but this kitchen isn't quite up to his standards, either. I hope you don't mind roughing it for a few days."

"A few days?" I scowled at him. "Is that how long you think we'll be here?"

With a hip propped against the counter, he hooked his thumbs in his pockets and studied me. "At most, yes. I'd love to get it over with sooner, but I do expect your father to be difficult."

I scoffed. "Difficult. That's a nice word for it. You expect him to be a miserly bastard with a mean streak a mile wide, you mean."

Nico nodded, then turned to one of the cabinets by the sink. He pulled out a bottle of Tylenol, then filled a glass with water and handed them both to me.

"I'll handle him. We have enough supplies to stay here for as long as it takes."

"I have a business to run, you know. I haven't missed a day of work in . . . well, ever."

"You've been working yourself to the bone for years, Kitten. I think a couple days off work will do you some good."

I scowled at him. "How do you know that?"

"Do you really think you can live in Spruce Hill and *not* have everyone know everything about your life? You might not live at The Castle anymore, but you're still the town princess."

"Whatever. Just how long have you been planning this?" I asked, tossing back the pills with a long swig of water.

"Since my father died. I really hoped to avoid putting you in the middle of it, but unfortunately, I've run out of options."

I wracked my brain, wondering what the hell my father had taken from Nico that was worth devoting two years of his life to pursuing. I'd get it out of him eventually, especially if we were going to be cooped up here for days on end. Deciding that I'd just have to be patient, I cocked my head at him.

"You know, this is not how I saw my weekend going," I informed him.

He grinned again. "No, I expect not. Your routines are legendary—work, home, yoga at the studio down the street. Then what, flea markets, yard sales? What do you call that part of the job?"

The glare I sent him didn't dim his smirk. "Scouting. It's called scouting. You know, you're starting to sound like a stalker. Are you obsessed with me?"

"Obsessed," he repeated, pushing away from the counter to stroll slowly toward me.

He pulled out a chair, turned it backward, and sat down facing me with his arms folded across the chair back. Those dark eyes locked on mine until I felt like all the air had been sucked out of the room.

"God knows I've never managed to get you out of my head, Kitten."

I remembered being irritated by the nickname when he'd first started using it—what, twenty years ago now? Twenty-five? As I got older and my infatuation with him grew, the name had become a stamp of pride, an inside joke between us, a symbol of his affection for me.

Now? Hearing his deep voice murmuring the word did odd, fluttery things to my insides.

His lips kicked up at the corners again. "You were always the one tying me up in knots. I guess I can't complain if you're a little tongue-tied this time around."

"Tied up in knots! You couldn't get away from me fast enough," I countered, frowning. "I barely saw you once you started high school. After—"

*After I threw myself at you,* I almost said. After I decided I was sick of waiting for him to notice I wasn't a little kid anymore and tried to kiss him outside the school during a football game. After I humiliated both of us when our teeth collided, when he had to grab my shoulders to keep us from falling to the ground and to force some distance between us.

That rejection still stung, even after all this time. It was the only time I'd expressed my true feelings for Nico, only to be shot down like the pathetic little mess I was that night.

Now, he was close enough to reach out and brush his knuckles along my jaw, close enough to see the shiver run through me as he did, though I tried valiantly to hide it.

"After that kiss, you mean?" he asked softly.

I wrinkled my nose. "That's a generous description for it."

"If I stayed away, Kat, it was only because I had no other option. Your father didn't exactly approve of me being around you to begin with."

There was something he wasn't saying—I could see it in his face. "What did he say?"

He rubbed his jaw. "A few days later, he told me my dad and I would be out on our asses if he ever thought I was so much as dreaming of touching his only child and sullying his reputation. Believe me, tangled up is putting it lightly."

Shock flooded my system at his confession, leaving me staring silently back at him until a low thrum of heat pulsed through my veins. Everything I thought I knew spun wildly inside my head like a Tilt-a-Whirl, until I was no longer sure which way was up. I'd always taken Nico's dismissal personally, assuming he had no interest in me.

Now here he was, pointing out something I should've seen for myself years ago.

Though I wanted to argue, I bit my lip to keep from saying anything more damaging to my own pride.

My father had never approved of Nicolas, I'd always known that much. Since having Nico's dad in his employ was a point of pride—some macho contest with my father's long-time rival, who'd hired a fancy chef from California—he'd never come right out and forbidden Nico's presence when we were kids, but the sentiment was clear.

I just hadn't known he'd paid enough attention to suspect we were anything but friends. Had I known he'd confronted Nico back then, I would've raised holy hell.

And Nico's family would have suffered for it.

Ashamed of my lack of awareness, I mumbled, "I didn't realize that."

The timer beeped from the kitchen and Nico rose to get the pizza out of the oven. While he sliced it, I watched him.

Watched, and remembered.

# Chapter Four

## Kat

*Selfish, spoiled little rich girl.*

What I'd seen as rejection at the time took on a new light now that I considered Nico's side of it. Not once had I even considered the position I might be putting him in, with both my friendship and, later, my shameless flirtation. What an idiot I'd been.

Nico set a plate in front of me, then held up a bottle of hard cider from the fridge. "I have this, Sprite, or more water."

I laughed, remembering that he'd gotten caught drinking one of those in the woods behind the house and been grounded for weeks. "Cider sounds wonderful right now."

He grabbed a bottle for himself, popped the tops, and handed one to me. "Drink it slow," he teased. "You might not think it was bad enough to warrant a doctor, but you did hit your head.

And I still remember when you got drunk on the champagne you pilfered from some fancy event your father hosted."

"I was tipsy, Nicolas, not drunk," I replied haughtily.

"So tipsy you tripped into a hedge in the garden and needed me to pull you back out?"

"Okay, maybe I didn't try very hard to remember that part of it. That was the last time I over-imbibed."

"Really?" His eyebrows lifted. "No college parties, no club-hopping?"

"Nope. I do love a good wine cooler, but only one of them and only once in a while."

Nico sat across the table from me and propped his chin on one hand, amusement sparkling in his dark eyes. "Jamaican Me Crazy? Sex on the Beach? Strawberry Daiquiri?"

This time, I stuck out my tongue. "I am an equal opportunist when it comes to fruity concoctions."

"If frozen pizza is an affront to my dad's memory, I'm pretty sure Katherine Willoughby sipping a wine cooler is the ultimate sin in your father's eyes."

"Yes, because running an online resale business for vintage toys makes me his pride and joy," I drawled. "This might come as a surprise, but I don't give a shit what he thinks. I haven't even seen him in years."

Nico blinked at me. "Years? Really?"

I tipped my bottle in his direction. "Your stalker game is clearly not up to snuff, Beaumont."

He gave a thoughtful hum and dropped his gaze to his pizza. Though I was a bit unnerved by his sudden silence, I was also completely exhausted and my head still ached, despite the painkillers. We finished our dinner with little conversation, then Nico took our plates to the sink to wash up.

By the time he looked over again, probably expecting to see me pacing around the small cabin with my usual restless energy, I was still seated at the table and beginning to droop.

"Come on, up you get," he said gently, pulling me to my feet.

He led me to the bedroom, flipped on the light, and showed me where everything was. I ignored everything but the bed—Nico's bed. The temptation of collapsing onto a mattress that smelled like him was almost too much to resist, but he took my hand and led me into the bathroom, where a packaged toothbrush sat on the counter.

"If you had let me explain, we would've had the chance to go home and pack a bag for you. I have plenty of t-shirts and some sweatpants with drawstrings that I guess will have to do for now, but I can wash what you're wearing. Anything in the dresser is up for grabs."

With a huffed laugh, I said, "Maybe next time you should mail out a handwritten invitation with full instructions before you show up unexpectedly. Then I can keep an overnight bag packed and be ready to roll at a moment's notice."

"Very funny. There won't be a next time. This is it, win or lose. I'll be out on the couch if you need me."

"So I get this big bed all to myself? What, Nico, are you afraid you can't keep your hands off me?" I taunted.

It was meant in jest, but my voice came out low and husky. Nico leaned down, so close that his cheek brushed mine in a whisper of sensation.

"Careful, Kitten."

The words vibrated against my ear and goosebumps rose along my skin. I bit back the smartass remark I wanted to make, but I couldn't resist turning my head a fraction of an inch, rubbing my soft cheek more firmly against the shadow of a beard gracing his jawline.

When he sucked in a sharp breath, I took a quick step back and smiled brightly up at him. Two could play this game.

"Right, then I'll just get ready for bed. Goodnight."

It was impossible not to feel his gaze burning into my back as I strolled into the bedroom and shut the door between us. As much as I wanted to collapse against it and relive that flare of heat, I suspected he was still standing there, still staring after me.

I gave myself a moment to take some slow, deep breaths, then moved to the dresser holding my meager wardrobe options.

*You're playing with fire,* I told myself, but the warning inspired a thrill of excitement rather than suppressing it.

After spending so many of my formative years dreaming about being alone in close quarters with Nicolas Beaumont, reality burned hotter than I'd ever imagined. Even more importantly, he wasn't immune to my charms, that much was clear.

As I pulled on a blue cotton pajama set I found in the top drawer, I contemplated our earlier conversation, his comments about not being able to get me out of his head.

This wasn't how I'd expected a potential reunion to happen, though. We had each gone away for college, but I kept an eye on his social media and knew he'd come back to town afterward. I thought he worked in computer programming of some kind, figured he'd be tucked away in an office somewhere.

When he said he'd remotely disabled those security cameras, though, I had to second guess that particular assumption.

For years, I'd envisioned a reunion between us—of course, most of my fantasies started there and ended up fairly explicit. Now, seeing him in the flesh, it was clearer than ever that I hadn't outgrown my feelings for him.

In truth, they seemed to have multiplied tenfold.

Just as I finished buttoning the pajama shirt, an amused huff came from the bedroom doorway and I jumped, startled. Nico had opened the door and leaned against the frame, arms and ankles crossed. When he only grinned, I scowled at him.

"You are a total creep," I muttered.

"I just came to see if you needed any help. Figured it might be difficult to get changed with a sore arm."

He slipped his hands into his pockets, smiling benignly as I humphed, turned away to fold up my discarded clothing, and tried to fight back the blush rising in my cheeks at the image his offer of help evoked.

"I managed just fine on my own, as you can see."

"Shame." The word was so soft, I wondered for a second if he'd really even said it. I shot him a glance, saw his lips curve upward for a moment, then his expression grew sober. "I meant what I said earlier. You know I won't hurt you, but I also can't let you leave once we set things in motion."

My mouth pressed into a thin line. "Is this you reminding me that I'm a prisoner here, even after all your reassurances that I haven't actually been abducted?"

The curve of his lips reappeared and deepened, showing off that damned dimple again. "Yes, I suppose it is. If you don't want to help me, this ends here and now. You go back to your life and I . . . well, I'll think of something."

Something in his expression—something bereft, almost hopeless—made the decision for me. This was Nico. His friendship had saved me from a childhood of loneliness and despair.

Helping him now was the least I could do to repay that.

"I'm in. I wish you'd explain what you're after, but you have to know I'd choose you over my father no matter what. What's going to happen if Erin tries to check in at my apartment, realizes I'm missing, and calls the police?"

"I'll take care of it. I'm sure she'll be worried about you, but that's unavoidable. Once I contact him, your father will step in and keep things quiet before word gets out, believe me." He turned away, then paused with his hand on the doorknob. "Do you remember that time you tried to steal my copy of *Firestarter* out of my bedroom?"

My lips parted in surprise when he glanced back over his shoulder. "Yes," I said slowly. "It was my favorite book and my father threw mine out like the asshole that he is. Not suitable reading material for a young girl, something like that."

Nico nodded. "Then you'll remember that if it comes to a physical contest, you won't win. Sweet dreams."

He left the room, closing the door behind him.

A startled laugh caught in my throat as I shook my head at the clear warning. It was true—he'd always been bigger, stronger, and faster, but I'd been more clever and far more devious.

Until I learned the truth about what Nico was after, I had no intention of trying to get away from him, not yet. Should I decide it was in my best interest to bow out of this adventure, however, I was confident I could outsmart him, even if outrunning him wasn't in the cards.

With that in mind, I went back to the bathroom to brush my teeth and splash water on my face, pausing to study my reflection in the mirror above the sink. Though the cut on my arm still stung and a fresh wave of annoyance rushed through me as I lamented my favorite jacket being torn, right now I wanted nothing more than to collapse into bed and sleep for a good long time.

*Let him enjoy the couch.* I left the bathroom and grinned to myself as I eyed the queen-sized bed with satisfaction.

Nico had topped out at a few inches above six feet, by my estimate, and the thought of him folding those long limbs onto the ancient sofa in the other room was an image that gave me no small degree of pleasure.

Served him right for deciding to use me as a hostage, willing or otherwise.

# Chapter Five

## KAT

Sleeping late wasn't something I did frequently, if ever, but when the clock in the bedroom told me it was after nine, I still couldn't quite drum up any urgency in jumping out of bed. My arm felt better and I'd slept shockingly well in a strange place.

Probably thanks to sheets that smelled like Nico, but I shoved that out of my mind.

At the moment, all I wanted was a hot shower. I slipped out from under the covers and assembled a passable if unattractive outfit of gray sweatpants and a black tee from Nico's dresser drawers. I spent an inordinately long time staring at my clothes from yesterday, which had clearly been washed and folded while I slept, and I wondered if I should be impressed or horrified that he'd been in and out of the room without me noticing.

After a moment of indecision, I shrugged and grabbed my bra and underwear from the pile. No point in wearing tight jeans if we were just going to sit around the cabin for days on end. I'd save my own clothes for a time when I needed them.

For half a second, I debated opening the bedroom door to tell Nico I was getting in the shower. Annoyance at the idea of even appearing to ask his permission won out, so I let myself into the bathroom, noted that the other door into the living room remained closed, and carefully unwrapped the gauze around my upper arm.

The cut didn't look as bad as I'd feared, just a jagged red line an inch or two long that curved around my bicep. I moved my arm around a bit to test it. The skin pulled uncomfortably when I straightened my elbow too quickly, but otherwise it felt okay, which seemed like a good sign.

I turned on the shower, waited for the water to warm up enough to cloak the bathroom in steam, and stepped under the hot, soothing spray. This break in my routine wasn't ideal, but I'd survive.

Nico might have won the first round, but now that I was rested and recovered from his unexpected return to my life, I prepared for battle. If I was going to linger here, missing work at the business I'd busted my ass to build up from scratch, Nico was going to spill his secrets.

Willingly or under duress, I didn't care which.

Maybe I should have burst out of the bedroom to demand answers the minute I woke up, but I'd rather face him on my own terms.

Twenty minutes later, washed and dressed, I went to leave the bedroom and found the door locked. It was only the span of a breath before I began pounding on it with my fists. I heard a muffled laugh before Nico's footsteps moved across the room to let me out.

"You son of a bitch, I'm going to *kill* you!" I yelled.

I was about to pick up the small metal trash can from beside the bed and hurl it against the door when it swung open.

"Good morning," Nico drawled, smirking at me.

His dark eyes glinted as he surveyed my ensemble. With my wet hair pulled up in a bun on top of my head and bare feet peeping out from under the too-long sweatpants, I doubted my responding glare carried as much weight as I would've liked.

"I'm going to kick your ass, Nico Beaumont."

Shooting daggers at him with my eyes, I brushed past, making sure my good shoulder nailed him square in the chest as I went. Nico grinned and followed after me, though he rubbed his palm against his sternum. I was stronger than I looked and he'd do well to remember that.

"You can try," he offered, "but after all the trouble I went to toasting you up some nice frozen waffles, violence seems a tad ungrateful."

I muttered a few uncomplimentary comments under my breath as I dropped into a chair at the table. When he set a plate of waffles and a glass bottle of maple syrup in front of me, I thawed ever so slightly, but I still ignored him while I cut into my breakfast. Nico sat down in the seat beside me, his knee nudging my leg under the table.

The frisson of heat that trembled up my spine was harder to ignore, so I covered it with sarcasm.

"So, tell me, oh kidnapper extraordinaire—what happens now? A ransom note made of letters that you painstakingly snipped out of magazines?"

"Come on, I would hope you'd give me more credit than that. Though if you want to play arts and crafts, I guess you're welcome to do it for me. As an alternative from the current century, I've got a computer program. Once you give me the go ahead, I'll set up an untraceable email to be sent to your father."

"Untraceable," I repeated, narrowing my eyes at him.

Nico gave a careless shrug, but his gaze locked on my face. "I'm a man of many talents."

I snorted. "So it would seem."

"That will be a first contact maneuver to warn him away from calling the police, but I expect he'll send his own people to your apartment and to Kat's Keepers to investigate. Presumably, if Erin speaks with him, he'll convince her to leave it to him to deal with the upcoming demands."

"So now what? We just sit here and wait?"

A boyish grin lit his face, nearly knocking the breath from my lungs with its familiarity. "Well, there's a deck of cards in one of the kitchen drawers, but I was thinking we could go for a walk."

"A walk with your hostage? Isn't that a little risky?"

"A willing hostage," he countered, "but I think you're too curious for escape, aren't you, Kitten?"

I pointed my fork at him. "You know, maybe that nickname was cute when I was little, but as a grown woman, I find it a little condescending."

"Do you? I think you enjoy it just as much now as you did when we were younger."

"What makes you think I ever enjoyed it?" I asked teasingly.

Nico leaned close and let his fingertips trail along my jaw. His eyes studied my face intently until I gave a tiny shiver, then he grinned again.

"Because," he replied in a low voice, "that's exactly how you respond when I say it against your ear."

I shook my head as he sat back in his chair, a smug expression plastered on his face. "You're impossible. Fine, let's take a walk in the woods, as long as your kidnapper duties are on pause for the time being."

It was a silly thing to be excited about, but the prospect of an adventure with Nico delighted me the way it always had. As children, we'd wandered every square foot of my family's extensive property and beyond—trekking through the woods to the creek where Nico showed me how to skip rocks, sprinting across the lawns to the edge of Lake Ontario, biking along the rocky coastline all the way to the Spruce Hill Lighthouse.

That was us: partners in crime, pirates seeking treasure, adventurers chasing their dreams.

A soft feeling of nostalgia crept over me as he stood to clear the table. Though I hadn't responded to his comment about my curiosity, I was sure he'd caught my anticipation at the promise of exploring with him.

"I didn't want to risk damaging it by trying to fix the hole myself, but I did get your jacket cleaned up. It should be dry by now," he said over his shoulder.

My eyes widened in surprise. "Oh," I replied, kicking myself for the stupid response. "Thank you."

A soft laugh escaped his lips as he turned back to me. "Well, it's apparently worth more than my life, so I wanted to make sure it wasn't ruined. How's the arm feeling?"

"I put more ointment on it, but the scratch actually isn't too bad."

Relief washed over his features. "I'm glad to hear it. Let me bandage it up before we go. I don't want to chance it getting infected."

I nodded, waited while Nico grabbed the first aid kit, and focused very hard on not reacting to the way his hand brushed against my skin as he wrapped gauze around my bicep again. The man practically radiated heat. It took everything in me not to lean into his warmth.

"There we go," he said finally, sitting back to admire his handiwork. "And your head?"

"It feels fine," I replied, but I wasn't quick enough to stop him from sifting his fingers in my hair to check my temple for bruising. Our eyes locked, held, then he dropped his hand again.

"Good. If you're ready to roll, go grab some socks and we'll head out."

Once I laced up my boots, Nico held out the leather jacket for me to slip on. A tiny sigh escaped my lips. At his questioning look, I gave a sheepish grin.

"I just really love this jacket," I said with a shrug.

He cocked his head as he looked me over. The jacket didn't offer quite the same effect as it had against my black jeans and clean shirt from the day before, but it seemed like he appreciated the benefits of subtlety, as well. My cheeks heated ever so slightly and his dimpled grin returned when he winked at me.

"You look good in it. I'm glad it wasn't ruined."

"Let's just go," I muttered.

The day was bright, though the morning air still held enough bite to make me grateful for the jacket. In some places, the forest grew dense enough to block out the sun, but then the trees would thin and brilliant streams of light trickled through the branches overhead. A chorus of birdsong drifted around us, slowly giving way to the sound of moving water.

When the trail opened up to the side of a wide creek, I gasped in startled pleasure at the beauty before us.

"Oh, Nico," I said softly.

A simple kind of joy warmed my chest as I walked forward and crouched down to trail my fingertips through the water where it tumbled over the rocks below. Nico stared at me, a smile playing on his lips, when I rose to my feet and faced him. My nose wrinkled when I saw his expression.

"What?" I demanded.

"Just admiring the view," he replied, but after the briefest hesitation, he added, "I've missed you."

It didn't seem to matter what else went unsaid; understanding rocketed through me before I moved away again. I wanted to return the sentiment, probably would have under any other circumstances, but pride had me clearing my throat instead.

"So, in addition to kidnapping, you've been working on computer stuff all these years?"

Nico snorted and walked up to stand beside me. "Computer stuff. That about sums it up, yes. And you're selling vintage toys online?"

"That about sums it up, yes," I mimicked, smirking at him.

"Seems like a far cry from joining your father's firm."

"Ugh," I muttered. "You know that was never an option. I started Kat's Keepers while I was still in college—it turns out I have an eye for finding hidden gems, I guess. It's like hunting for buried treasure."

"Maybe you're the one who became a pirate, after all," he teased.

I smirked at him. "Maybe. I really love that aspect of my job, though plenty of the items need to be fixed up before selling them. I've learned a lot about mechanics over the years."

"I remember how you used to take things apart just to put them back together. It always amazed me when you could remember where each separate piece went, even if it was something entirely new. Remember that old boom box my dad found in his closet? We couldn't believe you fixed it—I think you were nine at the time. I can take apart a motherboard, but only because I've had so much practice with it."

I nodded and flashed a quick smile. "I do love dissecting inanimate objects."

"And you made your passion into a career."

"Yeah. The business stayed small until I graduated, then I decided to focus on expanding my operation enough to make a living from it. A few years back, I was able to hire Erin on, though she only went full-time about eighteen months ago."

"You're a fascinating woman."

My business was something I was immensely proud of. I'd refused any financial assistance from my father through school and in starting my business, though I was sure Aidan Willoughby wouldn't be caught dead funding such a plebeian venture as the Keeper, even if I'd asked. I hadn't, because I knew better than to become beholden to my family.

To Nico, I gave a one-shouldered shrug. "I know what I want and I work hard to get it."

The dig didn't go unnoticed, given the spark in his dark eyes, but he didn't bother to argue. Until he told me all of the details of this fake ransom plan, I would remind myself the best course was to assume the worst of him.

Nico blew out a long, slow breath and looked out across the water, a pensive expression on his face.

"When are you going to tell me what's going on?" I asked quietly.

"Once it's safe. I don't want your father to have any reason to suspect your involvement in this."

My lip curled in annoyance and his own quirked, but he valiantly attempted to suppress a smile, probably knowing it would only piss me off further.

"You're really not going to tell me what this object is that's worth my life to you?"

"Dammit, Kat, nothing in this world is worth your *life* to me!" he burst out. My lips parted in shock, but he surged on. "If I thought for one second that you were in any real danger, I'd walk away without hesitation, no matter what the cost. Do you understand me?"

Wide-eyed, I searched his face. Standing before me now was my protector, my best friend, pirate and white knight all wrapped into one—everything he'd been to me so long ago finally erupting from the man he'd become.

Any question of whether that had dwindled during our years apart evaporated like mist on the breeze.

"I understand." The words sounded a little too breathless for my liking, so I repeated more firmly, "I understand."

Nico drew a deep inhale, like he was trying to get his emotions under control. After a second, he moved closer to cup my cheek in his hand.

"This isn't about money or revenge or whatever the hell you imagine it might be. I've spent every day since my father's death trying to figure out how to make this happen, and if I'd come up with any other feasible option that kept you out of it, I would've gone that route." When my brows drew down, he laughed softly and added, "And *not* because I didn't want to see you again, but because I hate the thought of putting you at risk."

I stared at him for a long moment. *Years,* I thought absently. So many years of my life had been spent imagining a moment like this, imagining Nico touching me like this, and it felt completely surreal now that it had come to pass.

Then, before I could think any more about it, he dropped his hand and stepped away. It left me feeling strangely hollow.

"We should get back," he said.

I could only nod and trail along a step or two behind him as we wove our way back through the forest toward the cabin. Every time he had his hands on me, I could see the edges of his careful control crumbling a little bit more.

Some wild part of me wanted to use that to my advantage, see where it led.

If I pushed the boundaries, what would he do? Lock me in the bedroom until it was over? Lock us in the bedroom together?

That thought sent a bolt of heat through me. I'd been crushing on him for a long time, long enough that I'd gotten used to the dull ache in my chest whenever I thought of him.

But now, of course, I had long since outgrown childhood crushes. I was very much a woman, one who knew her own mind. He still seemed interested, and my desire for him had never waned, not completely.

If I offered myself willingly, I might have a chance with Nico, now that my father wasn't standing in our way.

But I had to nudge Nico out of his own way, too.

Twenty yards before we reached the cabin, I set my hand on his arm, drawing him to a halt. It took a moment—or maybe longer—for him to draw his gaze from my lips, curved in a tiny smile, and finally meet my eyes.

"Nico," I said softly.

"Yes?" he croaked.

I leaned in close enough to catch a whiff of that scent that had soothed me to sleep, vanilla with a hint of citrus, then I peeked up at him and flashed a playful grin. Only then did he seem to note the devilish gleam in my eyes, narrowing his own in response.

"I'm going to kick your ass at cards this afternoon. First one to the cabin picks the game."

With that, I bolted toward the door. He would've won easily if I hadn't distracted him, given that he was in jeans and sneakers while I wore pants that dragged a few inches too long as they came untucked from my clompy boots. Unfortunately, it took him an instant too long to process the challenge in my words before he reacted and I heard his feet pounding into the ground behind me.

As it was, he reached the cabin door barely half a second after I did. His hand closed over mine on the doorknob, trapping me between the door and his chest.

"You cheated," he growled into my ear.

Though a shiver rushed up my spine, I turned in a tight circle to face him. It took a great deal of willpower to resist planting my palms against his chest. I knew he would feel as firm as he looked, as warm as those brown eyes promised. Better to keep my hands to myself.

For now, anyway.

"What happened to your advantage in a physical contest?" I asked sweetly, batting my lashes at him.

When his eyes flared, I knew exactly what kind of physical contest he wanted to engage in. Once he'd firmly locked down his reaction, he leaned close enough to brush the tip of his nose against mine.

"I am going to crush you at cards, Kitten. Prepare to lose."

# Chapter Six

## NICO

Kat's bright trill of laughter did nothing to quiet the emotions rollicking around in my chest—heady lust mixed with affection and a sharp undercurrent of regret—but it brought a goofy smile to my face anyway.

Even though I'd been missing her since the day I made the difficult decision to keep my distance, it hadn't been quite so clear until this moment just how badly I'd missed our friendship. We had always delighted in needling one another, challenging and celebrating together. After so many years apart, it felt like everything I'd missed was within reach.

For one sudden, glaring moment, my hatred for Aidan Willoughby burned hotter than ever. The loss of Kat's friendship might've been a greater sin than the theft of the painting.

A twinge of doubt niggled at me as her outburst replayed in my mind, particularly her insistence that Willoughby didn't value her enough to make a trade. Everything in my plans hinged on him agreeing to ransom her for the painting.

As brilliant as she was, Kat had a tendency to undervalue herself and to expect the worst, so it was entirely possible she underestimated her father's reaction to her being placed in potential danger. Knowing Aidan Willoughby, his reputation would always have been his first concern, anyway, and I intended to lean heavily on that weakness.

What concerned me now was the surge of protective anger that rose in my chest at the thought that her father might still be undervaluing Kat. Now that I had her close at hand, the instinct to keep her out of harm's way, whether the threat was physical or emotional, was almost too strong for me to resist.

I gave myself a swift mental shake—even if her father didn't care about her, I'd manipulate the threat to his reputation. I'd have to. Failure was not an option. Somehow, I had to make sure she was safe, both from my own course of action and from her father's disdain. It might complicate things, but I owed her that much.

As I basked in the glow of her smile, I started to think I probably owed her much, much more.

To my dismay, Kat wiped the floor with me through a dozen hands of rummy, but I managed to even the score when we switched to blackjack. Though I'd tried to teach her how to play poker a handful of times in our youth, she flat out refused to play against me, citing my ability to read her too easily for her to have any chance at beating me.

"Fine," I said, watching her shuffle the deck as competently as a casino dealer. "Your turn to pick the game. What are we playing next?"

Her reply was swift and assured. "Bullshit."

"That's not even a real card game," I protested, scowling, but she wouldn't be swayed. I dealt the cards, glaring all the while. "It makes no sense that you can't bluff to save your life when it comes to poker, but you can lie without a twitch in this game."

In response, Kat just smiled sweetly before turning her attention to organizing her hand. Since it was only the two of us, we removed a dozen cards from the deck in order to keep things interesting. I studied her intently during each turn, but she had no visible tell. Somehow, every time I lied, she was able to call me out on it with no hesitation, even when I was sure I hadn't reacted.

I was convinced she could read my mind, so I planted a few naughty images there just in case.

Her winning streak might have been infuriating if I'd been able to summon anything more than mild annoyance, which I played up outwardly for her benefit. Inside, I rejoiced at the experience. The brilliance of her grin when she got away with lying hit me square in the chest every time, no matter how I braced myself for it.

This was the Kat I remembered, the one who found joy in the simplest of things, who never hesitated to give herself over to the moment. That trademark impulsivity had been buried underneath a layer of rigid routine in adulthood, and relief swept through my limbs to learn it hadn't been fully quashed.

I couldn't quite tear my gaze away from her face. With the sunlight shining in the window, I noted each tiny freckle scattered across her nose, admired the way her long lashes curled against her cheeks, traced that delicious curve of her lips as she smiled over the cards at me.

*Stunning.*

I wished I had enough artistic talent to recreate that image—what a fitting companion it would be for the painting of my ancestor. From the stories passed down in my family from one generation to the next about Céleste Bicardeau, she was a woman filled with *joie de vivre,* in possession of a buoyancy that captivated those around her. That quality was something Kat had in abundance.

By the time she won her third round, I tossed down the cards. "I give up."

"Uh-uh, Nico," she sang. "You know what you have to do. Time for the Loser Song."

The force of my glare should have incinerated her, but she simply folded her hands on the table and waited.

"I am *not* going through the humiliation you insisted on heaping on me when you were twelve," I informed her. "There will be no singing, no dancing, and sure as shit no groveling."

When she pouted at me, I rose from my chair and stalked toward her. Kat eyed my approach, keeping perfectly still except for the flush creeping along her cheekbones. As I braced my hands on the arms of her chair and leaned close, she held her breath and had to tip her head back to meet my eyes.

I captured her gaze for a long moment, enjoying the way her tongue darted nervously out to run over her lower lip, the way her breath tickled my chin. Then I bent lower and slid my cheek along hers to murmur in her ear.

"Oh, Kitten. You are the least gracious winner I've ever met."

A choked laugh erupted past her pretty pink lips, but Kat dropped her head against the seat back and glared as I drew back.

"And you, sir, are a tease," she said primly.

Though dozens of potential responses floated through my head, all I could think to say was, "Teasing is all part of the fun."

Kat scowled, but it couldn't disguise her shiver of reaction. I smirked and, as a result, she closed her eyes until I moved away. When I returned, I set two bottles of water down on the table and slid back into my chair. Her expression changed as she sipped at the water, a calculating gleam appearing in her eyes.

I gazed suspiciously at her as I took a pull from my bottle. "I know that look. What are you plotting?"

She flashed a brilliant smile. "Plotting? Not a thing. So, my father will get his first message from you—then what? When do you demand the trade?"

"Are you that eager to get away from me? I'm hurt."

"Shut up," she muttered, rolling her eyes toward the ceiling.

I laced my hands behind my head, watching her gaze drop to the sculpted biceps that had most definitely not existed when we were in high school, and grinned at her.

"I won't know until he responds, but I imagine he'll want to do some digging first, mostly to make sure you're actually missing. Then I'll lay out the terms."

"So another comfortable night on your trusty sofa, huh?" she asked, her face the very picture of innocence.

"I thought you'd never ask," I drawled. "As a matter of fact, I was thinking I'd better keep a closer eye on you. Since I'm perfectly capable of keeping my hands to myself, I decided to take you up on that offer to share the bed."

Kat blinked at me in surprise. "Oh, you think so, do you?" she managed finally, though it came out in a sweet little squeak.

My smile broadened. "I do think so, indeed. I assume *you* can keep your hands off of *me?*"

"I'm sure I can manage." She narrowed her eyes. "Why the change of heart?"

"We're both responsible adults. I've known you most of our lives. And that fucking couch is the most uncomfortable piece of furniture I've ever had the misfortune of sleeping on."

Though I said it with complete sincerity, I let my eyes stroke over her features as I spoke. By the time my gaze landed on her mouth, lush and rosy, she smiled slyly.

I didn't trust that smirk for a single second.

There was no doubt in my mind that she was plotting something, regardless of her protests to the contrary. I would have to steel myself against her considerable charms, keep the ball in my court.

When it came to Katherine Willoughby, that was always the best course of action.

We spent the rest of the day lounging around the cabin, watching old DVDs, eating sandwiches, and throwing popcorn at each other as the evening wore on. By the end of the second movie, Kat was half asleep where she lay curled at one end of the couch. I switched off the television and held out a hand to tug her to her feet.

Neither of us said much as we prepared for bed, though I eyed her suspiciously when I came out of the bathroom and found her nestled under the covers already with her eyes closed. I turned off the lights and slipped into the other side of the bed, waiting for her to speak—or to make her move. It wouldn't surprise me if she simply reached out to take what she wanted. Every muscle in my body coiled in anticipation.

Instead, she sighed softly and murmured, "Goodnight, Nico."

For a moment, I stayed silent, staring up at the ceiling, then I rolled my head to the side to look at her. "Goodnight, Kitten."

Sometime before dawn, I jolted awake. A flash of annoyance shot through me, given that my dream—featuring Kat wearing very little clothing—was about to take an erotic turn. It was followed by a bolt of panic, thinking maybe an alert that one of the cameras scattered around the property spotted something had woken me.

I grabbed my phone from the bedside table and quickly scrolled through the camera feeds, but there were no notifications and I saw nothing of concern in any of the footage, not even a raccoon or deer passing through.

Just as I set the phone down again, I heard a soft whimper and realized that must have been the sound that had pulled me from the dream.

Carefully, I rolled back onto my side to face Kat. She was perfectly still, curled in a tight little ball with the blanket clutched under her chin. After a moment, another quiet whimper slipped past her lips.

"Hey," I said softly, setting my hand against her shoulder. "Hey, it's okay. Wake up, Kat."

She didn't flail or thrash, but her eyelids squeezed tight and she shook her head slightly. I gave her shoulder a gentle shake and her eyes suddenly flew wide, black discs against the pale oval of her face. She blinked owlishly for a minute before finally focusing on my face.

"Nico?"

"You were having a bad dream," I murmured, brushing her hair back from her forehead. "Do you want to tell me about it?"

She shook her head more definitely this time, then opened and closed her mouth twice before whispering, "No, I just . . ."

A trembling breath passed her lips and I couldn't help myself—I held open my arms. "Come here. I'll keep the nightmares away."

Without a word, she immediately scooted against my side to lay her head on my chest. I laced my fingers with hers at the center of my abdomen and ran my other hand gently up and down her arm, avoiding the bandage I'd wrapped around it earlier.

Though she didn't speak again, she nestled in, her ear resting against my heart. Something about that felt so intensely *right* that I had to keep myself from tightening my arms.

I couldn't tell when she drifted back to sleep, but her tension slowly eased, her breath evening out as her body softened against me. What I did notice was the contentment that seeped through my own limbs as I held her.

Like everything I needed was right here in this room.

I fell asleep with her hand still clasped in mine and my other arm tucked snugly around her.

## Chapter Seven

### Kat

When I awoke the next morning, sunlight peeked around the edges of the curtains. I was curled against Nico, my head still on his chest, my palm resting against rock solid abs. Though I vaguely remembered him holding my hand there, in sleep he'd flung that arm up above his head on the pillow.

I tilted my chin carefully to keep from waking him as I studied his features.

A faint growth of stubble shadowed the line of his jaw, making me itch to run my fingertips over it. He looked younger, more vulnerable, and terribly handsome with a lock of black hair tumbling across his forehead. The way his arm curved over his head revealed sleek, corded muscles that caused my pulse to trip over itself.

*Been doing more than just programming computers. What else has he been up to?*

He was as beautiful as ever, but I definitely appreciated the maturity of this look over his gangly adolescence or lean teenage years. A low hum vibrated against my cheek as he cracked open one eye to peer down at me.

"Morning," he said, his voice gravelly with sleep. "No more nightmares?"

I snuggled back down against his chest. "No, you really did keep them away. Sorry I woke you."

Though he tucked his bent arm behind his head, his other hand lifted to stroke lightly over my hair. I closed my eyes and tried to keep myself from uttering the appreciative murmur that rose in my throat.

For a moment, I thought I'd succeeded, but then he chuckled softly. "Are you purring, Kitten?"

"No," I grumbled.

When he laughed again, I buried my face against his neck. He made a soft sound that reverberated deep in his chest, beckoning me closer.

Maybe his resistance was lower than I thought.

I'd enjoyed a reasonably active sex life until the past year or two, when the business had taken over most of my free time and all of my mental energy. Combining that dry spell with the intensity of my desire for Nico was like tossing a match into a puddle of gasoline.

I knew he was a talented flirt, but I was no amateur, not anymore. It was clear his intention was to avoid getting involved with me, at least beyond his role as a criminal mastermind or however he saw himself now. As far as I was concerned, he'd involved himself enough when he set this plan in motion. Could he really blame me if I took the opportunity to wear down his resistance?

There were only so many card games one could play in the course of a weekend.

He said it could take a few days to work out the details of this whole debacle, so I had plenty of time. Knowing him, he'd be expecting me to make a move immediately—impulsive little Kat, ever impatient. I'd gotten him into trouble too many times to count by leaping before I looked.

*Joke's on you, darling Nico,* I thought, enjoying the feel of his heartbeat against my ear.

It would be much better to wait until he dropped his guard, or at least until anticipation began to get the better of him. No matter how impetuous I tended to be, I was perfectly capable of patience.

There was something intensely intimate about lying there with him, even though we were both fully clothed. In his arms, against his hard body, my limbs felt soft and languid. He continued to trail his fingertips through the wispy curls that had come loose from my ponytail during the night, and though I didn't make a sound this time, I melted against him.

When I swept my thumb in a tiny arc across his stomach, I felt him trying to stay still, to keep quiet, but each little movement ratcheted up the tension in those impressive muscles underneath my hand.

He managed to hold it together for another minute before shifting to face me, then he caught my chin in his free hand, stared long and hard at my lips, and said, "You're killing me, Kat."

Whether it was the low tenor of his voice, the husky quality of the words, or his use of my actual name, the statement ignited a ball of fire low in my belly. My gaze caught on his mouth before I managed to drag it to his dark eyes, burning with the same intensity that thrummed through the fingers touching my jaw.

I lifted my hand to his face, exploring the sharp planes under a rough shadow of beard, the contour of his cheekbone, the arch of a dark, smooth brow. For so much of my youth, he'd been my best friend in all the world. It was strange and wonderful to explore the man he was.

And Christ, the way he looked at me had my entire body ready to burst into flame.

"This is a bad idea," he said in a hoarse whisper, but the statement had no strength behind it.

I didn't bother to acknowledge it, just shifted up against the pillows so that my lips were close enough to torment his with each whisper of breath. His fingers slid along my cheek, then around to cup the back of my neck. For a heartbeat, he held me there, his eyes locked on mine as he kept me captive without a single ounce of force.

Just when I started to think he might pull away, might refuse to take the next natural step, he growled, "To hell with it," and brought his mouth to mine.

This kiss was heat and light and wave upon wave of emotion crashing over me, over both of us. My fingers clenched in the front of his shirt as I struggled to stay afloat.

Neither my teenage fantasies nor my more mature imaginings could possibly prepare me for the reality of kissing Nico Beaumont. Was it really only moments ago that I'd noted how perfectly we fit together? Kissing him now made it clear on an entirely new level as he tilted my jaw for a better angle. My breasts pressed snugly against his chest and I tangled one leg over his hip as our lips and tongues collided in a heated choreography.

All it took was a single kiss and Nico managed to obliterate the world outside of this intimate little bubble. Each sweep of his tongue and graze of teeth sent me spiraling into a completely different orbit.

A soft, frantic sound tore from my throat, spurring him to take the kiss deeper—though I doubted if he'd intended to let it go this far. Part of me thought he only meant to warn me away from this very thing before drawing back.

The rest of me laughed that idea into the next county.

His hand swept down my body to grasp my hip, tugging my pelvis flush against his, then his palm slid around to cup the swell of my ass.

That was all the invitation I needed. I rocked my hips against him, rejoicing in the clear evidence of his arousal. He growled against my mouth, but his fingers tightened into my flesh, holding me there, letting the heat between my legs sear us both.

When I gasped, breaking the kiss, his mouth cruised slowly along my jaw and down my neck as he shifted to balance on one elbow above me.

"God, you're soft," he murmured, rubbing his rough cheek over my collarbone and sending bolts of sensation rocketing through me.

I arched under him as his lips explored my throat and his free hand rose to toy with the top button of my pajama shirt. When his mouth covered mine once more, a single finger traced slowly back and forth along the skin above the cotton neckline.

Just as he slipped that first button free, his phone let out a series of staccato chirps. Nico dropped his forehead to my sternum with a groan.

"You cannot be serious," I breathed.

Nico's expression tightened, like he wasn't sure whether to laugh or cry. All of his muscles tensed to the point of quivering and the heat of his skin through that thin layer of cotton burned me like a brand.

"The universe hates me," he mumbled against my chest.

I hooked a leg around his waist and grabbed onto his face with both hands. "No! No, ignore the phone, Nico. That's an order. It can wait ten minutes."

A slow smile curved his lips. "Oh, Kitten, I'll need a lot longer than ten minutes with you. I've got a lifetime of fantasies to play out."

"I don't know how you can say things like that and then leave me here to suffer," I said, scowling. "It's inhumane."

Nico rolled his hips, watching as my eyes fluttered, smirking at my soft moan. I wasn't sure whether I wanted to punch him or strip him naked.

Probably both.

"This *thing* between us," he said, grinning when I opened my eyes to give him a pointed glare at the innuendo, "I'm done denying it. I want you, you want me. Believe me, this is just a temporary interruption. I intend to finish what we started."

I shut my eyes again and flung my arms wide with a frustrated groan. "Fine. Go."

He started to roll off of me, then dropped his head and nuzzled one nipple through the fabric of my shirt. My blood heated back to a rolling boil.

"Don't go anywhere," he whispered.

Though I was tempted to flip him the bird in response to that, I managed to refrain, instead simply listening to his footsteps as he left the bedroom. The man was positively masterful. After the intensity of that kiss, I had no doubt that he would prove himself an expert in the rest. My entire body had turned to liquid heat—certain parts more liquid than others.

Maybe there was some benefit to waiting until we weren't angsty, inexperienced teens anymore.

When he didn't return after several minutes, I groaned and rolled out of bed. I padded into the living room and found him sitting on the couch, frowning at his laptop. He shot me a cursory glance, then focused on the computer screen again.

"Trouble in kidnapper paradise?" I asked, cocking one hip against the doorframe.

"Just one of my monitoring programs," he muttered, fingers flying across the keyboard.

"Monitoring for what? My father?"

I crossed my arms over my chest and when he looked over again, his gaze lingered on the flesh forced upward to gather just where he'd unbuttoned my top only moments ago. I tried to hide a triumphant smirk.

"Ah. No. Keyword alerts. Mentions of the painting," he said, distracted, then his mouth snapped shut.

I straightened, the puzzle pieces finally clicking into place. My arms fell to my sides as I stared at him in horror. "The painting. He took the painting?"

Nico scrubbed a hand over his jaw. "So you do remember it."

"Of course I remember it," I snapped, but my frustration was short-lived. "Your father told me that story for the first time when I was eight years old. He found me hiding in the garden after I tore the stupid dress my mother insisted I wear for some party and he brought me back to the cottage for milk and cookies."

A swift jolt of grief crossed Nico's face, and I felt it echo in my own chest. Those moments had meant more to me than any time spent with my father, not that he'd offered much. In the Beaumont home, I'd learned what it meant to be part of a family. It had been my escape, a dream world where love lived on even after tragedy.

"I have to get it back," Nico said, looking grim and as determined as ever.

"Nicolas Beaumont, you can't seriously be hoping to bargain me for the goddamn painting!"

"It's the only way."

"Look, I know how much it means to your family, and I agree that it absolutely belongs to you. But he's not going to trade it. Not for me, not for anything. If he took it, he had a reason."

He shook his head. "He has to. It's a family heirloom. I have to get it back."

I wasn't sure whether to laugh or cry at the stubborn look on his face, but everything inside me softened in response to his predicament.

"Oh, Nico. I know it is. But this . . . it's not going to work, and he's going to know it's you."

"No, he won't. I planned it all out. This has to work. It's all I have left of my father." His voice broke and I went to sit on the couch beside him.

"I know, and I'll help you get it from him, but this particular plan is going to backfire," I said softly, looping my arm around his shoulders.

While he remained silent, my mind whirled with a series of progressively darker images involving my father's hired goons dragging Nico into the woods, beating him, leaving him for dead. I'd heard the stories—it was impossible to live in Spruce Hill and *not* hear whispers of how the self-appointed king had slowly conquered his adversaries, both personal and professional.

There might not be proof, but I'd heard enough snippets from behind closed doors in my childhood to believe it all, starting with that night under the desk. His mistress's husband had started getting suspicious, and he'd gone missing. Getting on Aidan Willoughby's bad side was dangerous, even fatal.

I couldn't let it happen. I'd just found Nico again. I couldn't lose him now.

"Look, why don't we take a nice hot shower and then make some breakfast? We can talk it all through over waffles," I suggested, keeping my voice low and calm.

When he turned his face toward me, eyebrows lifted, I tangled my fingers in his hair and kissed him, hard and swift. For once, I hoped he couldn't read the thoughts galloping through my head.

"Right. That's a sound plan," he mumbled against my lips.

I smiled and stood. "I have to brush out this tangled mess," I said, gesturing to my hair as I started toward the bedroom and prayed he wouldn't question the weak excuse. "Get the water going, would you? I'll meet you in there."

With that, I blew a kiss over my shoulder and shut the door behind me.

# Chapter Eight

## KAT

Once I reached the bedroom, I brushed out my hair even as my mind raced through the options before me. I listened to the sound of the water turning on in the bathroom, waited for an interminable minute to tick past on the bedroom clock, then swiftly and silently dressed.

I couldn't do it, couldn't stay here playing house with him, all the while knowing Nico was about to put himself in the line of fire the moment he made contact with my father. It was clear as day he wouldn't allow me to sway him from this idiotic plan.

Even if going through with it would put his life at risk.

My heart clenched in my chest. I didn't know if Nico had ever put it together, the conversation we overheard in the office that night and the mangled body found nearly three years later, but that was only the tip of the iceberg when it came to the rumors.

The best thing I could do was get the hell out of there and put as much distance between us as possible, for Nico's own protection.

If he didn't have me to bargain with, he should be safe enough. Hell, maybe I could get the painting for him on my own. If I could sneak out of my father's house as I had so many times in my teenage years, surely I could sneak back in and grab the artwork off the wall.

I would do whatever it took to keep Nico from putting himself in that kind of danger.

In under two minutes, I was dressed in my own clothes and tiptoeing out into the living room. I slung my purse across my chest, then grabbed my jacket, a granola bar from a box on the kitchen counter, and a bottle of water from the fridge before slipping out the door.

Hiking wasn't really my area of expertise, but I knew better than to set off without any food or water. Unfortunately, I wasn't sure how far we were from civilization. Hopefully not as far as the woods made it seem, because I didn't have a backpack to fill with more supplies.

The morning air was cool, though the sky was clear, and I thought I had a fairly good recollection of the path we'd taken the day before. I would need to pace myself, but since my head start was vital, I started off at a jog. It wouldn't take Nico long to figure out I was gone—a few more minutes, maybe? I needed to take advantage of every second to put some distance between us.

Of course, beyond that, I hadn't a clue what would happen next. I had no idea where the cabin was located, only that I hadn't seen any others during our outing the previous day. No signs of life, no indication of where the hell I was or how far it might be between here and home.

A web of tiny fractures spread within my chest, a heartbreak so poignant I couldn't hold back a strangled sob as I ran. Only the determination to protect Nico drove me on when I wanted nothing more than to curl up in a ball and weep.

*So close.* I'd been so close to finally getting what I'd longed for my entire life, but I couldn't sit there and wait for him to paint a target on his own back.

Nico was, at the very heart of him, the most honorable person I'd ever known. It was just like him to assume everyone else would act with honor, when I knew for a fact that my father would go to the ends of the earth to defend against an insult like losing something he considered his.

Why had he stolen it?

The question rattled inside my head as I ran until a stitch in my side forced me to slow to a walk.

"Oh, shit," I muttered, then made my feet keep moving.

I considered myself in reasonably good shape, but clearly I was wrong. With a vow to start exercising more frequently, maybe something more strenuous than yoga, I trotted along, weaving between trees along a path I prayed led toward the creek.

With my sense of time and direction now distorted by the endless trees surrounding my position, I guessed fifteen or twenty minutes had passed before I heard the distant sound of Nico yelling my name.

I froze for a second, listening, but he didn't sound terribly close. My heart hammered so loudly in my chest that I was afraid I wouldn't hear him coming even if he did manage to reduce the distance my head start had given me.

After another few minutes, the trees opened up before me so suddenly I almost stumbled. Instead of the creek, a steep, rocky incline rose in front of me, stretching like a wall as far as I could see in either direction. Another shout pierced the silence behind me, this one sounding much closer, and I swore colorfully as I scrambled up the rocks.

If the short stints of running had convinced me I was out of shape, trying to scale the incline made me feel like a helpless infant.

"Damn, damn, damn, damn," I muttered, turning the word into a mantra.

This was nothing like the movies. Each crumbling fingerhold took impossibly long for me to locate and even longer for me to use to haul my body another incremental inch upward. A branch sprouted from the split rock a few feet from the top—I focused on it with single-minded determination.

If I could reach that branch, I could use it to pull myself to the top.

"Go, go, go," I chanted, biting back a shriek when my left hand slipped and a spray of sediment rained down onto my face.

I closed my eyes just in time to keep the dirt out. Nico had stopped yelling my name, which I hoped meant he'd moved in another direction. This climb was taking far too long.

By the time I wrapped the fingers of my right hand around the tree branch, every muscle in my body trembled in protest. From there, it was only a short distance to the top, but I made the mistake of glancing down and realized my hands were clinging to the rockface ten or twelve feet from the ground.

The drop wouldn't kill me, but the thought of losing that painstaking progress made me want to weep. I'd just managed to swing my other hand over the branch when I heard Nico stumble to a halt somewhere behind me.

"Jesus, Kat," he gasped when he caught sight of me dangling against the rocks.

For a moment, I froze, unable—and unwilling—to turn my head to look at him, then I lifted one leg and braced my foot against a tiny ledge to boost myself up another twelve inches or so. If I could just get the other foot up, I'd be high enough to throw my body over the branch and hope it held my weight. From there, reaching the top would be simple.

If I let myself think about how much less time it would probably take Nico and all his impressive muscles to climb up after me, I would cry.

"Kitten," Nico called, his voice gentle as he slowly approached. "You've gone far enough. Let me help you down."

"Not a chance," I ground out, then I muffled a whimper as my fingers cramped.

Though the words were soft, I distinctly heard Nico mutter, "Stubborn as ever."

When I glanced over my shoulder at him, I saw he was out of breath from running after me, his arms and neck scratched from dodging through the underbrush. I refused to feel bad for putting him through that.

A few more inches, that was all I needed.

I managed to find a foothold, adjusted my grip, and tried to propel myself upward, but the rock crumbled beneath my boot and I dropped until my arms were fully extended, painfully wrenching both shoulders as the wound on my arm reopened and warm blood seeped along my skin.

The cry of dismay was past my lips before I could stop it.

"Kat, please," Nico said, standing below me.

My boots swung just above his head. He reached up to touch my ankle and I kicked out at him so hard he had to back up a few steps to avoid taking a boot to the face.

It was clear to us both that I was just about at the end of my endurance, I knew that when he stepped aside and planted his hands on his hips to wait me out. Sweat trickled down my temple, mingling with dust from the rock debris. If I fell now, the tumble would hurt like hell, but if I made it to the top, Nico might not be able to catch up to me again. The chance of losing him in the forest was both terrifying and exhilarating.

From the way my arms shook as I managed to crawl another few inches upward, the choice was very likely in the hands of fate at this point. Nico just stood there, watching, probably planning to catch me when I finally lost my grip.

It'd serve him right if I flattened him on my way down.

I would rather chop off my arm than admit defeat in front of him, but I was beginning to suspect this venture was doomed. If my arms gave out and I fell, I'd have very little control over the landing. If I accepted his assistance, I might save myself from bodily injury, though my pride was another story.

"Let me help you," Nico said softly, as though he'd heard my thoughts.

"I can't," I replied, the words coming out in a hoarse whimper. Even if I wanted to agree, I didn't think I could move my arms enough to let go.

With experience born of a lifetime spent saving me from various scrapes, Nico understood exactly what I meant. The bottom of the incline was a little less steep than the section I'd managed to make it to, so he leaned forward and picked his way up a few feet, until my knees were just above his head. Carefully, he wrapped one hand around my calf.

"Give me a second. Once I have a good hold on you, you can just let go. I'll catch you. Everything's going to be okay, I promise."

My response was a muffled snort. I didn't kick him again, which was as close to agreement as he was going to get. It took longer than a second, but his presence beside me was comforting, even if my sweaty palms kept slipping. By the time I felt his arm hook firmly around the back of my knees, I was afraid I wouldn't be able to wait for his signal.

"Come on, Kitten, let go," he said. "I'm going to try to keep you from tearing your skin against the rocks as you come down, okay?"

His grip on the wall didn't seem terribly secure, but he had a hold of my legs, at least. Before I could make a conscious decision to let go, my left hand slid loose of its own volition, so I closed my eyes and let go with my right as well.

For a brief second, my body slid down along his and it seemed like we would make it out of this unscathed. Then the momentum caused Nico to lose his footing on the loose rocks. He tumbled backward even as he clutched me against the safety of his chest.

The impact of us both striking the forest floor forced the air from his lungs in an audible rush. I landed on top of him, my head bouncing hard against his sternum as we hit the ground, then I scrambled onto my knees beside him. He lay still as death, eyes closed.

Terror rocketed through me, stealing my breath.

"Oh shit," I gasped, framing his face with my hands. "Shit, shit, shit. Please don't be dead. Don't be dead, Nico, open your eyes! Please, please don't be dead."

I released his face to run my hands over his skull, his arms, his ribcage, whispering the plea over and over until a harsh sob tore from my throat. Nico peeled his eyes open, caught my wrists in one hand, and tugged until I was sprawled across him once more. With a groan, he closed his eyes again.

"I appreciate your concern, Kitten, but I'm very much alive."

# Chapter Nine

## NICO

I EXPECTED HER TO respond with anger, to give me a taste of that fierce temper of hers, raging against me and my interference. What I didn't expect was for her to start trembling in my arms, the shudders intensifying until her whole body was wracked with sobs as she clung to me.

My back hurt from the fall, but it was the ache in my chest that threatened to overwhelm me now. With soft, murmured reassurances, I wrapped my arms around her and held tight while her tears soaked into my shirt.

After a moment, I carefully sat up, swallowing a groan of pain as I drew her onto my lap and cradled her against my chest.

"Hey, it's okay. We're both okay," I whispered, pressing my lips to the top of her head. "We're okay, I promise."

Tremors still ricocheted through her, but between the soothing words and the way she nuzzled her face into the pulse at my throat, the sobs seemed to have slowly worked their way out her system.

"I can't," she whispered. "I just can't..."

I waited for her to continue, but she simply shook her head and burrowed closer to me, so I prompted, "Can't what?"

Silence stretched for so long, I was sure she wasn't going to answer me.

"I lost you once, Nico, long before you even left. I can't lose you again."

Oh. *Oh.*

It hit me like a ton of bricks. She'd taken off from the cabin because she was worried about *me?* Risked getting lost in the middle of the woods for *my* sake? I struggled to wrap my mind around it, even as thick curls of warmth wound their way through my chest.

"I'm right here," I murmured against her ear. "I'm not going anywhere."

"You don't understand," she said dully, like the tears had washed all the emotion right out of her. "He's dangerous. More dangerous than you can imagine."

I swallowed my instinctive response, which was to assure her I could take care of myself, and instead tightened my arms around her limp frame and said, "I'll be okay, Kitten."

"You must have heard the stories," she whispered.

Oh, I'd heard them. I'd even pursued a few of them, wondering if there was any way to leverage knowledge of a crime for the painting, but there was never any proof. At least, no proof that wasn't already contained within the painting itself. Either the rumors were blown out of proportion, or Aidan Willoughby was a criminal mastermind.

I was inclined to believe the latter, which meant Kat was absolutely right.

"Please don't risk your life for this." Her voice broke on the plea, her body curling protectively into mine.

"Okay."

The word tore from my chest, searing a path from my heart straight through my ribcage. Losing the painting for good would be devastating in itself, but failing to retrieve the drive my father had hidden inside wasn't an option, especially now that I'd pulled Kat into this mess.

When it came to my own safety, I could brush off potential danger—hers? I couldn't chance it.

That drive contained something, some information my father had become privy to, something that I imagined must be evidence against Aidan Willoughby. If he thought I might have another copy, I was dead.

If he linked Kat to me in the meantime? Her life could be at stake, too.

She tipped her head back to look up at me. "Okay? That's it?"

Fuck, she was beautiful, even with dust and dirt coating the better part of what I could see of her. That burning in my chest eased bit by bit as I stared down into those big blue eyes.

"That's it," I agreed, nodding. "We'll find another way. I swear to you I will not make a single move without your approval. Can we go back to the cabin and discuss this after that hot shower we never got? I think we could both use it now."

She had the decency to blush a pretty pink under the layer of grime. "Right. Sorry about that."

I swiped a thumb across her cheek to better see the color. My thoughts had been scattered back at the cabin, bouncing between an image of Kat, sudsy and dripping, and the alerts from my computer. Letting her distract me in the shower would've given me time to assess the situation before deciding on our next move.

The monitoring I'd set up had caught chatter from art collectors about convincing Willoughby to sell—if they succeeded and the painting changed hands, I would never get it back. I didn't have anywhere near the funds needed to buy it, and even if I did, I suspected Willoughby would rather go broke than let the painting fall back into the hands of the little French brat he'd come to despise over the years.

And knowing the type of people he might sell to, I sure as shit didn't want my father's "leverage" ending up in the wrong hands.

Forcing Willoughby to give it up in exchange for his daughter might have ensured I had it back in my hands before he sold it, but Kat was right—while she'd be in no danger from me, no matter how it went down, both of us would have targets on our backs if we went through with it.

And, for her protection, I'd need to back off, stay away from her, so Willoughby had no reason to think she'd been in on it. Just the thought of putting distance between us made my chest ache all over again.

Could I really hurt her like that after just getting her back?

With the ransom plan off the table, I might have to steal the damn thing. And as soon as Willoughby imagined there was any risk of losing it, security would be locked up tight.

Still, if Kat was willing to risk her own life to save mine by disappearing into the woods, I would need to figure something out. I'd been so worried about putting her in danger that I hadn't given any thought to her doing it on her own.

I should've known better than to expect the ordinary out of this extraordinary woman.

The moment I realized she'd bolted had filled me with a near-paralyzing fear, not for the failure of my plan, but for her safety. The cabin was miles from everything, including neighbors, which was why I'd bought it years ago in a quest for solitude. Even if she'd picked the right direction—and managed to stick to it—it might've taken her days to hike out of the forest.

The terrifying images in my mind had nearly brought me to my knees before I forced myself to buck the hell up and rushed out the door after her.

"Come on," I said gently, helping her to her feet before climbing to my own. "I'm too old for this."

Kat's startled laughter brought a smile to my face, but before we started back toward the cabin, I set my hands on her shoulders and studied her. She winced slightly when I ran my palms down her arms to take her hands.

"I think I reopened that cut," she mumbled.

I grimaced. "We're in good shape, both of us. I'll take a look at it when we get home."

Fortunately, I knew the woods better than she did, and the direct route toward the cabin only took us twenty minutes of slow trudging. I could tell Kat was distracted by pain and exhaustion when she barely managed a scowl upon realizing just how much time she'd wasted in her aimless trek.

"I was shooting for the creek," she muttered, pausing to drum up enough energy to climb the three stairs to the cabin's front door.

"Veered too far north," I replied. "You were always shit with directions."

She shot me a quick glare, but I only grinned and took her elbow to help her up the steps. I paused in the living room just long enough to delete the scheduled message that would've reached her father a few hours later, then ushered her into the bathroom.

We were both aching and filthy, but my breath stalled in my lungs when she tugged her tattered tank top over her head. Even with angry scrapes marring her skin, blood seeping through the gauze around her arm, and streaks of dirt decorating her cheeks, she was so beautiful I could barely think straight. She'd just turned to toss her shirt aside when she caught me staring at her.

A rueful smile tugged at her lips. "I guess this morning's ship has sailed, huh?"

I knew I should agree, avert my eyes and nudge her into the shower alone, but I couldn't. Instead, I cupped her cheek in my hand and dropped a gentle kiss to her lips.

"Only until it doesn't hurt to move," I replied.

"Well, that much we can agree on. I think my arms are just about useless."

I managed to keep my eyes off her breasts, covered by pale blue lace, and turned her so I could unwrap the bandage from her arm. Only a small section of the cut had opened, presumably during her heroic monkey bar routine on that branch, but I cleaned it with antiseptic before tipping my head toward the shower.

"Go on, get in. It's going to take me a few minutes to bend far enough to get my jeans off."

It looked like she was about to offer her assistance, then she snapped her mouth shut and turned away to remove the bra and her black jeans, which she'd obviously decided were a better option to flee in than oversized sweatpants. I tried to focus on removing my own clothes, but then I saw the reflection of her bare back in the mirror as she stepped behind the shower curtain.

Certain parts of my body disagreed rather vehemently with the assessment that further relations needed to wait.

When had a woman's back ever intrigued me like that? The sleek curve of muscle on either side of her spine, the indent of her waist, the flare of those soft, generous hips—fuck, I was like a horny teenager all over again, still lusting after Katherine Willoughby.

*Plus ça change, plus c'est la même chose.*

My father's favorite phrase nudged at my brain as I leaned on the counter beside the sink and closed my eyes, trying hard to control myself in an attempt to not greet Kat with a raging erection.

From within the billowing steam of the shower, she gave a sharp gasp that went a good way toward quelling my arousal.

"Everything okay?" I called, kicking off my jeans faster than I'd thought possible.

"Yes, the water just stung for a second," she replied as I opened the curtain to join her.

Her mouth dropped open as she gave my naked body a slow once over, but she managed to shut it as I stepped in. With obvious effort, she forced her eyes to my face, smirking when she caught me in the same struggle.

She was nothing less than perfection. The coating of dust and dirt didn't even begin to detract from the fact that this woman was a dream come true. Our gazes locked and held for another beat, then I allowed myself a second perusal of her bare skin, watched as a pretty blush spread across her chest and cheeks, caught the way her breath lifted her breasts like an offering before me.

With immense effort, I kept myself from reaching for them and offered a crooked grin instead. "Turn around. I'll wash your back. You look like you took a bath in those rocks."

Shockingly, she did as instructed without any of the clever little quips I'd expect from her. My hands came down gently on her shoulders, smoothing away the layer of dust as water streamed over her skin. It would've been stunningly erotic if not for the pain radiating along my limbs, but when Kat let her head fall forward and allowed me to take care of her, I was overwhelmed by a flood of affection.

Even if landing flat on my back was certainly not the highlight of my day so far, I imagined she felt far worse after her climb. It had taken me too long to locate her, meaning she'd probably been trying to tough it out longer than she would admit.

I pressed my thumbs into the muscles just below her neck, easing the tension with firm circles until she dropped her chin to her chest and made a soft sound of pleasure.

In silence, I worked my way down her back, coaxing the sore muscles back to life even as I tried to ignore my reaction to the way she arched and swayed into my touch. When I paused to add another squirt of body wash to my palm, Kat peeked over her shoulder at me.

"You're good at this," she said.

I grinned and started back at her shoulders, this time moving my hands slowly down her arms. A tiny hiss escaped her lips when I rubbed her biceps, though I carefully avoided her injury. When I reached her hands, I laced our fingers together and tried to keep a respectful distance between us, no matter how much my own body complained about the space.

"You're stronger than you look. I thought for sure you were going to come crashing down any second from the moment I saw you hanging there. That was pretty impressive."

Kat snorted and leaned back against my chest, effectively ruining my gallant effort to hide my body's response to having her naked, glorious self so close.

"I'm sure it was pretty stupid, but it seemed like a good idea at the time."

I gave up on chivalry and rested my chin on her shoulder, finally allowing my gaze to drop so I could look down the front of her. A droplet of water rolled slowly from her collar bone over the swell of her breast, then clung for a second to the bud of her nipple before dripping downward.

"Well, shit."

"What?" she asked, turning her head to look at me.

The movement set her lips a fraction of an inch from my jaw. Her cheeks, already flushed from the steam, went scarlet.

"You have the most glorious breasts I've *ever* seen," I informed her, unabashedly watching as the dusky pink tips peaked under my gaze. "And my father was French. I've seen a lot of breasts in my life, you know."

She snorted a laugh and wiggled a little, like she could spur me to finally touch her, but my hands stayed right where they were, linked with hers. "If anticipation could kill, I'd have dropped dead by now, Nico."

"I told you teasing was all a part of it," I murmured, then my lips replaced my chin on her shoulder, brushing lightly back and forth across her wet skin.

I released one of her hands to wrap my arm across the soft swell of her stomach. One tug brought her body flush against mine. Kat dropped her head back onto my shoulder as my lips traveled up her neck to nuzzle her ear.

With my arm supporting her, she shifted her ass backward to cradle my cock, drawing a groan from deep inside me. When I lifted her other arm to hook it around the back of my neck, allowing me the freedom to slide my hand around to cup her breast, pleasure purred from her throat. My thumb circled her nipple and she arched, filling my hand.

"Oh, Kitten," I breathed against her ear.

*This way lies madness,* I thought, unable to keep from giving the same attention to her other breast.

Even as the hot water soothed my aching back, I didn't think I was in any shape to take her here, like this. God knew I wanted to—no, I *intended* to, when the time was right. Her body, wet and soapy and so fucking perfect under my hands, was everything I'd ever dreamed of and far, far more.

Kat gave another breathless cry when I rolled her nipple between my fingers, then I released her to stroke both hands soothingly down her sides before gripping her hips. With a gentle nudge, I set her away from me. She spun, ready to protest, but I gave her a knowing smirk, so she simply glared instead.

"Not here," I said, shaking my head. A spray of water droplets haloed my face. "If we're doing this now, it's going to be on that nice soft bed in the other room. This time, anyway. There will be plenty of time in the future for lifting you against this wall and driving into your hot, wet body."

I just hoped it was true—that we'd find our way through this mess with the painting and come out on the other side unscathed, with the rest of our lives stretching before us, because I didn't think any amount of time with Kat could ever be enough.

# Chapter Ten

## KAT

I SIGHED AS MY need spiraled higher, but then I nodded, taking the opportunity to let my gaze roam over Nico. Naked and dripping was an excellent look on him.

He was right about the bed, I would grant him that, so I kept my hands off him as I studied the way his sculpted shoulders topped that broad chest. His skin was dusted with dark hair that trailed down to the hard abdomen I'd stroked only hours ago.

And below that? The man was impressively equipped, no doubt of that. Desire flickered through my veins like electricity.

"If we don't get out of this shower right now, I'm going to ignore everything you just said and jump you right here, Nicolas."

There was no need to ask twice. Nico reached behind him to turn off the water, then caught the long strands of my wet hair in his fist and drew my mouth to his. I twined my arms around his neck, but after a moment he broke away, bundled me into a towel, and draped one carelessly around his hips.

"Now, this is a perfect look on you, Nico." It was only made better by the fact that I knew exactly what was hidden behind the thin layer of fabric.

"Let's go," he growled, grabbing my hand to tow me into the bedroom.

I practically skipped along behind him, laughing. He turned so abruptly that I crashed into him, but his arms locked around my waist as he captured my mouth once more. When my body sighed against his, he guided me down onto the bed, stretching out alongside me.

I couldn't remember anyone ever looking at me the way he did just then—intent, hungry, and utterly enthralled. The gleam of appreciation in his dark eyes brightened as he hooked his index finger between the knot in the towel and my skin, stroking in a teasing line between my breasts.

"This is what you want?" he asked, his voice low.

"Yes. Fuck yes. If your hands aren't on my naked body in ten seconds or less, I swear I'm going to turn violent."

"Only my hands?" Nico murmured.

He laughed softly at my scowl and tugged the towel loose, spreading the halves wide to reveal my skin, flushed pink from the hot shower. For a moment, his gaze caressed me, then he dropped his head to nuzzle the underside of one breast.

My entire body bowed beneath him when his teeth grazed my nipple. He grinned against my skin at the sound I made, something between a whimper and a moan.

"Should I take that to mean my mouth on your naked body is also acceptable?"

"Yes!" I gasped.

If I hadn't landed on top of him out there in the woods, I would never have guessed the man had taken a tumble so recently. He moved over me with all the grace of a jungle cat, his muscles bunching and coiling under my hands as I clung, unable to do anything but soak in the pleasure he lavished on my breasts.

By the time he returned to my mouth, I was trembling, this time in the best possible way. All the discomfort from my little escapade in the forest fled under his touch, and I assumed he must have felt the same when he propped himself on his elbow and drew my knee over his hip.

Dimly, I realized he still wore his towel, but when his palm roamed up the back of my thigh and around to cup the dark blonde curls between my legs, I promptly forgot everything else.

"Oh, Kitten," he groaned against my mouth. "So hot. So fucking wet. Do you have any idea how many times I've dreamed of this?"

I arched beneath him as his fingers parted my folds, stroked and circled until I was panting with need, then he slid one thick finger slowly into me. Why we'd both been wasting time dreaming about this separately instead of experiencing it together, I had no clue, but he was clearly not waiting for a verbal answer, since his teeth were now busy nipping at my lower lip.

In no time at all, I was sure he'd learned every intimate inch of me. His fingers, long and capable, teased and toyed, stroked and filled me until I writhed impatiently under him. All I could manage was a frantic whimper and a desperate tug at the towel between us.

Nico laughed, drew back until he stood at the side of the bed gazing down at me, and flung the towel to the floor. Flushed and breathless, I watched his eyes travel over me from head to toe and back again even as mine did the same to him.

"You are so beautiful," he said hoarsely, shaking his head slightly as though he couldn't believe his luck.

Slowly, he crawled back up my body, running his hands over my calves, catching the back of my knees to spread my legs wider. He paused halfway up, trailing his lips along the inner face of my thigh. When his tongue made the same exploration as his fingers, I choked out a strangled sound and my hips bucked off the bed.

His hands anchored me, holding me steady, but he'd brought me so close to the edge already that it only took a few focused sweeps of his tongue over my clit before I shattered against his mouth.

"Oh," I gasped, clutching one hand to my heart. "Oh, sweet lord. That mouth should be outlawed for the safety of humankind."

He pressed a laughing kiss to my hip bone and cocked his head up at me, looking altogether too pleased with himself. "You liked that, did you?"

I lifted my head to glare at him, then collapsed back onto the bed. "When you said you were a man of many talents, I didn't realize this was one of them or I would never have let you out of bed this morning. That would've saved us both a lot of trouble, you know."

His expression was one of pure satisfaction, along with more than a hint of smugness. He'd just settled beside me when my hand wrapped firmly around the base of his cock.

"I want *this*, Nico," I said pointedly.

He bit back a groan as my hand stroked firmly, just once, then I released him as my eyes shot to his face.

"Christ, what is it?" he asked hoarsely. "What's wrong?"

"You do have condoms out here in the middle of nowhere, right?"

"I do, yes, but I don't want you to think it's because I planned for this to happen," he said, rolling away again to grab them from one of the dresser drawers.

I turned onto my side, propping my head on one hand to watch him move across the room. Damn, but he looked good naked.

"You just happen to have them on hand for all the orgies you've been hosting out here in the boonies?" He shot me a sharp glance, as though trying to determine if I was serious, so I gave a slow smile. "Just teasing. I've been told it's all part of the fun, you know."

Nico tossed the unopened box of condoms onto the bedside table and leapt onto the bed, landing so I bounced right into him. He caught me, buried his face in my neck, and blew a raspberry against my skin.

"Okay, okay! I surrender," I yelped, laughing. I locked my fingers in his hair and drew him to me. "But I've had enough teasing."

The words came out sultry, breathless. He kissed me, deep and thorough, while his hand stroked down over my hip before reaching for a condom. I snatched it from his fingers, opened the package, and rolled it along his thick length, aware of every hitch in his breath along the way.

"Well, then," he murmured. "Far be it from me to contradict you."

He swirled his tongue over one nipple, then the other, humming at the soft sounds I couldn't possibly hold back. When I shifted restlessly beneath him, he settled himself between my legs and watched my face as he entered me with one long, slow thrust.

My lips parted on a sigh, then I hooked my ankles around his waist and threaded my fingers through his hair. With his eyes, dark as midnight and veiled under long lashes, focused completely on me, I felt like a goddess welcoming a supplicant.

Nico seemed more than happy to worship my body. It took every reserve of my self-control to let him set the pace, to resist the urge to hurry him along. For an instant, he stayed buried deep, his gaze stroking over my face.

Slowly, he began to move, withdrawing almost completely before thrusting home again. Every gasp, every moan, every purr that fell from my lips or rumbled low in my throat only served to make him seem more determined to prolong this.

I was drowning, or floating, or quite possibly both. The sensations he inspired both anchored me and guided me upward to another plane. I let him sweep me along as I clutched at his arms, dug my fingers into his shoulders, panted and writhed and marveled at his unending stamina and patience.

For his part, Nico seemed to be holding on by a thread, determined to wait until I hit another peak. When I whimpered against his lips, he must have known I was close. He gave two more slow, deep thrusts, then raised himself up on one elbow.

"Let go, Kitten. Come for me again," he whispered, adjusting the angle of his hips so he could reach a hand between us.

One stroke of his thumb was all it took after those dark, hoarse words. I arched, cried out, and clenched hard around him as the orgasm shook me. Nico groaned, burying his face in my neck. After a flurry of deep, hard thrusts, he shuddered through his own release and collapsed carefully onto me.

"Holy. Shit." I panted the words, curling my arms around him.

His low rumble of laughter tickled my throat. "I'll second that."

As soon as he caught his breath, he shifted off of me, took care of the condom, and drew me back into his arms. Limp with satisfaction, my entire body was infused with soft, relaxing warmth. I draped myself across his chest, one leg tangled in his, utterly boneless and languid in my bliss as he trailed his fingers lazily up and down my spine.

After a moment, I mumbled, "Not that your ego needs the boost, but you are very, very good at that."

"I've had a lot of years to think about it," he replied, "but reality exceeded every single fantasy."

For a long while, we stayed like that, cocooned in the quiet and the shared glow of satisfaction. A lifetime of childish daydreams and more mature fantasies still couldn't prepare me for the soul-deep contentment that seeped from every pore, coating every inch of my body.

This? This was worth the wait. It was worth *everything*.

Every moment of neglect, however benign, every second of loneliness, every ounce of rejection—Nico's careful attention swept it all away, like brushing cobwebs from the rafters.

Whether he'd planned to stay in my life after this was over or intended to slip away into the shadows again, I didn't care. I wouldn't let him walk away again, not now that everything had changed.

As the sunlight coming through the window shifted and changed, I had no idea what time it was, only that my empty stomach couldn't win out against the comfort of Nico holding my naked body against his. I'd stay here and starve, as long as he was with me. Eventually, I wondered if he'd dozed off, but then he shifted slightly and I couldn't bite back the words any longer.

"Why didn't you tell me he took the painting?" My voice was low, my breath warm against our cooling skin. There was curiosity in the question, but I hoped no trace of accusation.

Nico's eyes flew open. "I—I don't know. When I think about it now, I tell myself that I didn't think it was fair to involve you."

"But that's not true. I've always been involved and you know it."

"I guess you're right." He frowned when I peeked up at his face. "It was a hard time. I was grieving and desperate and felt so, so alone. Everything from that period of my life seems cloudy and distorted, everything but the pain."

I lifted my head, propping my chin on his chest to look at him. The words hurt before they even left my lips, but I had to say them.

"You weren't sure you could trust me."

One corner of his mouth curved upward, soothing that wound before it could fester. "No, that's not it. To be honest, I wasn't sure you could trust *me*. I was angry, angrier than I've ever been in my entire life. It had been a long time since we'd seen each other, even longer since I'd been a halfway decent friend to you. How someone like you came from someone like your father, I'll never understand, but I was afraid, terrified that I would do anything I had to in order to get it back, including turning you into a pawn."

The irony had us both huffing a soft laugh, but I laid my head back down. "So here we are, only now I'm a willing pawn."

Nico heaved a sigh. "I still don't like putting you at risk. Not for my sake."

"Good thing I'm not doing it for you then," I replied.

"Oh, really? Then why would you choose to be involved in this mess?"

"I'm doing it for your father's sake. He was the only adult in that house who made me feel like I wasn't a complete and total failure."

Startled, Nico lifted his head. "A failure? Why the hell would you feel like a failure? You're the smartest person I know."

I tried to disguise the stab of pain in my chest with a bright smile. "Oh, the usual. Not born male, to start with. Never classy enough, girly enough, or obedient enough for the daughter of a man like Aidan Willoughby. Too cozy with the household staff, which I'm sure is how he viewed you, even though we both know that was a giant crock of shit."

"Kitten," he murmured.

*Do not cry.* My father didn't deserve my tears, but the tenderness of Nico's expression threatened to draw them straight to the surface. I shoved them back down and let gratitude for having Nico and his father in my life fill in the crumbling gaps of my resolve.

"Oh, and my mother leaving me with him was definitely a point against me, though who knows how *that* became my fault. After she moved out, he told me she trapped him into marriage by getting pregnant with me. Since he was caught cheating on her with a dozen witnesses, she took him for every penny she could get. I don't think he ever got over that."

"Christ, I'm sorry. That sounds so inadequate, but it's true. I knew you weren't exactly happy there, but I always thought your father's disdain was directed at me, not you."

I shrugged. *"C'est la vie,* I guess. I got the hell out of there as soon as I could, and I made a life for myself. I don't need his approval or his permission, not anymore. Your dad, though . . . I always felt appreciated when I was around him, like he valued all the quirks my father hated."

"He always felt you were part of the family. You're right, I should've told you about the painting as soon as it happened. It was a family matter."

"Yes, you should have."

"And I definitely should've roped you into my nefarious plans earlier on."

"Well, I probably could have saved us both some time and stress."

I saw the flash of guilt in his expression, but he covered it by kissing my forehead. "I really am sorry about that. I'll make it up to you."

"Damn right you will, and I have a few ideas on how," I replied, smirking at him. "But first, you're going to feed me. I've worked up quite an appetite."

"Far be it from me to deny you anything. Let's eat."

# Chapter Eleven

## NICO

Although it hurt—a great deal—to abandon my carefully laid plans, I reminded myself that flexibility had always been a priority in this venture.

And, if I were completely honest, the prospect of having Kat at my side moving forward was a comfort. I'd been on my own since my father died, but now she was here with me, a partner instead of the pawn she'd called herself.

Her brilliant mind would be an asset.

I threw together a haphazard brunch, laid the spread across the coffee table, and we sat down on the sofa to eat before getting into a more serious discussion about what the hell to do from there.

Kat, dressed in only one of my t-shirts and a pair of my boxers, wiped a drop of syrup from her lip with a paper towel.

"So," she said, tucking her feet under her as she turned toward me. "Tell me what happened, from the beginning. How did my father get his hands on the painting in the first place?"

I leaned back against the cushions. "I didn't know my dad was sick, not until the day before he died—even then, I had no idea the illness was that serious. I talked to him on the phone and he insisted it was just a bad cold."

"Unsurprising. I don't remember him ever taking a day off."

He had, but only rarely. It'd been a bone of contention between us, especially after I finished college and was able to view the situation from the outside. We'd argued about it—he insisted he had no need of vacations, but I knew he missed France, missed his family. Only once, for my sixteenth birthday, had we made the trip back to visit my mother's grave.

It was the only gift I asked for that year.

"As it turns out, it was a lot worse than that. Some woman called me the next day, your dad's assistant or secretary, I think, to tell me he died that morning. I couldn't believe it. He was only in his fifties."

*If anything happens to me, anything strange . . .*

My father's words from that night had hit me the second I hung up the phone. Now, I had to bite the inside of my cheek to keep from spilling it all to Kat. If she knew what was at stake, she'd throw herself headlong into danger before I could blink.

Her fingers curled around mine in a silent show of support. That period of my life had been bleak, to say the least. With a single phone call, everything changed. The only member of my family who lived on the same side of the Atlantic was gone. Looking back, I wished I'd realized how great a loss it was to Kat, too, but I'd been too tangled in my grief—and then my rage—to consider how she would feel about my father's death.

I forced myself to shove down the emotions those memories drew to the surface. "By the time I got to the cottage, the painting had been swapped out for some generic piece of crap like you'd find at a doctor's office. As you might imagine, I had some choice words for your father, but his security guards forcibly removed me from the premises."

"So he's had it for what, two years now?"

"Yes."

"Why now? What changed?"

"A while back, I was sitting in a cafe when the news came on. There's an exhibit in Rochester coming up, featuring Hugo Clément's work. The guy started talking about the number of unsigned paintings Clément left behind, then mentioned the discovery of a piece belonging to your father. I guess he claimed he hadn't known who the artist was before then."

"It's a Clément?" she whispered.

"Yes," I said, smiling at her awed expression. She'd always loved that painting, which had inspired years of fascination with other Impressionists. Not telling her the truth when I learned it had been nearly impossible.

Kat frowned a little. "Why would he have even bothered with that particular painting?"

"Right." From her expression, I knew she was puzzling things over.

"Then he should have had no idea who the artist really was. It's beautiful, don't get me wrong, but my father's not exactly a connoisseur of fine art. Anything owned by one of his household staff would've been considered below him—he wouldn't have taken it just because it was pretty."

For a long moment, I stayed quiet. When I looked over at her, my brows drawn low over my eyes, I said, "I hadn't really thought about that, but you're right. I don't know why he would've taken it, if he didn't know it was worth anything."

"Your dad must have known who painted it though, right? He never said as much to me, certainly never gave me a name. Not that the name of an artist would've meant much to me at the time, but it always seemed like there was more to the story. He'd get this smile on his face, like he was feeding me clues, waiting for me to figure it out. I never did, though."

"Yes, he knew, and he told me, though he warned me that it needed to stay secret. Probably for this exact reason."

"I always hoped he'd loop me in, make me part of your family instead of my own."

I felt another twinge of guilt for not realizing how unhappy she had been all those years ago, but I nodded. It hadn't occurred to me just how helpful it would be to have someone to talk this through, someone who knew the people involved as intimately as I did.

"Kitten, you have to know that he did consider you family, whether he told you the whole story or not. I was sixteen before I heard the name Hugo Clément. He told me while we were in France."

I watched her swallow the hurt flashing in her eyes before she asked, "When did the news first break about Clément being the artist?"

"About six months ago," I answered, studying her now with interest.

For as long as I could remember, Kat always got a certain look on her face when the wheels in that brilliant mind turned at full tilt, and she wore it right then. Anything was better than the note of sadness that crept into her eyes, even if the alternative meant she'd gone into her most devious state of mind.

"Did you ever look into the source of the leak?"

My mouth opened, then snapped shut before I finally shook my head. "No. I didn't think it would matter, but I guess I assumed some hoity-toity guest had spotted it at the house or something. Your father runs with a pretty ritzy crowd and art collecting seems like a rich person's hobby."

Kat smirked. "That's true, and I guess it's a plausible explanation. But what if *he* leaked it? What if he knew the painting was done by Clément when your father died, and that's why he took it in the first place?"

"My father wouldn't have told him that," I replied quickly, but she shot me a soft, sympathetic glance.

"Nico, your father was ill. Dying. Do you remember that time I got food poisoning in seventh grade?"

My brows lifted. "Yeah, from that seafood buffet I told you not to visit."

"Yeah, yeah, you're a genius. Anyway, in between bouts of puke, I was rambling—you recorded some of it because I kept talking about ocean insects and aliens. We listened to it by the creek a few days later and I thought you were going to sprain something laughing so hard."

"Okay," I said slowly, still unclear about where she was going with this.

"What if your dad was feverish or delirious? What if he thought he was talking to you in those final hours while my father or one of his minions was nearby? Who knows what he might have said?"

She reached over to lay a hand against my cheek. I knew it broke her heart to speak so callously, but what she said made sense. I managed a weak nod, considering the ramifications of the scene she'd just painted.

"It would be more believable than my father pulling a random painting off a wall just to spite you, no matter how much he hated you," she finished.

"Son of a bitch," I whispered.

Everything she'd proposed was far more likely than my own assumption that Aidan Willoughby had recognized a treasure when he saw it. In truth, I was a little embarrassed I hadn't thought of it myself. I sighed heavily and realized I should've asked for her help much sooner.

"You're a genius, Kitten. If you're right about this, then your father has known all along how valuable that painting is."

She wrinkled her nose. "Which means he's playing the long game, which in turn means he has a plan. Whatever that plan might be, I can assure you it is *not* going to involve trading the painting for something as useless to him as the daughter he never wanted."

I grabbed hold of her arm and pulled her onto my lap, scowling down at her. "Look, I'll agree to exploring other options, Kitten, but only if you stop referring to yourself like that. It breaks my heart."

Blue eyes wide with surprise, she leaned back to look at me. "It does? Why?"

"Because," I murmured, placing tiny kisses from one corner of her mouth to the other, "while my father might have been the one who made you feel like you weren't a failure, you've always been that person for me."

"Oh," she said, the word escaping her lips on a soft exhalation.

When I continued to kiss a line down her throat, she lifted her chin and closed her eyes. It hadn't been a long conversation, but I was already tired of talking about artwork and secrets and plots. Here she was, straddling my lap, warm and soft and inviting. With her head tipped back, her hair fell nearly to my thighs in a waterfall of silky golden curls.

"Sweet Kitten," I whispered, making my way back up the other side, "do you have any idea what you do to me?"

She shifted her pelvis against mine, smirking as she lifted her head. "I think I'm getting the idea."

I took her hand and pressed it flat against my chest. "Here, too."

With a sharp intake of breath, she dropped her forehead to mine and closed her eyes. I'd always assumed she knew how important she was to me, knew how much I wanted her. Now I felt like I had years of misunderstandings to correct, oceans of feelings I needed to convey.

"You don't have a fireplace here," she said after a minute, twisting her head to glance around.

I laughed, unfazed by the sudden change of subject. Her brain had always worked at a faster speed than anyone I knew. Just because I couldn't always follow the connections in her head didn't mean they weren't there.

"No, I don't. What made you think of that?"

She flushed. "Nothing."

"Oh, you cannot possibly believe I'll let you get away with that."

After biting her lip, she finally said, "Just one of the things I used to daydream about."

"You mean fantasize?" I studied the pink staining her cheeks and neck. "I'm going to need to hear more about these daydreams."

"Just, um, things I thought we'd grow up and do together. Champagne on New Year's Eve, reading in front of a fireplace."

"What else?"

"There might have been a hot tub version after I started reading romance novels," she admitted.

"No hot tub here, either. I hadn't realized just how lacking this place was until you got here. Maybe I'll upgrade one day."

Instead of replying, Kat slumped down against my chest, her forehead resting to one side of my Adam's apple. My hands left her hips to stroke slowly up and down her back. The sudden silence didn't bother me any more than the zigzagging conversation.

I knew exactly what she felt, because I felt it, too. After half a lifetime of simply accepting what was between us as children, we'd spent the other half denying it, ignoring it, trying to get past it. Now here we were, in the middle of nowhere, together.

It might have been funny if it wasn't so strange and overwhelmingly potent.

While I held her, my thoughts tangled and meandered. After two years of planning and plotting, could I just . . . let it go? Accept that I would never see the painting again? Leverage aside, it had been in my family for generations, passed down from firstborn to firstborn, the tales told like a bedtime story from one cradle to the next.

I'd spent my life loving it—but the same could be said for loving Kat.

If the tradeoff of accepting defeat was a chance at a real relationship with her instead of a series of stolen moments like this one, then I'd have to think long and hard about what I would risk to get the painting back. I wouldn't have considered it before that exact moment in time, but now I had to.

I wanted the painting, *and* I wanted Kat. I just didn't know if there was a way for me to have both.

A few minutes later, I set the conundrum firmly aside. She was involved now—beyond serving as a willing hostage, beyond being collateral damage. Knowing her as I did, there wasn't a chance in hell *she* would ever agree to just let the painting go.

If anyone held a more intense grudge against Aidan Willoughby than I did, it was the man's only child.

Kat gave a soft sigh against my throat. "Should we make a list of options?"

"Not yet," I said, twirling a lock of her hair around my finger.

"Are we just going to hide away here and have lots of wild sex?"

I laughed and drew back to bounce my eyebrows at her. "Fuck, you're onto me. Now that I've had a taste of you, it's all I can think about."

"While I'd be delighted to give you more opportunities for carnal bliss, we need to sort at least a few things out, Nico dear. Most pressing, in my opinion, is informing Erin that I'm okay and she doesn't need to check up on me. If she shows up at my apartment with soup and cold medicine and I'm not there, she's going to think I was abducted by a serial killer."

I grimaced. "I know. Just give me a second to mourn the death of my ransom plan."

"Would you rather have a SWAT team show up outside?" she asked dryly. "If you're not sending a message to my father and letting him be responsible for keeping Erin from calling the cops, we'll need to do it ourselves. I've almost never taken a day off of work, nevermind being randomly out of touch for days at a time."

I knew she was right, but shutting the door on all my years of planning was still a harsh blow.

"You never take a day off?" I asked, fully aware that I was stalling.

Kat was equally aware, if her glare was anything to go by. "Not really. Look, we'll come up with a plan, Nico, I promise you. But it's not going to be trading me for the painting."

With a groan, I conceded. "Fine. You can use my phone to call or text her if you really have to."

She leaned forward and kissed me, the kind of kiss that sent all conscious thought straight out of my brain. When she finally pulled back, I must have looked as dazed as I felt, because she grinned.

"We'll figure this out. Together."

I ran my hands along her bare legs, from knee to hip. "You're right. But first, I don't think I'll be able to focus on the problem at hand until you put some pants on."

Laughing, Kat obliged.

# Chapter Twelve

## Kat

After I returned, Nico seemed just as distracted as before. When I questioned him about it, he said it was because he was all too conscious of my naked body hiding beneath a layer of cotton. He even closed his eyes while I made the call to my assistant from his phone.

Erin answered on the first ring, acting like I must be at death's door to have taken a day off—which was fair, since my last sick day had involved a dangerously high fever and a bout of dehydration requiring IV fluids. It happened only three weeks after Erin started working for me, and it had taken her hours to convince me to go to the clinic in town.

Shit. Maybe Nico was right to mock my rigid routine.

"Boss! I was getting ready to call the hot firefighter down the hall to come check on you. How are you feeling?"

"Better. I should be back on Monday. Everything's going okay there with the auctions?"

"I'm all over it. If you need another day to recover, I can handle things Monday, too. I don't want you pushing it when you're sick."

Guilt slithered through my belly. "I'll be okay, but I'll let you know if things change. Enjoy what's left of your weekend, boss's orders."

She called a cheery farewell that made me feel even worse for lying.

When I tossed Nico the phone and dropped down beside him on the couch, I asked, "Is Pokey just sitting around, waiting for your next instruction or something? Standing on call for your orders?"

Nico burst into startled laughter. "Oh, shit, I can't wait to tell Gumby you're calling him that, but no. I sent him home. I just didn't want your father or any of the neighborhood gossips seeing my car at your shop."

"So Pokey knows about the painting?"

"He does."

"And what does he think I'm doing here?" I asked, certain he was hiding something.

"I might've given him the impression I was planning some kind of romantic little getaway the entire time, enacting a fantasy of yours. You know, being whisked away to a remote location for a little tryst."

He was lying—I knew it as surely as I knew he'd lied about putting down two aces during our game of Bullshit. Still, there was something in his eyes, a certain vulnerability, so I was willing to let it slide.

For now. Gumby, Pokey, whoever he was, knew more than Nico was willing to admit.

"You're the one here making cute little quips about tying me up, you jerk. If anyone's fantasy is coming into play, it's yours," I replied.

He bounced his eyebrows. "Don't knock it until you try it."

My cheeks flushed hot, but I continued to glare at him. "Now you're just trying to distract me," I accused.

"Not at all. If I wanted to distract you, I would use my hands. And my mouth. And my—"

I slapped my palm none-too-gently over his mouth. "I get the picture, thank you very much. Are we discussing the actual situation or not?"

Nico waited patiently for me to remove my hand. Once I did, he nodded solemnly.

"You're right. Time to focus on work. I suppose pleasure can wait. When's the last time you were inside your father's house?" He pulled his laptop out, along with a notebook and pen, and laid them on the coffee table in front of us.

"It was six months after your dad died, so I guess a year and a half or so?" I answered. "I stopped by to drop off a birthday gift for Beardsley. No one even bothered to tell me your dad was gone. There might have been an epic screaming match involved when I found out."

His eyes widened. "Screaming match?"

"Well, yeah. I always considered your father part of the family, and even if I hadn't seen you in a while, you were one of my best friends, Nico. What kind of self-absorbed asshole neglects to mention that kind of news to his only child?"

"I should've told you myself. I'm so sorry." Guilt twisted his mouth even as sorrow filled his dark eyes.

"Yes, you should have," I said simply, "but you had enough on your plate at the time. There was no reason he couldn't have told me. I was living across town, not on the moon. But in any case, I didn't see the painting, not that I spent much time wandering around the house. I delivered Beardsley's gift, ran into my father on my way out, screamed until my throat was raw, and stormed away from the house. I haven't been back inside since that day."

"Kitten." Nico swallowed hard as he laced his fingers with mine on the couch between us. "The image of you swooping down into that cavern of a front hall like a Valkyrie on my behalf . . . it means more than you know. Thank you"

I scowled slightly, though I did love the feel of his big hand enveloping mine. "It's really nothing to thank me for. Believe me, he deserved every word I threw at him. In any case, neither of us can turn back time so I could be there when you needed me the most, and it gives us no insight about the painting, either."

He lifted our joined hands and kissed my knuckles. "I still appreciate what you did. I wish I could've seen it, though. You really are something special."

For a long moment, I was silent. Regret was a heavy thing, as was grief.

Maybe, now that we'd found each other again, we could help to lighten one another's load. I leaned my head against his shoulder and sighed softly when he pressed his lips to my temple.

Already, I felt lighter with him by my side.

"So, our options are straight up burglary, maybe some blackmail if we can find enough dirt, your truly terrible ransom scheme, a prolonged legal battle if we could prove the provenance of the painting belonging to your family . . . what else is there?"

Nico snorted. "If we had ten or fifteen million dollars on hand, convincing him to sell could be an option, maybe, but I still don't believe he'd agree to that, not with our history. And no offense, but your father's the shadiest lawyer I've ever known, so I think the legal battle is off the table, along with the ransom. If he knew you were involved in conning him, I'd be terrified of what he might do to get revenge."

"And blackmail would require concrete proof of something."

"Which I spent a long time searching for, with nothing to show for it. He covers his tracks too well."

He paused, like there was more he wanted to say, but he fell silent.

"What about your computer programs?" I asked, studying the laptop.

"What about them?"

"Do they save information about the alerts you get? Like, any news footage mentioning the painting and my father, for example?"

Nico nodded slowly. "Yes. Most of the articles or news segments I've seen just showed a single photo of it in the frame, nothing that stood out to me as a clue as to where it might be hanging. I have logs of everything, though."

For a second, I tapped my bottom lip. "What if we could arrange an interview with him in order to get some current footage of the painting from inside the house?"

"How would we do that?" he asked.

I shot him a sly grin. "I know a journalist who, with a few tips on the right wording to use, might be able to convince my father to agree to it. Unfortunately, her number was in my phone contacts. I don't want to reach out through any official channels."

"And then what? We break in and steal the painting?"

Humming thoughtfully, I said, "The thought did cross my mind, though maybe that option should be kept as a last resort. You've obviously been doing plenty of research, but the specific location is one thing we don't know for sure. There's no way I'm letting you break into the house—if we have to steal it, I'll be the one going in. I snuck in and out all the time in high school. My father's not going to have his goons beat me to death if I got caught inside, but you? There's no guarantee."

I watched as Nico's urge to tell me there was no way in hell he'd allow me to put myself in danger rose and died before it reached his throat. This was no time to be macho or heavy-handed; he clearly knew it would certainly do more harm than good.

"Agree to disagree," he said in a low voice.

Stealing the painting was firmly relegated to the role of last resort, because I was right and he knew it. It would make more sense for me to be the one to go in, even if we ended up just needing reconnaissance, and he'd probably cut off his own arm before he'd put me at risk.

I squeezed his hand because I knew just what was going on inside his head.

"Look, as much as I'm enjoying this little love nest you've got here, I think it would be smart to combine forces back home so we don't draw too much attention to ourselves. Erin might forgive the aberration from my schedule for a day or two, but if I'm gone longer than that, she's going to get suspicious. I told her I should be back at work Monday."

"Love nest, huh? I like the sound of that. How about we keep *enjoying* this little love nest until tomorrow afternoon, if I promise that I'll get you back to your apartment in time to get a good night's sleep before heading to work Monday morning?

God forbid I throw you too far off schedule," he murmured, nuzzling my ear.

My annoyed humph turned into a sigh as his lips traced my jawline. "I like my routine, is that a crime?"

"No," he replied, nipping lightly at my chin, "but maybe we can throw some new routines into the mix."

"You know, Nico, I think you might just be able to convince me."

## Chapter Thirteen

### Nico

By Sunday afternoon, I knew I would never look at the cabin the same way again. From my solitary bachelor escape to our own delightful love nest—it was an evolution I hadn't foreseen but definitely didn't regret. There'd been a few scattered brainstorming sessions involved, but for the most part, Kat managed to keep my mind completely off of the painting.

As a result, I felt curiously lighthearted as we packed a small cooler with the remaining perishables from the fridge, even if I suspected she'd done plenty of silent scheming in her own head.

"Where's your car?" Kat asked suddenly. "I didn't see it, not even when I took off."

I grinned. "Parked about fifty yards south, in the underbrush. I was afraid you might have learned how to hot-wire a car over the years and didn't want to tempt fate by parking right outside."

"Hmm. That's unfortunately not in my skill set," she mused, then cocked a brow at me. "Do *you* know how to hot-wire a car?"

"Sadly, no. Maybe we should learn together."

"It would've been a useful skill that time your dad caught me stealing keys to my father's Corvette in high school."

I choked on a laugh. "He never told me about that."

"I swore him to secrecy."

Her brilliant grin filled me with an oddly buoyant feeling of hope. After carefully placing the last two bottles of hard cider into the cooler, I flipped the lid into place and pulled Kat into my arms. She immediately snuggled in, rubbing her face against my chest like that was right where she belonged.

As far as I was concerned, it was exactly that.

For several long moments, we stood there together, soaking in the simple comfort of each other's presence. Finally, I loosened my hold, tipped her chin up, and kissed her soundly.

"Let's get you home, Kitten."

The drive back to Spruce Hill felt like a blast from the past, a comfortable, intimate interlude far removed from our real lives. We sang along to the radio, slowed down to let a small family of deer cross the road, and eventually stopped at a yard sale just outside of town.

I smiled indulgently as I watched Kat explore the goods. She looked like a kid in a candy shop, exclaiming over cheap but nostalgic junk as much as she did over the one or two items she thought might be worth fixing up to resell. Those blue eyes were alight with enthusiasm, her pretty lips curved in a near-constant smile as she studied the two folding tables full of toys.

"I still can't believe you broke my phone," she muttered under her breath as she set a toy car back down again. "I could be looking this stuff up, but no, it had to be tossed into the damn dumpster."

I took the two items from her hands, held them up to show the middle aged woman behind the table, and handed over a ten dollar bill.

"Problem solved," I said, winking at the saleswoman before turning the goods over to Kat. "And I'm very sorry about your phone, for the tenth time. I've already ordered a replacement for you. It's a newer model, better camera."

Kat scowled at me, but the delight in her eyes softened it. "Yeah, yeah. You just want to play hero so I'll fawn all over you."

I held open her car door and bowed as she sat. "I'm counting on it. In fact, anything you want to do all over me is perfectly acceptable, in case you need any encouragement."

When she glared, I only laughed and closed the door behind her.

The rest of the drive was quieter, signaling the end of our peaceful escape from reality. As we finally neared her neighborhood, Kat opened her mouth to give me directions—then snapped it shut, apparently remembering that I knew more about her adult life than she knew of mine. I parked the car out front and watched the debate in her eyes as she decided whether to dismiss me here or let me walk her in.

In the end, she pursed her lips and kept quiet, so I assumed I wasn't being barred from the premises. I cocked a brow as I joined her on the sidewalk, the barest hint of a grin teasing at my lips.

"Just shut up," she muttered.

I laughed. "I didn't say a word."

Kat rolled her eyes and handed me the yard sale finds so she could fish the keys out of her tiny purse. Her home was the lower left side of a slightly rundown old Victorian that had been converted into four apartments. The place might have been considered charming if somebody took the time to replace the broken porch railing and slap on a coat of paint here and there.

Oddly enough, despite its obvious state of disrepair, it suited Kat in a way the Willoughby estate never had.

"I can hear the gears turning, Nico," she said as she locked the front door behind us and led me into her apartment.

"Just thinking this place is very on brand for you." I peered around as she flipped on the lights. "Which seems strange, since I wouldn't have pictured you somewhere like this."

Kat snorted. "Because it's not up to my father's standards?"

"Well, that part is obvious, but that's not why it suits you," I replied easily, placing her treasures on the kitchen counter.

"No? Then why?"

"It's because I know how you love to find those dirty, broken, hidden gems so you can fix them up and make them pretty again."

Warmth softened her expression, though I couldn't quite tell if she was annoyed or pleased with my insight. I realized in that moment she was doing the same to me—taking the broken pieces of my existence and carefully gluing me back together, one shard at a time.

"Ah, yes. Well, I did tell the landlord not to be surprised if I take care of some cosmetic issues on my own dime. I just haven't had a chance yet."

I reached out and cupped her chin with the tips of my fingers. "It wasn't a criticism. In fact, I think it's one of your most endearing qualities. You are incredible."

She sucked in a breath, even as some part of me wondered why that innocent touch affected her so profoundly after these past few days of having my hands all over her body. I smiled down at her, sweet and comforting, knowing it would either soothe her or rile her up enough to sharpen her claws against my skin.

Within the space of a heartbeat, she closed the distance between us, sliding her arms around my waist.

For several long minutes, we stood like that in the silent apartment. I wasn't entirely sure who was comforting who—I knew she wanted to reassure me that we would get the painting back, would figure out some way to return my father's legacy to my possession, but empty platitudes had never been Kat's style.

I tried to imagine how this all might've played out if I'd proceeded with my plan, but every time we talked through the possibilities, I could hear the panic rising in her throat. She'd confessed to the nightmarish images that threatened to choke her, vivid pictures of finding me bloodied, beaten, rotting in a jail cell or left for dead in the woods.

"Hey," I said softly, pulling back to look her in the eyes. "You're trembling."

"It's just been a long few days," Kat replied.

She forced a quick smile and turned away, focusing instead on the old toys we'd brought home. That particular ploy wouldn't work, not on me. I moved to stand behind her at the counter and set my hands on her shoulders.

"I'll find another way, one that keeps you out of it, if that's what you want."

She shook her head without looking at me and said, "In for a penny, in for a pound, right? Besides, someone with half a brain needs to keep you from making any other idiotic decisions."

I laughed softly and wrapped my arms around her. "A deal's a deal. I won't make any moves without your approval. Kitten . . ." I trailed off, turning her back to face me. "If I could walk away from this, I would."

"I would never ask you to. Just give us some time to think, and we'll figure it out. I owe your father at least this much. And you, too," she added.

Even though she hadn't missed the funeral by choice, it was one thing she apparently couldn't forgive herself for.

"Together," I promised, pressing a kiss to her forehead before brushing my lips across hers. "You have an early morning tomorrow. I'll get out of your hair."

I saw the debate flashing through her expressive eyes, recognized that part of her wanted to protest, to ask me to stay, but our cozy little adventure in the woods was over. It was better to readjust to real life sooner instead of later.

Kat's pragmatism and practicality were as familiar to me as my own heart.

"I'll get in touch with my journalist friend as soon as I find a way to contact her under the radar," she said finally.

I cupped her cheek and she rose up on her toes to kiss me more thoroughly. When she finally drew back, I chucked her under the chin and smiled fondly.

"Sweet dreams, Kitten. I'll get that new phone to you as soon as possible, I promise."

Kat poked a finger into my ribs. "You'd better, or I'm keeping every cent of profit from your investments today."

With one hand clutched over my heart, I heaved a dramatic sigh. "You are a cruel woman, Katherine Willoughby, and I am entirely at your mercy."

If only she knew how true that was.

# Chapter Fourteen

## Kat

By the time I bid him goodnight and closed the door fifteen minutes later, I was still too keyed up to sleep. I treated myself to a hot shower and a mug of tea, did a little bit of research on the painting from my laptop, and then carefully sewed an embroidered mermaid patch over the tear in my jacket sleeve.

With a contented hum, I set it all aside and finally went to bed.

Though there was one hell of a highlight reel playing through my head, I thought back to the way Nico had spoken about his feelings for me, his reasons for staying away. How was I supposed to respond to that? I'd loved him as long as I could remember, had spent most of my childhood dreaming of fancy magazine-worthy weddings and imagining all the clichés—barefoot walks on the beach, cozying up in front of the fire together.

That last one had distracted me into commenting on the cabin's lack of a fireplace, for fuck's sake, and the man had simply smiled like I was some kind of prize. Where other people might get huffy or roll their eyes at my abrupt change of conversational direction, Nico had always followed along seamlessly, like it was a gift instead of a fault of mine.

As I lay in my own bed, it felt strange not to have him there at my side: holding me, kissing me, teasing me, making me feel like I finally had everything I'd ever wanted. Except . . . I wasn't really sure *what* I had. Our lives were a tangled mess, twisted up in the painting and with my father. We were stuck in limbo, unable to move forward with any kind of real relationship until those threads unraveled.

If we succeeded in getting the painting back, what then? Would Nico want me around, a constant reminder of what my father did to him? Would he even stay in town, at constant risk of discovery?

Would he ever truly be safe?

And if we failed, how long before he started to resent me for all that he'd lost, especially if he sacrificed the chance to get it back in exchange for keeping me safe?

When I finally dozed off, I dreamed about being inside the Beaumont cottage. Like a scene from a cartoon, the painting on the wall grew and grew until Nico and I walked right into the field of lavender ourselves, never to return.

Monday morning dawned far too quickly. I was disoriented by waking up alone instead of beside Nico, even though it had only been a few days—maybe a lifetime of anticipation was the reason it felt so normal.

Under typical circumstances, it would've felt like moving at warp speed. With him, it seemed so *right*.

Still, I delighted in rolling out of my own comfortable bed, selecting clothes for the day from my own wardrobe instead of Nico's extras, and following my usual morning routine. As I left my favorite coffee shop with breakfast in hand, a familiar broad frame ranged easily beside me on the sidewalk.

"You know, if you were anyone else, I'd be calling the police to report a stalker," I said lightly as I lifted my chin in an attempt at haughty disdain.

Nico wasn't put off by it, not in the least. He simply handed me a gift bag and gave a lopsided grin.

"I just thought you'd be eager to get your hands on your new phone, that's all."

Even as my eyes lit with pleasure, I shot him a suspicious glance. "And will you be monitoring all my phone calls? Tracking my whereabouts?"

"Only the calls you make to me," he vowed. "Pinky swear."

I choked on a laugh, but I believed him. "Yeah, yeah. Is it 'bring your lover to work' day, or are you just killing time walking to the office with me?"

"Your lover, hmm? I like the sound of that."

Though I rolled my eyes, Nico caught a glimpse of the smile on my face before I managed to school my expression. He gave me a world class puppy dog look, batting the long, black lashes that framed his dark eyes.

I'd forgotten how cute he could be.

"If you want to invite me in to see this remarkable business you've been building, I wouldn't say no."

"Consider yourself invited, though it's not nearly as exciting as it might sound. I hope you had breakfast already, because I'm not sharing my bagel."

Nico only grinned and strolled along beside me. When we reached the back door of the warehouse, my gaze caught on the stack of pallets next to the dumpster and he grimaced at the broken wood.

"I'm really sorry, Kitten."

I turned suddenly to beam up at him. "In good news, the trash doesn't get picked up until tomorrow, so while you're here, you can dig through and find my old phone. Then I can get the SIM card out of it, since you didn't ask me before tossing it into the dumpster, and I won't need to play cloak and dagger to find Evelyn's private contact information."

"I should've expected that," he grumbled, but he slid one hand around to the small of my back and kissed me. "But for you? Anything."

Fierce heat infused my cheeks as I turned to open the door. When it swung in, I gestured for him to enter. Nico took a few steps forward to survey the space and I tried to see it through his eyes. It was large and bright, lined with shelves. Along each shelf were stacks of labeled boxes, loose merchandise, and a huge array of packing supplies. His gaze paused on a row of garage sale finds, ranging from a wind-up circus lion to a vintage Ouija board to the Teddy Ruxpin I'd just repaired.

"Oh, this is just beautiful," he said, grinning at me. "I don't know what I was expecting, but this—it's so *you*. Absolute chaos contained in tidy little rows."

When I scowled at him, he took the bags and coffee cup from my hands and set them aside so he could tug me into his arms.

"I'm not chaotic," I mumbled.

"I mean that in the best possible way. For such a competent, organized woman, you've always had a touch of chaos inside you. Such a delicious study in contradiction."

I made an impolite sound, but everything he said was true, so I nestled myself more comfortably against his chest. The business was something I'd always thought he would appreciate, something so quirky and peculiar compared to my father's lifestyle that it couldn't help but be an affront to the man's sensibilities.

It gave me a feeling of accomplishment and I truly loved what I'd built, but it had often been a lonely venture. Though Erin's bubbly presence helped mitigate that, Nico's approval warmed me in a way that little else could.

"Hey," he said, smiling broadly as he fingered the patch on my sleeve. "You fixed the tear."

"I am a woman of many talents, Mr. Beaumont." I lifted my chin proudly, but a grin snuck through. "Besides, I've been waiting six months to find a reason to use that patch, so it seemed like a match made in heaven."

"Or a match made through gross negligence and idiocy on my part?"

I laughed. "That, too."

Nico tucked a curl behind my ear and smiled. "This might sound patronizing as fuck so please don't punch me in the balls for saying it, but I am so fucking proud of you."

For a moment, I was simply trapped in his gaze, warm and gentle and just the tiniest bit misty as he looked down at me.

"Nico," I said softly, but whatever else I'd been about to say flew out of my head.

His mouth dropped down to whisper over the curve of my ear. "Yes, Kitten?" he breathed.

The shiver that ran up my spine rippled under his palm like lightning. Instead of answering him, I tipped my head back. Nico willingly obeyed my unspoken request and I sighed as his lips trailed down my neck. My hands curled into his shirt, tugging him closer.

Just when a soft purr of pleasure from my throat caused a noticeable response from his lower body, the door swung open and a startled Erin gaped at the sight of us.

"Oh! I'm sorry!" she gushed, averting her eyes as though we were standing in the middle of the warehouse naked.

I laughed—a little breathlessly, even to my own ears—and shook my head. "It's fine, Erin. This is Nicolas Beaumont. Nico, this is Erin."

Erin's enormous green eyes widened. "You mean *the* Nico?"

Nico, damn him, turned to me with raised brows. He caught me making a frantic "stop talking" face at my assistant, so I forced my expression into a pleasant smile despite my flaming cheeks.

"My childhood friend, Nico. Yep. That's him. He was just leaving, weren't you?"

The man gave Erin his most charming smile and nodded. "I was, actually. I have a date with a dumpster."

Erin's bafflement was evident, but she returned the smile. "I'll just go check on our auctions," she said, moving away from the pair of us. "Nice meeting you, Nico, and I'm glad you're feeling better, Kat!"

Nico waited until my assistant had closed herself in the office before turning to me. "Been talking about me?" he asked, eyes wide with mock innocence. "I'm flattered."

"Shut up," I muttered.

He couldn't hold back a broad grin at my discomfort. "Don't get all shy on me now. What did you say? That I'm tall, dark, and handsome? That you've been dreaming about making love to me since you were sixteen? Give me just one morsel to get me through my lonely dive into that dumpster."

I glared at him. "I told her you were a worthless swine. I hope that will keep you company, darling."

"You're adorable when you're annoyed," he murmured.

His hand tangled in my hair as he tugged me against him for one last kiss. Even an expert grudge-holder like me couldn't resist the lure of his mouth. I melted into the embrace so quickly I might have been embarrassed, had it been anyone other than Nico.

"Better get to work, you're already off schedule," he teased when he released me.

"And whose fault is that?" I replied, shooing him toward the door.

He threw a wink over his shoulder as he went outside, leaving me standing there in the silence I usually appreciated but now found curiously empty. After a few calming breaths, I grabbed my breakfast and the gift bag containing my new phone and joined Erin in the office. My assistant had booted up the laptop and was pretending to be busy checking the filing cabinet when I dropped into the chair behind the desk.

"Please, please tell me that you weren't really sick and actually spent the weekend banging that gorgeous hunk of man-flesh out there," Erin said immediately, clasping her hands to her chest like it was the most romantic thing she'd ever heard.

I lowered my head to the desk with a groan, which Erin clearly took as confirmation.

"Oh, thank god. He is just beautiful. And *built*. And clearly way better suited to you than that dusty old professor, anyway. I'm so glad you ignored me about texting him so you could sleep with Nico instead. You've only been in love with him for what, ninety-five percent of your life?"

"Please stop talking," I begged, not bothering to lift my head.

Erin huffed good-naturedly. "Fine, but my sex life is a pitiful desert right now so you could really do a girl a favor by sharing some exciting details in the near future—and don't even bother trying to convince me that a man like that doesn't have some amazing tricks up his sleeve, because I could see it in his eyes when he looked at you. Definitely a step up from the professor."

The problem, I realized, was that even after Erin left me alone, those little details my assistant had mentioned continued to play through my mind. A tremor crept up my spine as I sipped at my coffee.

*Tricks up his sleeve, indeed,* I thought, allowing myself to savor the memories for two solid minutes before forcing my focus back to my work.

I'd finished breakfast and done some research on the items from the yard sale when I heard Nico talking to Erin out in the warehouse. After giving myself a quick, bracing pep talk, I rose to join them.

Nico looked only mildly disheveled, but I could smell him from across the room. He grinned when my nose wrinkled.

"Not the most glamorous aroma, but I found the phone. You might want to, ah, sanitize it first."

"I'll do you one better," I countered, grabbing a plastic baggy from one of the shelves. I held it open for him, then zipped the foul odor inside. "I'm afraid I don't have any bags big enough for you, so you'll have to go home and shower."

"Shame you can't join me," he murmured, "but do try to enjoy your day, Kitten. Don't work too hard."

He raised a hand in farewell to Erin, who smiled radiantly as she waved, then he winked at me one last time before leaving the warehouse. I stared after him for a moment, just long enough for Erin to start laughing to herself across the room.

When I shook myself out of the trance Nico managed to put me in, I shot a useless glare in Erin's direction and we both got down to work.

# Chapter Fifteen

## Nico

Freshly showered back at home, I was seated at my kitchen table when a text from Kat popped up on my phone. I grinned—before turning over the new device, I'd programmed myself into her contacts.

*This is quite an upgrade. Hope you're not expecting to be paid in sexual favors.*

I laughed aloud. *Well shit, there goes my afternoon. Much better camera on this one, perfect for sending appreciative, scantily clad selfies. Or so I've heard, anyway.*

She sent back a selfie, but she was fully dressed and making a peace sign with her fingers. I studied it for a moment, appreciating the reluctant smile on her lips. It was cute and silly and the realization that this was what I'd been missing in my life pierced me like a knife between the ribs.

I didn't have it in me to joke at the moment, so I replied with a simple, *You are so beautiful, I can barely stand it.*

It was a few minutes before the bouncing dots indicated she was typing. *So are we, like, dating now?*

Tentative was not generally a word I associated with Kat—she lived her life with gusto, with boundless enthusiasm. I figured she was teasing me and was tempted to reply in a similar tone, but I wanted too badly to be on the same page about the answer.

*You are every dream I ever had come true, so yes.*

Her response came through almost immediately. *Sappy, but same.*

When a new picture of Kat with a lollipop in her mouth appeared on my screen, I decided that dating Katherine Willoughby was exactly what I needed. I studied the image, noting the familiar sparkle of humor in her eyes, the slight tinge of pink in her cheeks, those sweet, full lips that always tasted faintly of some kind of fruity lip gloss, the thick honey curls that tumbled halfway down her back.

I wanted her more fiercely than I'd ever wanted anything, even the damn painting. It was a physical ache centered in my chest, a sense of longing that flowed through me as surely as the blood in my veins. This was a dangerous, tangled web I was plunging myself into, but I could no sooner walk away from Kat than I could the painting.

With a sigh, I rubbed at my temples, then picked up the phone again to text her. *If we're officially dating, can I take you to dinner tonight?*

Her reply was swift and satisfying. *As long as you'll come home with me after.*

*It's a date. Pick you up at six.*

---

WHEN I PULLED UP in front of Kat's apartment a few minutes ahead of schedule, she was seated on the front steps wearing a short, ruffly white dress with her leather jacket and boots. This look was like one of my teenage fantasies come to life. Her hair was twisted up with little silver clips, a few curling locks falling artfully free. A dark gray cat wove back and forth in front of her bare legs, purring so loudly I heard it from three yards away.

"Is it wrong to be jealous of a cat?" I asked, shoving my hands into the pockets of my jeans.

I'd traded my usual tee and sneakers for a nice shirt and leather dress shoes; the appreciative feminine gaze that traveled over me from head to toe made me glad to have put forth the effort.

"Well, if it makes you feel any better, I paid to have Tempest's balls chopped off last month," she replied, rising to her feet and brushing cat hair from her skirt.

I gave an exaggerated grimace as I held out a hand, curling my fingers around hers when she took it.

"You look extraordinarily beautiful," I said quietly.

She paused on the bottom step. "You clean up pretty nice, too. It's a good thing you weren't dressed like this when you came to the Keeper earlier, or Erin would've thrown herself at you then and there."

"Oh, really?" I mused, then leaned in to kiss her.

Whatever she had on her lips, it tasted different today, more like vanilla. Only Kat could be so addicted to routine in some ways and so unpredictable in others.

"You should tell your assistant I'm into this hot blonde, really hoping she'll let me stick around awhile."

With a mischievous grin, Kat said, "I guess we'll have to see how an actual date goes first, won't we?"

I slid an arm around her waist, lifted her from the step, and twirled her around before setting her to her feet on the sidewalk. "Challenge accepted. Excellent date starts now."

"Where are we going for dinner?"

"The Mermaid," I answered, laughing when she squealed in delight.

It was a nice, family-owned restaurant in the middle of Spruce Hill's main drag, but Aidan Willoughby wouldn't be caught dead in a place without Michelin stars to its name. Back in my teens, Kat and I had been there together a few times with mutual friends, including the current owners, Jake and Sam. The twins took it over from their father several years ago.

For me, a trip to The Mermaid meant a tasty meal in cool surroundings, maybe a chat with Jake if he was tending bar or working on his ledgers at an unoccupied table. For Kat, it was something else entirely: another jab at her father's snobbery, another experience he'd denied her, another memory made in spite of his neglect.

Being the one to give that to her made me feel like less of a failure despite my plan for the painting crumbling to dust.

"I'm still working on getting into my dear, departed phone," Kat said as I paid the bill. "I have a college friend I could ask for Evelyn's number, but I feel like the fewer people involved, the better."

I nodded. "If you can't get your contacts from the old phone, I can do some digging."

"You mean hacking?" she asked, arching a brow.

"I'm not a hacker, Kitten."

"Shame." She scooted out of the booth and looped her arm through mine. "I was hoping for a chance to yell, 'Hack the planet!' at you."

"You're a goofball," I told her, but I couldn't hold back a grin. She'd always had a soft spot for nineties movies.

"Give me one more day, then you can hack to your heart's content. The sooner we get Evelyn on the case, the better."

She was right. I debated doing a little digging before that day was up, but then she jabbed me in the side with her pointer finger.

"Give me another day, Nicolas."

I frowned down at her as I rubbed my sore ribs. "Fine, fine. I'm just eager for this to be done."

"It will be. I promise."

After dinner, we wandered a few blocks from the restaurant to peek in the windows of cute little shops lining Main Street, then picked up dessert from Caboose Creamery, an old train car that had been converted into an ice cream parlor. Watching Kat savor her cone of Brake Line Bubblegum, an impossibly bright pink ice cream with blue and purple gumballs mixed into it, was both torture and bliss.

If the sly grin on her face as we strolled back toward my car was any indication, she knew exactly what she was doing.

"Are you spending the night?" she asked, unbuckling her seatbelt when I parked in front of her apartment.

I raised a brow. "I am ever hopeful, so I brought a change of clothes, but it's entirely up to you."

She hummed thoughtfully before shooting me a grin. "Better bring them in, just in case."

As Kat locked the door behind us, I silently applauded my decision to invite her out on a real date, and not only because she'd gotten dressed up. The evening had been filled with laughter and the familiarity of our old friendship, along with that new, sharp undercurrent of desire. It felt like redemption, like a second chance at everything I'd ever dreamed might be possible between us.

Whatever happened with the painting, I was determined not to lose my hold on her, not this time.

"You're looking very serious," Kat teased, unlacing her boots so she could kick them off beside the door.

I leaned against the wide archway leading into the kitchen. "What's on your socks?"

An actual giggle bubbled out of her. While I stared at her in shock, Kat lifted her leg and propped her foot on the wall beside me.

"Read it and weep, handsome."

"They're actual kittens. And rainbows. You have rainbow kitten socks."

She fluttered her lashes at me. "I do. Regret asking out a nerd like me yet?"

"Not even a little."

My hand wrapped around her ankle and a wicked grin curved my lips. Before she could lose her balance, I caught her behind the knees and swept her into my arms.

"What's it going to take to get you naked?" I asked.

This time, it wasn't a giggle, but a throaty laugh that rocketed straight through me. "To start with, the bedroom is that door at the back left. Then I'm going to need a few minutes to get these stupid clips out of my hair so I don't shred my scalp while we roll in the hay."

"Fair enough," I said, depositing her at the foot of the bed. "I'll go brush my teeth and put on my footie pajamas for beddy-bye."

She snorted. "If you don't actually have footie pajamas, I know exactly what you'll be getting for your next birthday."

I winked and left the room, whistling cheerfully as I grabbed my backpack and located the bathroom. When I came back into the bedroom, Kat was on her hands and knees, peering under the dresser. Her leather jacket hung on a hook by the door, her pretty silver hair clips lying on the dresser above her. I had a perfect view of the lush, round globes of her ass as the ruffled hemline of her skirt crept upward.

"Not that I'm complaining about the view, but what exactly are you doing?"

"Trying to find the back to my stupid earring. This is the third one I've lost and it was the last of the replacement pack."

She didn't bother to glance at me, not until the silence stretched as a series of progressively dirtier fantasies paraded through my head. When she pulled her arm out from beneath the dresser to look over her shoulder, I was still at the doorway, staring at her with a burning intensity that she read immediately in my expression.

Kat licked her lips and looked at me in question.

"You have an absolutely magnificent ass," I said softly.

"Oh," she breathed. "Well. Thank you?"

"I think this floor would be a little rough on your knees, though."

Understanding swept over her features, darkening the blue of her eyes as her pupils went wide. She let her gaze travel over me across the room. It lingered where I'd unfastened the top two buttons of my shirt, trailing heat over my skin.

"Fortunately, I have this nice big bed here at our disposal," she replied.

As I approached, she sat back on her heels and I held out a hand to help her up. As soon as she was on her feet, I kissed her, glorying in the way she welcomed me, opened for me, the way she clung to me like I was an anchor in the storm raging around and between us.

With one hand tunneled through her hair, I let the other slip under her skirt, skating over her hip to cup her ass, kneading lightly as I pressed her against my body. Her hands were busy unbuttoning my shirt, then sliding across my chest as she shoved the sides apart.

Kat had just managed to unbuckle my belt before she twirled and presented me with the zipper of her dress. Slowly, so slowly that she wriggled impatiently against my fingers, I drew it down, caressing each revealed inch of skin with my lips. Each shiver sparked a path along my own as well.

I pushed the straps over her shoulders, realizing she wasn't wearing a bra. As I watched the dress pool at her feet, I couldn't hold back a groan.

"I want you," I whispered. "From behind, just like this. What do you say?"

Kat nodded, dropping her head back against my chest when my hands slid around to cup her breasts. Over those few days at the cabin, I'd learned just how much pressure made her gasp, how much made her moan, and I used that knowledge until she writhed against me, her satin-clad backside shifting restlessly back and forth against my jeans.

Hooking my thumbs into those sinful panties, I slipped them down over her hips, then guided her forward until she knelt at the edge of the bed. I grabbed a condom from my pocket before dispensing with my clothes, then trailed my lips from one softly rounded shoulder to the other while my palms coasted up the backs of her thighs, smoothing over the soft curve of her ass.

When she dropped forward onto her hands, I made a hoarse sound of appreciation.

"So lovely," I murmured. "So fucking perfect."

With one hand, I stroked my fingers between her legs, finding her more than ready for me, impossibly hot and slick. After a few teasing brushes of my fingertips, I sank two fingers into that welcoming heat, curling them against her inner walls until she moaned. I let my other hand roam up the long muscles of her back before returning to her ass, squeezing gently while I continued to thrust slowly with my other hand.

"I've never seen anything quite so erotic," I told her. My voice came out in a low rumble that sent a visible shiver through her.

"Jesus, Nico. Enough talk," she gasped, wiggling as though to prod me into action.

It worked. I withdrew my fingers and immediately plunged deep, holding her steady, her ass flush against my hips. A guttural cry was my reward, but she tried to shift, to encourage me to thrust again, and I clucked my tongue.

"Oh no, I want you to keep perfectly still," I instructed, tightening the fingers of one hand around her hip as the other glided across her skin.

With a breathless laugh, she shook her head. "I don't know if I can."

I grinned, though she couldn't see it, and ran my free hand up her spine. "Lean down for me."

Once she'd done as I asked, folding her forearms under her cheek and resting her chest against the mattress, I drew back and returned with a hard thrust that made her moan. Using both hands, I stroked over her heated skin, tracing lazy shapes across her back and bottom before returning to her hips, then I drove home once more.

The sequence repeated again and again, until Kat was trembling and breathless before me. After another deep, hard stroke, she gasped, "Not. Enough. It's not enough. Please."

Though I stayed buried within her, I slid my hands up her sides, lifting her torso until her back was pressed against my chest. I let my thumbs sweep across her nipples, then locked one arm low across her hips and reached down to stroke idly through the damp curls between her legs.

"Is that better?"

My voice was hoarse, tickling her ear as I teased her sensitive flesh. When her pelvis rocked against my hand, my restraining arm tightened. She growled in annoyance and I bit back a laugh.

"Oh no, stay right here with me. I want to feel you around me, every ripple. You're going to come for me, Kitten, just like this."

My hand moved away, drawing a frustrated whimper from her, but I hooked it around her knee and positioned her to my satisfaction, with one foot on the bed and her thighs spread wide. Despite her clear disapproval of the interruption, the new position gave me greater access when I started stroking again, circling her clit with my fingertips. Kat groaned, arching back against my chest, though her hips remained locked against mine.

When my teeth grazed her shoulder, she came apart under my fingers. A sharp cry burst from her lips, the sound echoing in my blood. I eased her back down to the bed, my touch soothing now, caressing the muscles that still quaked with her release.

The next few thrusts were lazy, languid, as I gauged her recovery. Eventually, I felt her shift to brace herself against the mattress, pressing her hips backward. She made a sound somewhere between a purr and a moan, and my lips tipped upward.

Lightly, as though it wasn't killing me to maintain my last shred of control, I said, "How do you want this? Say the words, and I'll give you whatever you want."

Kat bit her lip and rocked back against me. "Harder!"

*Thank fuck.*

Hearing her say it was almost as erotic as the sight of her flushed skin shivering in the throes of passion. My hands locked on her hips and I took her, hard and fast, just as she'd requested.

Every gasping breath, every muffled groan drove me closer to the brink. She met me thrust for thrust, and when I knew I couldn't hold out much longer, I took advantage of the leg I'd shifted to reach around and tease her again, to drive her toward another peak.

It took barely more than a press of my finger for her to convulse around me, her muscles squeezing so tight it triggered my own orgasm. My shuddering groan layered over her hoarse cry. Kat managed to keep her arms braced underneath her only until the pulsing within her faded, then she collapsed forward onto the bed.

"I'm never moving again," she mumbled, her voice muffled by the bedding.

I laughed softly as I crawled into the bed alongside her, then I gathered her boneless limbs against me, tucking her head under my chin and smoothing damp tendrils of hair back from her face.

"I think I can get on board with that," I replied.

"That was . . . hot. Incredibly hot. Don't you dare think it means you can boss me around outside of the bedroom, but holy shit. In bed, I think I love it."

My low hum of agreement reverberated under her ear, so she snuggled in closer and didn't bother trying to keep her eyes open as I stroked her hair. Every inch of my body relaxed against her loose frame, floating on complete and utter satisfaction.

"It's different with you," she said drowsily.

My fingers paused for only a heartbeat before continuing the soothing path along her wild tumble of curls. "What is?"

"Everything," she mumbled, exhaling a long, exhausted sigh. "Everything is different."

My arms tightened around her as she drifted into sleep, but those words echoed in my mind for a long time while I lay there in the dark.

They were terrifying, exhilarating—and almost certainly true.

# Chapter Sixteen

## KAT

My alarm clock, one of those old-fashioned types with the clanging bell on top that I picked up from a yard sale a few years back, startled Nico into bolting upright the next morning, dislodging my sleepy self from where I'd been curled into his side. I merely mumbled a few choice words as I grabbed the clock and made the obnoxiously loud ringing stop.

Nico panted like his heart might beat straight out of his chest. "How the hell can you stand that thing?" he asked, flopping back down beside me.

I shrugged one bare shoulder and buried my face against a pillow. After a few minutes, he recovered enough to start drawing lazy swirls over my shoulder blade with his fingertip until I inched closer and tugged at the blanket he'd covered us with sometime during the night, exposing more of my back to his ministrations.

"You really are a kitten at heart, just begging to be petted. Every time I touch you, you start purring. It's satisfying to know I have such an effect on you."

"Just keep rubbing," I muttered, but the soft rumble of pleasure in my throat brought a broad smile to his face as I peeked up at him.

When I shifted onto my side, his caresses grew increasingly intimate and his lips followed the twisting paths his fingers had sketched across my skin. I hadn't strayed from my morning routine in years, barring our weekend together, but I couldn't summon a word of protest, either, as I arched into his touch.

After finally playing out Nico's shower fantasy, which resulted in us running even later, we walked to the Keeper together. He grinned smugly when I ordered a heartier meal than usual at the coffee shop, choosing a breakfast burrito over a bagel.

When I magnanimously waved my hand for him to pay for both our orders, I lifted my chin. "Seems only fair. It's your fault I worked up an appetite."

"I'm more than willing to take responsibility for my actions, especially when I enjoyed every single second of it." He smirked as he held open the door for me.

"Mmm. Me too."

When we set off down the sidewalk, he slipped his arm through mine in a gesture of such casual affection that I almost stumbled before recovering. He responded to my misstep by kissing the top of my head.

It was sweet and affectionate, blissfully natural, as though the intervening years had evaporated between us.

For once, I found the walk to work was too short, though Nico's obvious reluctance in removing his arm in order for me to open the door consoled me. We ate breakfast at my desk, but he snorted when I left the office door open so that Erin would walk in on a respectable scene instead of a repeat of the morning before.

As I savored the last few sips of my coffee, I leaned back in my chair and studied him—he looked a little scruffy, a little sleepy, and appealing as fuck.

"Don't you have to work? Like, ever?" I asked.

Nico grinned around his last bite of a breakfast sandwich. "I work from home and set my own hours. You know, you do own your own business, Kitten. You could choose to come in at ten instead of this ungodly hour. It would give you more time for various . . . extracurricular activities."

"But then we wouldn't have to save time by showering together." I blinked at him, a picture of pure innocence, then my expression morphed into a sly grin and he laughed.

"Excellent point. It's worth your heart attack-inducing alarm to experience your sweet, wet body wrapped around me in the shower. Do you even know how fucking beautiful you are?"

He laced his fingers behind his head while his heated gaze stroked over my limbs. Though we weren't touching, I felt the words as surely as if he'd painted them on my skin. My cheeks flushed hot, but I managed to keep my gaze steady on his face.

"I'm not actually sure what you see in me, except that I'm clearly addicted to you now."

As he dropped his hands and leaned toward me, his expression sobered and those dark eyes grew intent on my face.

"I can't argue with that part, but fuck, Kitten. There's so much more. You're beautiful, yes, but you're also brilliant and loyal and fierce. I don't know if I'll ever be able to forgive myself for walking away from you, or for letting you walk away from me. All that time we could've had together, if I hadn't let your father and my own stupid insecurity scare me away."

Tears burned at the back of my eyes, but it was nothing compared to the feeling of being knocked completely breathless by his words. I could only stare for a long moment while I struggled to make my lungs start functioning again. Before I could speak, Nico was out of his chair and crouching at my side.

"Hey, I'm sorry," he said softly, running his knuckles along my jaw. "I'm sorry, Kat, I didn't mean to upset you."

"I'm not upset. I just . . . that's the nicest thing anyone's ever said to me."

My voice broke just a touch and his arms went around me. Nico held me while I tried to gather myself back into some semblance of calm.

"You can cry all over me tonight, if you want. Why don't I bring over a pizza and a box of tissues?" he offered.

My wobbly laugh made him flinch ever so slightly, like I'd driven a stake through his heart. "That sounds perfect," I said, pressing my fingers against my eyelids. "I should probably get to work."

He trailed a row of kisses across my forehead, murmuring, "You do that. Tonight, pizza. And if you happen to open the door wearing only a silk robe, I won't complain."

At that, I laughed outright, clearing some of the tension from his expression.

"I'll see what I can scrounge up from my closet. And Nico," I said softly as I laid a hand on his cheek, "thank you."

With a smile, he turned his head, kissed my palm, and stood.

"Better get used to it, Kitten. I won't be so easy to shake off this time around. Not by a long shot."

I watched him go, those long legs of his covering the space from the office to the parking lot in half the time it took me. I was still staring after him when the warehouse door opened again and Erin fluttered in.

"Aw, c'mon, Kat. I was hoping to get at least some vicarious action this morning," she called as she wandered into the office. A sudden frown creased her forehead when she saw my face. "Is everything okay? Do I need to chase after him and kick his ass?"

"I'm fine, I promise. No ass-kicking required."

Erin dropped down into the chair Nico had vacated. "You look . . . conflicted," she said carefully, studying my expression.

*Conflicted.*

It was a good descriptor for how I felt. For so much of my life, I'd longed to be in this position, with Nico at my side—but I was afraid to be too happy about it just yet. Everything was still unsettled, at least until the painting was sorted out.

I'd lost him once before; losing him again would destroy me.

"I think I'm in love with him." The words poured out of me before I could stop them. I covered my face with my hands and moaned, "What am I going to do?"

"Do? Besides the obvious, which is to continue letting that stud kiss you like he's been wandering the desert and you're a cold glass of water?"

"I'm not sure it's that simple."

Erin smirked at me. "Do you really think he's not just as in love with you as you are with him, Kat?"

"Yes. No. I don't know!"

Her smile went soft. "I know enough for both of us."

"I think I've loved him since I was in kindergarten and it certainly wasn't reciprocated back then. Things are just really complicated right now."

"Life is complicated," Erin replied, but her expression was gentle. "I see the way he looks at you, honey. It might be complicated, but you have to know he's head over heels in love with you. Believe me, I can tell these things."

I nodded—somewhere deep down, I knew it, too.

Part of me wished I could waltz into my father's house, pluck the painting off the wall, and hand it to Nico so we could move forward, but it would continue to hover at the horizon until we came up with a better plan than burglary. Preferably something that one or both of us might be more qualified for.

Except...

"We've got work to do," I said, flashing a bright smile at Erin and ignoring my assistant's sudden suspicion. "I've got to make some calls. Can you update this week's spreadsheets?"

Erin nodded and closed the door behind her as she left the office. I grabbed a notebook and made a sketch of my childhood home, taking care to map the grounds of the estate as well. Once upon a time, Nico and I had tromped through the woods, explored every inch of the house, raced and roamed and made the entire property our playground.

When he left for college and I decided to test the practically invisible boundaries of my teenage years, I'd used that knowledge to sneak out for dates and parties—not because my father would've said no, but simply to flex my own youthful power.

I'd never been caught, either.

Ten minutes later, I had a fairly decent blueprint of the property in front of me, along with a few jotted notes and arrows detailing the best paths in and out. I didn't know the intimate details of my father's security team these days, but at least I could guess based on my previous knowledge of them.

Experienced burglar I was not, but I had more confidence in my ability to slip in and out of my father's home undetected than Nico seemed to have. It was the aftermath that concerned me; Aidan Willoughby was not the type to stand by and let something be stolen out from under him, not something of actual value. I could steal the painting, I was sure of it, but I didn't want Nico to be swept up in the manhunt that might follow. He'd never be able to enjoy his inheritance if he had to spend the rest of his life hiding it away.

Or if he was one of those adversaries who went missing without a trace, or one of the mangled bodies found in the woods years later with no evidence of a crime.

With a sigh, I tucked the map into my purse and convinced myself to stick to the plan. I spent the next half hour fiddling with the broken pieces of my old phone until I finally convinced it to boot up, then I swallowed down a hoot of victory.

Once my data was safely transferred over to the new one, I pulled up my contact list, uttered a silent prayer that this might actually strike gold, and made the call.

# Chapter Seventeen

## NICO

Though I hadn't expected to actually find Kat in a silk robe when I showed up with dinner, I threw back my head and laughed when I caught sight of her pink flannel pajamas and matching fluffy slippers.

"Oh, now this is a look I could get used to," I teased, setting the pizza on the kitchen counter to take her in my arms. "Soft and cozy. You did make one mistake, however."

"And what's that, pray tell?"

"You're the most beautiful woman I've ever seen. And no matter what you're wearing, I want you all the same," I murmured against her ear. "So bad that I ache."

With a snort, she nudged me back a step. "Well, if the jammies didn't do their duty in killing your libido, I'll have to do it myself. I'm hungry, so we're eating before anything else."

"It's my dearest wish to cater to *all* your needs, even basic nourishment. Food first, then I intend to find out just how soft those jammies are."

I loaded our plates, then traded her one for a bottle of soda. We sat on the couch instead of at the small dining room table she told me she'd picked up at a yard sale down the street a few years ago.

"I'm glad you understand my priorities so clearly," she said. "Besides, I have some good news."

"Oh?"

"I got in touch with Evelyn, the journalist I mentioned. We were roommates in college. She put in a call to my father's secretary and texted me back just after five to say he agreed to an interview at the house. I'm sure he looked her up and saw that she's young and gorgeous, which probably helped convince him."

I flinched a little. "I hope you warned her about him."

"Oh, I did," Kat said, grinning. "She carries pepper spray and has a black belt in some martial art or another, so she wasn't overly concerned."

"How much did you tell her?"

"Shockingly little. She'd already heard about the painting and the exhibit, so she was eager to have an in. I told her it was okay to mention we were roommates, but not that I'd contacted her. I think she's used to anonymous tip-offs so she had no problem with that."

I didn't like Kat being connected to this in any way, but there wasn't much to be done about it. "Good. That's good."

"The interview is set for tomorrow afternoon and Evelyn will be sure to get footage of the painting, wherever it's hanging. I said I was curious about where it was, because I didn't remember it. I'm sure she realizes there's more to the story, but she didn't pry. She's hoping the piece will air tomorrow night."

"You truly are a goddess," I said, impressed.

This version of Kat, alight with excitement and glowing with success, was a far cry from how I'd left her that morning. It also went a long way to soothe the guilt I'd been carrying around with me all day.

She sat back and raised her soda in a toast. "One step closer, at least."

Cozying up with her in the evenings was becoming a habit I knew would be hard to break, though I sincerely hoped there'd be no need to do so. This was the closest thing to family that I'd experienced in a long time, and I knew it was the same for Kat. When we finished dinner, I took the plates to the sink and held out my hand to her.

"I want to take you to bed," I said softly. That now-familiar sizzle coursed through me as soon as she laid her hand in mine.

"By this time tomorrow, we should have more brainstorming to work through, which will leave less time for sex," she teased.

My lips nuzzled her throat. "There's always time for sex."

Peeling the flannel pajamas from her body was just as enjoyable as the silk robe would've been, I decided later. More so, maybe, because these particular pajamas were so quintessentially *Kat*: soft, warm, and pink.

Revealing the equally soft skin underneath as I unbuttoned the top was like opening a Christmas gift designed especially for me. I felt like I was making up for lost time, so I gloried in soaking up every opportunity to spend time with her, both in bed and out of it.

Late in the night, when she was curled against me, sated and sleepy, a surge of emotion caught in my throat. I loved her—Christ, how I loved her—but I was so damn terrified of putting her in danger that it threatened to choke me.

Smoothing a hand over her hair, I wondered what the hell I'd gotten us into and how I could navigate us safely back out of it again. When I finally dozed off, my dreams were unsettled, a flashing amalgam of memory and nightmare where we huddled under her father's desk during a raging storm, but we were no longer children. Kat sobbed soundlessly in my arms as thunder shook the house and our fathers screamed at one another in a mix of English and French.

Long before her alarm clock could startle me into another heart attack, I jerked awake, yanked from the dream like someone had pulled an invisible thread. Kat murmured sleepily, unaware of my rioting pulse, so I eased my way out of bed and tucked the blanket around her.

In the kitchen, I poured myself a glass of water and chugged it down, my unseeing gaze falling to the countertop. As I set the glass aside, my elbow knocked over Kat's purse, spilling bits and bobs of random junk, accompanied by a folded sheet of paper that fluttered open at my side.

"What the fuck?" I whispered into the silent kitchen.

It was a drawing of the Willoughby estate, perfectly to scale in a way that only Kat could manage from memory alone. I leaned down to read the notes in the light of the street lamp outside and a fresh string of curses fell from my lips.

Memories pounded inside my skull of Kat's sudden whims throughout our youth—sometimes brilliant, always impulsive. Late-night excursions into the woods to see if there were really ghosts where the old carriage house had burned down decades ago, spy-style missions into the kitchen to sneak forbidden snacks, challenging a middle school bully to a battle of wits that resulted in Kat getting a fat lip and me having to threaten the kid within an inch of his life.

I couldn't be sure she wouldn't put her own safety at risk in order to achieve our goal, and that was unfathomably terrifying.

"Nico?"

At the soft sound of her voice, I squeezed my eyes shut to control the urge to rage at her, shake sense into her, demand her solemn vow not to go anywhere near her father without me at her back.

"What is this?" I asked instead, my voice as tight as the muscles I kept clenched in restraint.

Her warmth teased my senses as she came to stand beside me, but even my panic couldn't resist the pull of her. It loosened its grip on my heart when she threaded her arm around mine and tipped her head against my shoulder.

"It was just an idea, in case we don't come up with anything else. I wasn't going to do it without talking to you, I swear."

There was a timid little trill in her voice that dissolved the rest of my anger, though it left behind an aching chasm of fear. I turned and wrapped my arms around her, nuzzling my face into the top of her wild curls.

"I'm sorry," she whispered.

"It's okay. It's okay, Kitten. I just need you to be safe. This isn't a game."

Her breath hitched as she mumbled, "I know."

My arms tightened around her, and we stood that way for several long, quiet minutes before my fear fully subsided, leaving behind a clarity that was at once simple and earth-shattering.

I chose her. I would always choose her.

Kat was it for me. No family heirloom could replace this perfect, gloriously frustrating woman in my arms. No hidden leverage could be worth losing her.

"Let's get you back to bed," I murmured into her hair.

She nodded against my chest and let me guide her back into bed, where I curled my body around hers in a protective cocoon. I waited until she drifted back off before I turned my attention to some of the ideas I'd considered in the past for retrieving the painting.

Unfortunately, most of the options I'd come up with over the years would require me and the painting to disappear afterward—something that I no longer considered an option. I would no sooner leave Kat behind than I would force her to abandon the life she'd created for herself.

Even if it meant going back to the drawing board a dozen times over, I was determined to find a solution that didn't necessitate leaving town or putting Kat in any degree of danger.

# Chapter Eighteen

## Kat

By the time Nico arrived at my apartment the next evening with a bag full of groceries so he could make dinner for us, I was ready to burst with excitement. I still wore my work clothes, which today featured rainbow striped knee socks, a twirly black skirt, and my leather jacket.

"Oh, come on. We've only been dating for three days and you've given up putting on those sexy pajamas for me already?"

I scoffed and poked him in the ribs. "You're a jerk, you know that?"

"Who, me?" Nico grinned. "This outfit is really doing it for me, just so you know."

"Oh?" Momentarily distracted, I glanced down at myself, then flashed a wicked grin. "Good to know."

He proceeded to unpack the grocery bag, setting out ingredients with a precision that I found as sexy as he apparently found the knee socks. Finally, he looked over at me and shook his head indulgently.

"All right, spill. What is it that has you bouncing and bubbling like this?"

I dragged him to the dining room table, popped my laptop open, and gestured to the image on the screen. "Evelyn emailed me a photo she took at the house today."

It was my father's office. I knew Nico would never forget it, not after that night we'd spent hidden under the desk, the night that had changed my life forever. Standing before the fireplace was an older, slightly grayer Aidan Willoughby, smiling against the backdrop of the Beaumont painting.

"Son of a bitch," Nico muttered, but his eyes swept from the computer screen to my face. When he caught sight of my expression, he shook his head. "We still can't steal it. It's too dangerous. Too many risks."

"You had no qualms about trading me for the painting, but theft is what, too illegal for you?"

He caught my chin in his hand. "I wouldn't trade you for anything, Kat, not then and not now. And I had qualms aplenty, just so we're clear. Seeing you bleeding and disoriented at the cabin was the most terrifying thing I have *ever* experienced. I won't go through that again."

I wanted to argue—I'd snuck into that office a dozen times over the years, pilfering everything from pens to bottles of whiskey—but Nico's expression halted my protest.

"Whatever you did in high school, you were starting out *inside* the house. We sure as shit can't just waltz in unnoticed to grab it. I've learned enough about your father's security protocols to know that breaking in would get us both shot."

Everything inside me softened at his concern. "Point taken."

"We'll find a way. You cannot break into that house, Kitten."

"Okay. Evelyn said the story will run at seven. Plenty of time for you to make us a fancy dinner," I teased gently, hoping to wipe that fiercely protective look from his face.

"Promise me," he said, not releasing his grip on my chin. "Promise me you will not go into that house without me."

My heart fluttered in my chest. "I promise, Nico."

I didn't like it, and I didn't agree with his assessment of the danger, but he'd never forgive me if I went against his wishes in this—and he'd never forgive himself if something happened to me because I did.

Before he released me, his other arm slipped around to the small of my back, pressing me to him. By the time his mouth landed on mine, my lips were already parted in invitation. He was definitely being a bit overbearing by demanding my word like that, but I knew I was impulsive enough to terrify him at times. I'd done it often enough in my youth to recognize the fear in his eyes.

It felt strange to have someone concerned over my safety, and stranger still to like it.

Once I was breathless and flushed in his arms, Nico drew back and grinned. "Plenty of time for an encore later. If we want to eat, I better get started on dinner."

It turned out Nico had learned a number of things about cooking from his father, despite his own professed disinterest in the culinary arts. I watched him as he worked, trying not to let my nerves over the interview get the best of me. Even though I was sure he must be feeling the same, he didn't show it, not anymore. He looked calm, capable, and impossibly at ease in my kitchen as he chopped vegetables and whisked sauce on the stove.

"You really never thought about following in your father's footsteps?" I asked, propping my chin on one hand as I leaned against the countertop. "Chef Nico sounds pretty hot, you know."

"I thought about it, sure," he replied. "It was just never my passion, not the way it was his."

"But hacking is?"

He pointed a spatula at me. "Not a hacker."

"You know what I mean. I remember when you started bringing a laptop on our adventures instead of a book. I just thought you were messing around."

"I started programming maybe a year before high school. It just made sense to me, the way mechanical stuff makes sense to you. Writing a really beautiful set of code, that's what makes me feel like I'm on top of the world. For my dad, it was coming up with a truly stellar recipe. He loved watching people enjoy what he made. Especially you. I think he got more joy out of cooking for you than for anyone else. You're very enthusiastic in your responses, you know."

I rolled my eyes at his innuendo, but then I cocked my head, considering. "You know, I always thought he was just offering me a haven from my father, but he would make me sit and keep him company when I was at the cottage, and he'd always put a plate of something or other in front of me."

"He loved you," Nico said simply. "I hope you know that. Even if your father would choose to swim with electric eels rather than see us together, I'm pretty damn sure my dad always dreamed you'd be his daughter-in-law someday."

"I miss him. I wish . . ." I trailed off, then refocused my gaze on him. "Well, I wish a lot of things. I'm just glad you're here now."

He added a pinch of seasoning to the pan and turned down the heat before crossing over to me. With one hand curled around the back of my neck, he tilted my face up so he could kiss me. This wasn't a sizzling demand or a gentle reassurance, but a slow, thorough reminder that we were together, here in this moment. As my soft sigh whispered across his lips, Nico lifted his head.

"I'm glad I'm here, too." He kissed the tip of my nose and moved back to the stove.

We ate in relative silence, apart from the low moan of pleasure I made upon my first bite of chicken chasseur. It was a dish his father had made time and again, sentimental and delicious, and it had always been one of my favorites.

"This is heavenly," I purred, choosing to ignore the pointed look he leveled at me.

It wasn't that I didn't know how to cook, I simply detested it—cooking was a necessary evil in my world. I'd never found the same joy as Pierre Beaumont had in what I viewed as a survival skill and I certainly didn't have one iota of Nico's unconscious talent for it, but I knew a good meal when I tasted one.

After dinner, we moved to the couch and I turned the TV to Evelyn's news channel. Nico was silent but tense, though he tried to hide it by draping his arm along the couch cushion and toying with the curls at the back of my neck. I couldn't think of anything to say that might distract him for the few minutes remaining before the news came on, so I just leaned my head against his shoulder and set a hand on his knee.

When the anchor on screen started talking about the upcoming exhibit of pieces by Hugo Clément, my stomach clenched. Under my palm, Nico's thigh muscles were taut.

The anchor gave an introduction and cut to Evelyn's interview. She was petite and exquisitely beautiful, with long black hair and delicate features, and she was seated diagonally from my father in his office. I fought back a bubble of nervous laughter as I thought about squeezing under that desk again now, with Nico's long limbs and my own curves.

"How did you come by this magnificent piece of artwork, Mr. Willoughby?" Evelyn asked, gesturing up to the wall behind them.

My father gave her what I'd always called his schmoozing smile, wide and patronizing. "I purchased it at an estate sale when my daughter was born and it's been hanging in the house ever since. We had no idea that it was anything more than a beautiful piece until recently, when an art collector friend saw it and questioned who the artist was. Imagine my surprise to learn it was painted by Hugo Clément."

Nico growled, but I squeezed his knee in warning. I didn't want to miss a word of this, even if it was all lies—and even if my father was dragging me into the dirt along with him.

Evelyn smiled, then followed up with, "Have you been asked to lend the painting to the Warner Museum of Fine Arts for the duration of their Clément exhibit? It seems they're very eager to feature such a newly discovered piece."

My father's expression turned almost mournful. "They've asked, certainly, just as a number of collectors around the world have asked if I'd ever sell it. The fact of the matter is that this painting is very sentimental to me, given its connection to my daughter. I simply couldn't bear to part with it."

The interview ended soon after, but I barely paid attention. My mind whirled with possibilities, shifting the puzzle pieces back and forth, tilting them every which way.

"Well, that was the biggest load of bullshit I've ever heard," Nico muttered, turning off the television and tossing the remote onto the coffee table. Even his voice didn't quite cut through my distraction until he waved a hand in front of my face and said, "Earth to Kitten, come in?"

I jerked, startled from my tumbling thoughts, and blinked Nico back into focus. He stared at me intently, waiting.

"Sorry," I mumbled. "It was bullshit, yes, but that might be just what we need."

"How do you figure?"

"He's saying he's owned that painting since I was a baby, right?"

He blinked at me. "So?"

"So," I continued, "if a painting worth millions of dollars was in my father's possession the last time you and I were together in that office . . ."

Nico sucked in a sharp breath as he followed my train of thought. "Then it would be subject to the divorce settlement, unless it was written into their prenup, which obviously it was not."

"Exactly." I tucked my knees under me, turning toward him. The excitement sparkling in his dark eyes mirrored my own. "And while you and I might not have the funds for a long legal battle, I know someone else who would be extremely happy to take his ass back to court over it. That will leave him to either reveal he's lying about ownership or fork over millions to my mother for her half of the asset. Either way, it buys us time to make our own move."

"You're a genius," he said, leaning over to kiss me. "An evil genius, in this case, which I'm finding almost disconcertingly attractive right now."

I grinned. "Why, thank you. I even surprise myself sometimes. I was thinking, though, that maybe we should pursue another angle once we turn that information over to my mother. When's the last time you went back to France?"

"France," he repeated, frowning in confusion. "We went back just once since I moved here when I was what, four, five? For my sixteenth birthday."

It was a long shot, I knew, but if Nico hadn't found anything useful in his father's belongings after the funeral, it was the only other option.

"Nico, if we can find anything, literally anything proving the link between that painting and *your* family, we can discredit him completely."

He was silent for a long moment.

"Discrediting him might have to be enough," he said finally. "I don't know if there's any chance of that painting being returned to me, and I may have to accept that."

I'd come to the same conclusion, though it pained me. As much as that painting symbolized family and history to Nico, to me it represented the only place in my entire childhood where I'd felt like I belonged.

Losing it would hurt. A lot.

I squeezed his hand and nodded. "I want to see him pay for what he did to you. But if we can't get the painting back, we can at least ruin him."

"There's something else you need to know, Kitten."

His solemn tone freaked me out. "What?"

He drew a deep breath before speaking. "There's something hidden in the back of the painting, an SD card, embedded in the frame. I don't know the details, but my father called it leverage."

My lips parted in surprise. "Leverage. Like, dirt on my father?"

"I assume so. He said if something suspicious ever happened to him, I should take the painting and use that information to protect myself. He told me to get far away from your family if it came down to that."

A tiny fissure of hurt zigzagged through my chest. "Were you going to leave?"

"No. Kitten, even when he told me about it, I wasn't willing to leave you behind, and that was before all of this happened. If your father stumbles across whatever it is, though, he may assume I'm the one who put it there."

"Shit," I whispered.

"Yeah. And at this point, you're linked with me, which means it might put you in danger, too."

Something he'd said caught inside my head. "Something suspicious," I murmured.

Nico stayed silent, watching me closely.

"Your father was a fit man in his fifties. He told you he had a bad cold, and then he died the next day. Doesn't that strike you as suspicious?"

*Double shit.* I didn't want to believe it, but given the evidence of my father's other misdeeds, it wasn't beyond the realm of possibility.

Nico shook his head. "He didn't kill him, Kitten. There was an autopsy. He had pneumonia and developed sepsis. Your father might be powerful, but that's not something he could orchestrate. Believe me, it was the first thing I considered when I got that phone call."

My eyes flew to his face as relief flooded my veins. My father's hands weren't clean, but I hated the thought that he'd had something to do with Pierre's death. "Are you sure?"

"Unless he had the autopsy faked. But I think you're right—he might've taken the painting because my father said something while he was delirious."

"I was thinking it was about the artist, but what if he said something that made my dad suspect the painting housed whatever evidence he had? It might not have been about Clément at all."

"That's possible," Nico conceded. "I hadn't considered that."

"If that's why he took it, though, he must have realized you weren't involved. It's been two years, and he hasn't come after you yet."

"True."

The relief sweeping over me was overwhelming in its intensity. Maybe Nico was safe from my father, after all—at least until we poked even harder at this hornet's nest.

"Right. So finding proof your family owns that painting is still the only chance we have of knowing whether he uncovered what's inside or not."

"And maybe," he mused, "even if we can't get our hands on it, we can manipulate things in a way that might get the painting donated to a museum. That would be almost as satisfying as having it in my possession, and it would keep whatever's in the back safe from him, if he hasn't found it already."

He tugged me onto his lap and nuzzled my throat until I was laughing and breathless. "So we have a plan?" I asked.

"We have a plan. You really are a goddess."

"I am pretty fantastic," I agreed. "But let's not get ahead of ourselves."

Nico stood, lifting me easily into his arms. "We'll get working on the details tomorrow. I have plans to celebrate my evil genius girlfriend tonight."

# Chapter Nineteen

## NICO

THINGS MOVED QUICKLY AFTER that. At Kat's request, I sent an anonymous email with a link to the interview, along with a few pertinent details, to both her mother and the lawyer she'd run away with following the divorce. After the way the former Mrs. Willoughby's lawyer had raked her former husband over the coals during that process, there was no doubt the two of them would know exactly what to do with this new information.

If our only choice was to make Willoughby's life miserable, the man's ex-wife would serve as the perfect proxy.

Kat arranged for Erin to handle things at Kat's Keepers while she was away and booked our flight to Avignon for that weekend. I was stupidly proud of her for being willing to take that time off, even if I felt guilty for pulling her away from her livelihood.

Though I would rather have stayed in a hotel, I contacted one of my cousins about the trip and we were offered a guest room with the family. Jérôme was the cousin closest in age to me and we'd kept in touch over the years, especially after we met up on my sixteenth birthday trip, but I couldn't for the life of me remember our exact relation. Second cousins? Third? Twice removed?

It didn't matter. I only knew that our fathers had been some degree of cousins but had grown up as close as brothers. The last time I saw Jérôme and his father, affectionately called Uncle Philippe despite the confusion over how we were actually related, had been at my father's funeral.

Finishing out the week and getting things ready for her absence barely made a dent in Kat's excitement. It radiated from her like a palpable aura, shimmering around her in a halo of joy. Despite his riches—and his recently purported love of art—Aidan Willoughby had never been the type of man who wanted to spend his vacations exploring museums instead of schmoozing on a golf course, so this would be Kat's first trip to Europe. She'd never met any of my extended family, either, and I was looking forward to seeing things through her eyes.

There was nothing like Kat Willoughby's sense of wonder to make everything more enjoyable.

Of course, I was also nervous. Part of me felt like I was going home to announce my own failure. I'd hoped our next conversation about the painting would be to inform them it was safely back with the family, not to confess it might be lost to us for good.

Even though I'd always considered myself an American, at least since I started kindergarten here in Spruce Hill, France was my father's homeland, spoken of with such affection that it developed into a magical place in my mind, a haven of love and laughter and the kind of family ties that didn't exist for me in the States.

The prospect of admitting defeat hung over my head, threatening to drown me in shame.

Having Kat at my side was the one thing that held me together. She shone like a beacon in the darkness, sparkling in her usual way and keeping me sane through it all.

On Friday night, I picked her up after work, stopped by her place to get her luggage—all of which she'd decorated with glittery rainbow kitten stickers that made me guffaw when I saw them—and brought her back to my apartment for the first time. It was located in a slightly more modern section of town than hers, one of a dozen apartments in a nondescript brick building.

When I opened the door to let her in, she took two steps inside and halted so quickly that I bumped into her.

"This is where you live," she stated, looking around.

The place was spacious enough, but I knew it was bland, devoid of color and lacking, as far as one could tell from where we stood, a single personal touch. Sad beige furniture, blank white walls, shining but bare wood floors.

"Yes. Home sweet home." I skirted around her to set the suitcase off to one side, then studied her critical expression. "What's wrong with it?"

"Nothing, I guess, if you like generic and cold."

I laughed and wrapped my arms around her middle, drawing her against me so I could bury my face against her neck.

"Does this feel cold to you?" I asked softly.

Though she gave a soft hum of pleasure, she refused to be distracted. "I want a tour. Let's see the rest of this pitiful bachelor pad, hmm?"

I acquiesced only after twirling her around and kissing her soundly. For the most part, the remaining rooms were more of the same, though the master bedroom showed evidence of at least a few strokes of color, thanks to the plaid comforter I kept on the bed.

The second, smaller bedroom had been turned into an office where I spent the most time, and as such, it was the only room in the entire apartment that looked remotely lived in.

"This is rough, Nico," she said, shaking her head. "When's the last time you brought a woman back here?"

I considered it, then shrugged. "Four years, maybe."

Kat's jaw dropped and she said, "You cannot be serious. When did you become a monk?"

The smirk on my face had color rising in her cheeks before I even spoke. "I didn't say I haven't gotten laid in four years, just that I don't bring women here. And before you ask, it's been almost a year since I did even that much, okay?"

"No wonder you're such an enthusiastic lover," she quipped, smiling brightly at me.

My smirk widened into a teasing grin just before I picked her up and tossed her over my shoulder, letting her helpless laughter wash over me like a balm.

"No wonder," I drawled. "Now let's go add a personal, *enthusiastic* touch to my nice big bed."

---

BENEATH THE BRIGHT VENEER of Kat's excitement, the fact that she was nervous about the flight flared into evidence several times before we finally settled into our seats on the plane. I laced my fingers through hers and leaned over to peer out the window beside her. When I drew back, I frowned at her tense posture.

"Kitten," I said gently, "are you afraid of flying?"

Her forehead wrinkled in an expression that looked more troubled than thunderous. "No, I'm not afraid. I just don't like it."

"I could distract you," I offered, angling myself toward her to block the view from the aisle.

Now her expression darkened enough for her eyes to shoot daggers at me. "Or I could disembowel you. That would make a good distraction. You just keep your filthy hands to yourself."

When I feigned offense and tried to withdraw my hand from hers, she tightened her grip and laid her head against my shoulder.

"Except this one. I'm keeping this one."

I laughed and kissed her temple. Though her fingers squeezed mine painfully tight as the plane took off, she relaxed enough to enjoy the view once we rose above the scattered clouds and into a brilliant blue sky. For the first part of the flight, we chatted in low tones about random topics—nothing pertaining to the painting or Kat's father, nothing that might bring back her tension—and then dozed for a few hours with our arms linked and heads tilted together.

By the time we landed, I was fairly sure her nerves had faded into the background, leaving that starry-eyed excitement front and center. Christ, I was ready to offer her the world just to keep it there.

It wasn't until we found Jérôme outside the airport that I suddenly realized Kat had greeted my cousin in beautifully spoken French. I cocked a brow when I caught her eye, but she only grinned at me. Since she insisted I sit up front with Jérôme during the drive out to the house, I didn't have a chance to question her until we were unloading our suitcases from the trunk.

"When did you go and learn French?" I murmured against her ear.

Mischief sparkled in her eyes. "I actually minored in French in college, thank you very much. Seriously, your stalking skills are crap. Besides, my father might not have cared to communicate with your dad in anything other than English, but I'd learned enough to stumble through conversations with him by the time you left for college. I'm just a little rusty."

"You don't sound rusty. I've barely spoken any French since I was in high school, so I'm sure I'm even rustier. You, however, sound hot as hell." I chucked her under the chin, then the introductions began.

While Kat was swept off by Philippe's wife, Camille, to get settled in, I sat down in the kitchen with Jérôme and Uncle Philippe. The older man, more gray than blond at this point, didn't look much like my dad, but he had that same knowing expression in his dark eyes. It even inspired the same response in me as it had from my father, so I straightened my shoulders to steel myself for the third degree.

"Tell me why you're really here, Nicolas. You were vague enough on the phone, but we all know this isn't a social call."

I rubbed my hands over my face. Though Kat spoke fairly fluent French, she always pronounced my full name the American way. Now, though the conversation was in English out of deference for their poor American relation, hearing my name as my father always said it filled me with a wave of grief so overwhelming, I needed a minute to gather myself before I replied.

As succinctly as possible, I relayed the story of how Aidan Willoughby had gotten the painting before my father's funeral, our suspicions that my father might have revealed the truth about its origins, my long quest to get it back, and the hurdles still before us.

Then I described the night my father hid his "leverage" in the back of the frame.

Philippe and Jérôme listened without a word, nodding here and there. When the tale was over, my uncle regarded me steadily for a long, quiet moment.

"Nicolas," he said in a low voice that reminded me so clearly of my father that my heart clenched again, "sometimes things happen that are beyond our control. Your father wanted you to have that painting, *oui*. He would never have expected you to break the law to get it back, not even to retrieve what was hidden. I think you already know this."

The knot of tension that had taken up residence in my chest loosened. "I do know it. He would never have wanted Kat involved, either. He loved her like she was his own blood."

Philippe leaned back in his chair as he studied me. "Before me, I see the boy I've called nephew for more than thirty years, the boy who turned into a man so much like Pierre that it brought tears to my eyes to see you again after all these years. He would be so proud of the man you have become."

I blinked back tears myself, inclining my head in silent acknowledgment. If I spoke, I knew I'd end up crying like a baby.

"Tell me what help I can give to you and your *copine*, and it is yours. We are delighted to have you here, but tell me, what is it that you seek?"

I gave a strangled laugh. "That's a loaded question right there," I replied. My uncle only smiled, so I blew out a breath. "For once, I want the villain to lose a round. If we can find any documentation of the painting's origin or the fact that it belonged to our family, then we can prove Willoughby is lying."

"And even if you do this, you may never get that painting back. Can you live with that?"

Kat's laughter drifted in through the open windows. Everything in me turned toward the sound, drawn to the warmth of her presence like a heat-seeking missile. When I forced my gaze back to Philippe, his smile was soft, his expression knowing.

"Ah, I see," he said quietly.

"Yeah." I wasn't surprised my uncle understood. We were French, after all. "She's . . . everything. If I hadn't already been on this path when I found her again, I would've abandoned it for her."

Jérôme clapped me on the shoulder. *"Elle est si belle,"* he said, grinning. "Why a beauty like that would choose *un connard* like you, I could not say, but I am happy for you, cousin."

When the women came into the kitchen after another few minutes of ribbing from the two Frenchmen, I felt like the sun had just come out from behind a cloud. My aunt was a stunning woman, with blonde hair several shades lighter than Kat's, but it was the brilliant smile Kat sent my way that quite simply illuminated the entire room. The warmth of it soaked into my veins, untwisting any remaining tangles of the knot in my chest.

She fit into my family as easily as she fit in my arms. Even though I hadn't seen most of them since I was a child, Philippe's quiet mention of the painting to the right parties caused my other aunts and uncles—some of whom weren't any blood relation at all—to circle the wagons around both of us.

It wasn't an experience Kat or I had ever had before, but it filled me with appreciation, with love and a touch of wistfulness.

The next day, after several back-breaking, eye-blurring hours of rifling through boxes from three different attics and storage areas, I called for a break. As I relaxed with Kat in a hammock strung between two trees in Philippe's yard, I twirled a lock of her hair around my fingers and stared up at the leaves overhead.

I'd never considered moving back to France, but for the first time in as long as I could remember, I did start thinking about what the future might look like—a future that included Kat at my side. Images of a little house tucked away from town, with trees for a hammock and room for children to explore, danced before my eyes.

"I had an email from Evelyn," Kat said, sounding sleepy. "The shit is starting to hit the fan over there. My mother is in Florida at the moment, talking to various reporters and news outlets. Apparently she and her lovely second husband took the bait."

I kissed the top of her head, nestled as it was in the crook of my shoulder. "That may have to suffice. We haven't found so much as a reference to the painting so far."

Kat twisted to peer up at me. "Is it terrible that I'm still really, really glad we came, even if we don't find anything helpful? Your family is amazing."

"I was just thinking the same thing," I murmured. My sigh was one of contentment, not disappointment—having Kat in my life changed everything for the better. "I still can't believe you're fluent in French and I didn't know."

She gave an indignant huff and muttered, "I have a great many secrets. You don't know everything about me, *monsieur*."

"No?" I nuzzled her ear. "I know enough, enough to realize you're everything I ever wanted."

Kat drew in a sharp breath at the words, then released it, sinking against me. "Oh?"

*"Je t'aime,* Kitten."

The whispered words shivered across her skin, raising goosebumps before my warm palm smoothed over them. A tear spilled over her cheek, landing in a damp circle on my shirt. I immediately lifted my hand to her face, urging her to look at me.

"Oh, Kat. Don't cry, please don't cry," I murmured.

When her lips lifted to touch mine, I knew I was lost—my heart belonged to her. It always had. She drew back and smiled in that soft way that made her blue eyes shimmer with joy. Emotion flooded my chest, threatening to burst forth like shooting stars. Never in my life had my heart felt so gloriously full.

"I think I've always loved you, you know," she said quietly.

My arms tightened around her. "Believe me, I do know, because I've loved you just as long."

Contentment cloaked us both as surely as the dappled sunlight that danced across our skin. Kat closed her eyes and I let the warmth of her body and her words sink through me.

Not all quests ended with success, I knew that well enough, but now that we had found one another, it certainly felt like we'd cleared the biggest hurdle of all.

# Chapter Twenty

## Kat

That night, Nico made love to me slowly, tenderly, like he was taking particular care to show me just how precious I was to him.

When we first arrived, we'd both thanked our lucky stars that Uncle Philippe hadn't been so cruel as to insist on separate bedrooms under his roof. We had only one more full day in Avignon before flying home and, despite having little to show for our efforts, I knew we both felt like we'd been handed a second chance.

Even as we settled down on the living room floor to sort through the last of the boxes the next morning, Nico seemed to be feeling optimistic to an almost unsettling degree. How long had it been since he'd looked to the future and seen a chance at real happiness?

I noticed his bright mood right away and tilted my head at him.

"You're awfully chipper this morning." I leaned close and whispered, "I can't possibly imagine what might contribute to such a sunny outlook first thing in the morning, dear Nico."

He winked at me. "I have the most beautiful woman in the world by my side, what more could I ask for?"

I shuffled through a stack of papers, shaking my head. "Solid legal proof of ownership of the painting, maybe."

"I wouldn't turn it down, but I don't think we're going to find anything along those lines here. I'm prepared to accept defeat."

Still, we worked side by side until the final box was emptied and repacked. Despite Nico's resignation, I had to fight against the wave of disappointment rising in my chest. Too often, I'd seen my father win because of his money, his connections, or his willingness to play dirty.

It would've been beyond satisfying to beat him at his own game.

Philippe and Camille insisted that the two of us spend the rest of the day playing tourist, so Nico dragged me off to see some of the sights in Avignon. It was every bit as glorious as I'd hoped, especially with him at my side. We toured the Palais des Papes, wandered through the museums, and strolled hand in hand through the Place de l'Horloge.

Nico seemed to glow brighter throughout the day, as though the wonder in my eyes fed some spark within him as well.

"We'll come back someday soon," he said softly, kissing my temple as we returned to his uncle's house. "As often as you want."

I nodded and leaned into him for a moment. We hadn't found all that I'd hoped for, but the trip felt almost like a honeymoon, a little bubble of solitude and beauty so far removed from our regular lives that I was tempted to just hide away here forever.

"Your father must have missed this, after you moved to the States. The place, the people. Even the language," I mused.

"He did, I'm sure. But no matter how much he loved it here, after my mom died, there were just too many painful memories for him. That's why he took your father's job offer."

"Did he ever regret leaving?"

"No, I don't think so. While I was growing up, he told me so many stories, about her, about the family. I barely remember living here, but when we showed up, it felt like coming home. Having you at my side this time just made it that much more meaningful."

I squeezed his fingers. "I'm sorry we didn't find what we were looking for. I really hoped there'd be something for us to use against him."

"Don't be sorry. Everything works out the way it's supposed to—my father always said that. I used to think it was ridiculous and sentimental, but now I'm beginning to realize maybe he knew what he was talking about."

He tugged me in for a quick, fierce kiss before we entered the house.

We were home just in time for a boisterous family dinner that included Jérôme's girlfriend, Angélique, Philippe's sister and brother-in-law, and their son, François, who was a few years younger than me. Though Nico gave the young man a sharp look when he lingered over kissing my cheeks, François had an infectious grin and accepted the admonishment good-naturedly.

"Before you two go home, Katherine should see some pictures of baby Nicolas. Best to know what to expect before your own little bundle comes, *non?*" Aunt Camille smiled slyly at Nico's startled expression and my crimson cheeks.

"Oh, I really don't think that's necessary," Nico protested, but he was immediately overruled by the ladies at the table, including me.

There was no way I would miss this chance. Nico had been gorgeous from my first memory of him—I was willing to bet he was a ridiculously cute baby.

He allowed himself a groan when we cooed over the photo albums that were conveniently at hand, but after a moment, he sat back to watch me smile with delight as I turned the pages. That particular joy dissolved into shock about three minutes later, and Nico jerked to attention as my expression shifted.

"What is it?" he demanded, leaning toward me.

"Nico . . . look."

My finger landed on a photo of him at age three or four, sitting on his mother's lap as his father looked proudly down at his little family from behind her chair. At first, Nico's gaze lingered on his mother's image, but I knew the moment he saw it.

Hanging on the wall behind them was the Clément painting.

"Holy shit," he breathed, earning himself a sharp jab in the ribs from his aunt. "*Pardon, Tante Camille.* This is it, Kat. This is our proof that your father was lying. This was right before *Maman* died, which refutes his story about buying it when you were born."

A flurry of activity rose up around us even as Nico and I continued to stare at one another. At Camille's insistence, I carefully removed the photo from the album, then we pored over every remaining page, searching for more. Within minutes, everyone at the table had been handed a photo album from various generations and we scoured the images, some in color and others black and white, looking for any that captured the painting in the background.

Every so often, a triumphant exclamation rose from one relative or another, and a small pile of photos showing the painting through the decades formed at the center of the table. The level of excited chatter grew along with the collection, which gave a clear glimpse of the family growing and changing over the years under the watchful eye of Céleste Bicardeau.

Both Nico and I took pictures of each photo found, in case anything happened to the originals.

"I'm an idiot for not thinking of this sooner," Nico muttered.

François and Jérôme exchanged grins before Jérôme spoke. *"Oui, cousin.* It is very lucky you have such a brilliant family to assist, *n'est-ce pas?"*

I snorted, but I understood Nico's comment all too well. What better proof of provenance than several generations' worth of photographic evidence? Our focus had been on the kind of things my father dealt in—paperwork, wills, insurance records. It hadn't occurred to either of us to search the very heart of an extended family history like Nico's, namely the countless albums piled beside us, consisting mostly of childhood photos.

Twelve more hours and we would've set off home without ever seeing these pictures, without a single speck of proof to contest my father's lies.

By the time the group finished, I was fighting tears—tears of relief, of satisfaction, of the overwhelming love I felt not only for Nico, but for all of these people who'd welcomed me into their home and into their lives.

The sun had long since set and the pile of photos had been carefully packed up for us to take home when the guests departed. Each warm embrace threatened to tip me over the edge of letting the emotion loose, but I managed to hold it together until Nico and I finally crawled into bed.

He'd seen the sheen of moisture in my eyes during the family's farewells, so he simply opened his arms. Within seconds, I was curled against his side, tears cascading soundlessly down my cheeks and trailing over his bare chest. There were no murmured words of reassurance this time, just his warm embrace, his lips against my hair.

I let out a long, shuddering breath as the tears dried on our skin. Maybe we could win this, after all.

# Chapter Twenty-One

## NICO

Hours passed before I let myself follow Kat into sleep. There were decisions still to be made, ones that involved her as much as me, but all I wanted to do was enjoy the feel of her in my arms, to lie there and breathe in the soft scent of her. Reality would hit all too soon; for now, my entire world was right here.

The true test would be whether I could keep it that way once we got home. This battle wasn't over, not by a long shot.

By unspoken accord, we didn't discuss what to do with the photos during the flight home, nor during what I'd teasingly termed our "recovery day" before returning to our real lives. Kat insisted we spend it at her place, though she'd reluctantly conceded that my bed was entirely tolerable.

The following morning, however, we decided that it was finally time to talk through the options as we ate breakfast. I ticked off each potential plan on my fingers.

"One: we go to your father directly, tell him we can prove he's lying, and give him the chance to do the right thing. Two: we go to the media with the photos and let that put pressure on him, see what he does from there. Three: we hang tight to wait and see what happens between him and your mother. Or four: we go straight to the police and let them sort out the mess."

"You think that would work?"

"No." I made a face. "And I'd rather we not choose that one because it will both shine a light on some of my more questionable hacking *and* take things completely out of our control."

Kat's lips quirked at my use of the word *hacking*, but her tone was gentle and her gaze intent on my face as she said, "What do you want to do, Nico? What's our end goal?"

*You,* I wanted to say. *You are the beginning and the end for me.*

The stubborn set of her jaw made me think she could see the truth written in my eyes. It wasn't that I thought she'd disagree with that particular sentiment, only that I knew she was determined to come out on top in this battle with her father, for my sake.

"I still want the painting back," I said quietly. "But if I can't have it, I'm petty enough that I want to make sure he doesn't get to keep it, either. The longer he has it, the greater the chance of him finding what my father hid."

There was a look on her face that I didn't like, one that said she would do battle on my behalf if it came down to it.

"No matter what, Kitten, I will not put you in harm's way. You are more important to me than the painting."

Kat rolled her eyes. "Fortunately for us both, I'm a grown woman and fully capable of making my own choices. My father might be a sleazeball and a cheat, but he won't hurt me."

Of course, that didn't mean she believed I was safe from her father's underhanded methods of retribution. I wondered if I'd have an easier time keeping Kat safe if she weren't so focused on doing the same for me.

"Are you sure of that?" I demanded. "Really, truly, one hundred percent sure? You ran away from the cabin because you were terrified of what his thugs might do to me. Can you really be so certain that he wouldn't send them after you, once he knows you're working with me? That he won't want to punish what he sees as your betrayal, because you're siding with me over him?"

For a moment, her gaze flickered away from me, which was confirmation enough. She'd been grounded for weeks once after standing up for me to her father when he accused me of scratching some antique side table in the library.

No matter how much she hated that I was right, my point stood. Aidan Willoughby had stolen a family heirloom from a man who'd worked for him for decades, then lied publicly about that painting's origin for his own gain. There was a greater plan in play, I was sure of that, one most likely rooted in money.

What was worth more to the man, the daughter he'd cast aside so easily or millions of dollars? It was an easy answer, but how far would he go to keep what he'd falsely claimed as his own?

"I still say it's safer for me than it is for you," she insisted, scowling at me.

I surprised her by laughing instead of arguing my point. "Fine, we'll have to agree to disagree, but I'm going to take this standoff as a sign that we shouldn't get directly involved. Either of us. That leaves us with waiting it out to see how your mother gets on, or slipping the photos to the press. Which one sounds like a better plan to you?"

The flash of defiance drained slowly out of her as she thought it over. "Let's give it a few days, at least, to see if anything else happens between my parents. I'm not sure leaking the photos to Evelyn directly would be the best course of action, since I don't want to paint a target on her back, either. He'll be pissed enough as it is if he realizes it was her interview that brought my mother down on his head."

Nodding my agreement, I slid an arm around her shoulders. Tomorrow, we'd both return to our regular lives. Another few days would give me more time to analyze the risks of both options and work through any hiccups I might be able to foresee.

Hopefully, the best path forward would become clear.

After I walked Kat to work the next morning, lingering just long enough for Erin to walk in on another searing embrace, I headed back home and sat down in my office. While half my brain worked on a problem for a client, the other part considered the variables at hand.

Ultimately, it came down to one simple fact: confronting Aidan Willoughby was a dangerous proposition.

The photos would make it abundantly clear who was behind the discovery. There was simply no way to hide that if we went public. Still, I thought it was safest to poke the bear from a distance—and to accept that the outcome wasn't likely to be what I hoped for.

*Leverage,* I mused, thinking about the SD card and my father's cryptic explanation.

The photos provided leverage, especially once public opinion got involved. Willoughby liked to present himself as the white knight of the legal world, the rehabilitated bad boy who'd seen the error of his wild ways after he was caught cheating on his wife, the family man who'd raised his daughter alone after a very public, very messy divorce.

He was going to be angry if made to admit he'd lied. Wouldn't it be better if that anger were directed toward his ex-wife, rather than his daughter's lover? Or, worse yet, his daughter herself? Waiting for him to speak out would certainly be safer for Kat than forcing him into action.

By lunchtime, I'd finished my work for the day and was able to focus all of my attention on the problem at hand. I scoured news sites, social media, anything that might indicate where things stood between Willoughby and his ex-wife. It had only been a few days since Julia Willoughby-Chesterfield arrived back in the United States, and she'd made good use of her time.

I'd always found the woman terrifyingly beautiful, the ice queen running The Castle of my youth. Never anything less than perfectly coiffed and garbed, her dyed blonde hair was several shades lighter and harsher than Kat's honey locks. She had blue eyes the same color as her daughter's, but they'd always felt entirely different when they landed on me—which hadn't been often, thankfully. Where Kat's sparkled with intelligence and good humor, Julia's had forever been cold, calculating, constantly seeking some kind of advantage out of every situation.

Of course, I realized I was probably biased, looking back on my childhood. As a motherless child, I'd longed for the warmth and love my father had so frequently described when he talked about my mom.

Kat's mother was nothing of the sort, even before she went away.

On the day she left with Ferdinand Chesterfield for St. Croix, I could still recall with perfect clarity the desolation in Kat's eyes. I never understood how anyone could simply walk away from their own child, especially one as easy to love as Kat.

I rubbed a fist against my chest, fighting the ache. If the wound still felt so raw for me, how did Kat bear it? Could I really ask her to face down not only her asshole father, but her heartless mother, as well?

I forced myself to stop dwelling and turned back to my search, replaying each clip I'd found of Julia speaking to reporters about the painting. She looked just as I remembered her, though perhaps a bit tighter around the mouth and eyes. Even with a megawatt smile for the handsome young newscaster, she seemed as cold as ever. I closed my eyes to focus on the words instead of the image.

"My ex-husband, as you know, broke our marriage vows while I entertained his illustrious coworkers. He publicly humiliated me, Mr. Carlson. Am I surprised he hid something as valuable as a painting by Hugo Clément during the divorce proceedings? Of course not. I should have noticed its absence on the divorce papers, but as you can imagine, I was terribly distraught."

She sniffed and dabbed delicately at her eyes with a handkerchief and answered a few more of Jeffrey Carlson's questions before the clip ended.

Though I didn't think she had the brains to orchestrate a true battle against Willoughby, she might still be a means to an end. Her new husband had won her an impressive divorce settlement, but that was largely due to the iron-clad prenuptial agreement already in place. Still, it was entirely possible the man had picked up a few new tricks over the intervening years.

On the other hand, Aidan Willoughby had not yet spoken publicly about the painting or Julia's crusade, not since his interview with Evelyn. I wasn't foolish enough to believe that silence signified he was ready to admit defeat. It was likely just the opposite. Maybe the man held enough sway among judges now to simply brush off his ex-wife's claims, or maybe he'd try to handle it quietly, away from the spotlight.

Whatever the case, we'd find out soon enough. Willoughby would eventually have to show his hand.

While I busied myself with reviewing keyword alerts, I considered Kat's adamant belief that her father wouldn't hurt her. If Willoughby hoped to keep things quiet, releasing the photos was going to shred that goal into tiny little pieces. Once the man was backed into a corner, whatever scruples he might possess were likely to fly out the window. We hadn't been hiding our relationship, so all it would take was one careless word from someone in Spruce Hill to inform Willoughby of his daughter's connection to me.

I felt trapped between warring sides of the equation. It might be safer for Kat if we kept our distance from one another for a while, but if I wasn't close by, how could I possibly protect her?

# Chapter Twenty-Two

## NICO

IN STANDARD KAT WILLOUGHBY fashion—stubbornly and with no small hint of that fiery temper of hers—she immediately shot down my suggestion of keeping her distance from me, even temporarily. I'd tried to broach the subject as diplomatically as possible when I arrived at her apartment that evening, but the fury that rose within her was truly a thing to behold.

If it hadn't been directed at me, I might have been impressed.

"Don't be an idiot," she snapped. "I'll be damned if I let him ruin another single thing for me, Nicolas Beaumont. Whatever your macho sensibilities are telling you, I suggest you shut them the hell up."

With a long-suffering sigh, I raked my hands through my hair. "The painting is just a *thing*. An important thing, sure, but it's just canvas and paint. You're a living, breathing human being who I am madly in love with. If something happens to you, if *anything* happens to you because of my role in all this, I will never forgive myself."

Despite her annoyance, there was still a crystal clear image in my mind of patching up her bleeding arm at the cabin, of how I'd taken care of her, fussed over her, soothed her. I'd already caused her harm by involving her in this mess. The thought of hurting her more was like an arrow in my heart.

"The more obvious the connection between us, the more likely it is your father will lump you in with me when shit hits the fan."

"I am not staying away. Not from this fight, not from you. We're in this together."

"I need you to be safe." The alternative was unthinkable.

"Look, Nico," she said softly, her tone conciliatory now, "you know that I'm safer with you watching my back than I would be alone, and vice versa. And anyway, I have a gift for you."

I blinked at her in surprise, but I waited quietly while she disappeared into the bedroom. Knowing Kat as I did, it was just as likely to be an antique toy that reminded her of my eyes as it was to be something bizarrely useful. She possessed a knack for gift-giving that had always intrigued and enchanted me—like when she was fourteen and happened upon a signed copy of my father's favorite vinyl at a consignment store in town.

It had been so long since we'd spent a holiday together, I hadn't even realized just how much I'd missed those goofy, quirky gifts of hers.

Kat returned after a moment bearing a stiff manila envelope, which she handed over with a slightly misty smile. "I wasn't sure I had anything of use, but after our success in France, I decided to take another look."

I lifted the flap and slid out three glossy photographs. The first featured my father with one arm looped playfully around my ten year old neck and the other knuckling the top of my head. Fighting a wave of grief, I spent a minute staring at the image, then set it aside to look at the other two pictures.

The next one was me by myself, taken just before my junior prom, dressed in an uncomfortable rented tuxedo and holding the magenta corsage my date insisted I buy for her. The last was a picture of Kat at fifteen or so, her golden locks still long enough for a bouncing ponytail, pecking my father playfully on the cheek.

All three photos had been taken inside our cottage behind the Willoughby mansion. All three showed the painting clearly in the background.

"It might be just canvas and paint," she said quietly, "but it's also family and connection and legacy. Even if you didn't want it back, I would go to war with my father just to see that returned to you. This is airtight proof it belonged to your family during the years your father worked for him, in case he claims he misremembered when he bought it."

I laid the photographs carefully on the coffee table and yanked her into my arms, crushing her against my chest. As I buried my face in her hair, I wondered what the hell I'd done in this life to deserve her.

"I regret a lot of things in my life, Kitten, mostly related to walking away from you all those years ago, but I will never be able to regret the way you came back into my life, even if my stupidity made you think you were being kidnapped."

Her laughter was muffled against my shoulder. "There's been more excitement in my life these past few weeks than in the past decade," she joked.

"If anyone is going to war for me, I'm glad it's you. He doesn't stand a chance against the two of us."

It settled me somewhere deep inside, that simple statement, settled both of us if her soft sigh was any indication. Even if I was still concerned for her safety, having her by my side was a comfort, a strength I simply didn't have on my own.

It was also, I had to admit, sexy as fuck to see her turning so fierce on my behalf.

"Look, I'm going to scan the photos in and work up a program to send them out when we're ready. If you've got any particular news outlets in mind, let me know. I think it's probably best if we scatter them to make sure your father doesn't take it out on any one reporter or organization. We'll need a message to send along with the photos, though—I think aiming for subtle rather than combative would be in our best interest," I said, tugging her across my lap as I sat down on the sofa.

Kat drew back and let her jaw drop. "Are you calling *me* combative?"

"I would never," I deadpanned. My steady gaze held hers until she smothered a laugh with her palm, then I grinned. "I would, however, describe you as tempestuous, ferocious, and just the tiniest bit impulsive at times."

She sniffed delicately and hiked her chin in the air, but her eyes glinted with amusement. "And you, Mr. Kidnapper, are just an even-tempered sweetheart, huh?"

I grinned. "Clearly."

Despite the particularly pleasant form of distraction Kat offered, my mind continued to circle back to the photos. Once they were released, that was it. There would be no taking it back. Willoughby would know for certain who was behind it.

I wished I could predict exactly how the man would react, how much danger we might be in, whether her father would try to hurt Kat in retaliation.

*Maybe*, I thought just before I dozed off later that night with Kat spooned in front of me, *maybe I can convince her to take a long weekend at the cabin.* When I finally fell asleep, memories of our time at the cabin filled my dreams.

I spent the following day setting everything up for the release of the photos, but my suggestion of a weekend retreat was met with a flare of annoyance and not-so-subtle disdain from the woman in question. No matter how I pitched it, Kat brushed off my concern and insisted that she needed to spend the weekend scouting out new items.

"Nico, for fuck's sake, just give the program the green light and let's get on with it," she said, leveling a knife at me from where she stood chopping vegetables in her kitchen. "The more we delay, the more on edge you get. If I have to murder you for my own peace of mind, I'm going to be really pissed, but I can't take it much longer."

That sentiment I certainly understood. I squeezed the bridge of my nose between my fingers.

"Fine, you're right. I'll make sure it goes out tomorrow, then. But if you think I'm leaving you to traipse through garage sales and antique malls alone this weekend, you're very much mistaken. I'm sticking to you like glue as soon as those photos go public."

Kat leaned over and gave me a smacking kiss on the lips. "I happen to like when you stick it to me," she teased, waggling her eyebrows at me.

I laughed, but even her light-hearted quips couldn't dissolve the knot of nervous energy in my gut when I sent out the photos just before lunchtime the next day. I'd held back the one of Kat and my father, choosing instead to turn that one into the wallpaper on my phone screen. Maybe I could pick up a frame for the printed version while I tagged along on her scouting expeditions.

As soon as the slew of anonymous messages were launched into cyberspace, I grabbed my overnight bag and headed to Kat's Keepers.

Erin, for one, was delighted to see me. "Kat's busy with some repairs at the moment. Can I get you some coffee? We have a fresh pot brewing."

I gave her a broad smile. "That'd be great, thank you. If I don't touch anything, is it okay to poke around and look at this stuff?" I asked, gesturing to the shelves lining the big warehouse space.

"Oh, of course! Make yourself at home. I'll be right back." She slipped into a break room beside the office, the door to which was still firmly closed, and I stuck my hands into my pockets as I wandered the perimeter.

They had an impressive array of old toys, ranging from iconic to quirky to downright bizarre. My phone pinged as I studied a mechanical tin shepherdess, and I let out a tight breath—the first news site had thrown a slapdash headline together and published some of the photos. By the time Erin came out with a mug of coffee for me, three more had gone live as well.

For a brief moment, I considered storming the office to inform Kat, but Erin managed to convince me to sit down in the break room with my coffee and a slightly stale donut leftover from what she called their "TGIF morning splurge."

By the time Kat emerged from the other room, her fingers streaked with some kind of grease that required dish soap to remove, a dozen more alerts had come through my phone. She paused just inside the break room doorway, hands aloft to avoid staining the vintage movie tee she wore under her beloved jacket, and raised her eyebrows in question when she saw the look on my face.

"It's done," I said simply.

It seemed to take a great deal of effort for her to move her feet, but she eventually made it to the sink so she could scrub the grease from her hands.

"It's done," she repeated, nodding slowly. "So now all we have to do is wait."

I nodded. I was tired, weighed down in a way that I wasn't sure even she could lift. Kat dried her hands on a towel and then came over to wrap her arms around me. Without hesitation, I rested my head against her soft stomach and slid my own arms around her waist. We stayed that way for a few minutes, sharing our strength, until Kat finally stepped away.

"Now, if you're finished fueling up with coffee and donuts, let's get out of here," she said, tugging at my hand. "We're playing hooky this afternoon. I sent Erin home already, but you and I have a couple yard sales to hit."

Whether she seriously wanted to start her weekend of scouting early or, as I suspected, she simply wanted to distract me from the impending fireworks, her plan worked. There was nothing quite like watching her haggle over a few grimy and often broken hunks of plastic or painted metal.

"You're one cool customer," I told her, impressed, as we left the first sale with an armload of goods.

Kat beamed at me and dropped a little curtsy. "I do try. I'm sure half of these people think I'm completely ridiculous for bargaining over toys like that, but whatever. This one will probably sell for close to a hundred after I get her cleaned up," she said, holding up an ugly doll who looked like she'd gotten a nightmarish makeover from a toddler.

"Not once did you let on that any of this crap is worth more than a couple bucks. Very smooth, very collected. It's a hell of a turn-on, you know."

She laughed, a bright, musical sound that warmed me to my toes. "Well, I'm glad I'm not boring you, Nicolas."

"I don't think you could ever bore me, Kitten, even if you tried. And you know, I like the way it sounds when you say it."

She smirked at me as we headed down the street to the next sale. "What, your name? You mean like an American instead of the French way, like your family? I'll admit I found that pretty sexy."

My lips curved. "Oh, you can speak French to me any time, *mon cœur*. We already established just how hot I find that."

Kat devoted our scouting excursions to keeping my mind off of the buzz generated by the photos using any means possible. She teased, cajoled, flirted—and for the most part, she was successful. I appreciated it, even during the moments when I couldn't quite stop myself from looking at the alerts.

Aidan Willoughby had still not made any public statements, nor had he tried to contact me or Kat directly, but our anxiety grew throughout the weekend, knowing the other shoe was bound to drop.

On Sunday, Kat dragged me out to an antique mall almost an hour away, but even her own focus on the expedition was scattered. We still left with a canvas tote bag full of items, half of which I could barely recall seeing her pick out and which she confessed were probably worthless.

The most memorable purchase of the afternoon was a velvet painting of Elvis Presley wearing a sequined jacket, which she'd only agreed to buy because it had us both in stitches when we came across it.

I turned the radio to something soothing for the drive home and kept her laughing with some fond memories of our childhood adventures. Kat was still wiping tears from the corners of her eyes when she caught me frowning at the rearview mirror. All trace of laughter evaporated as she turned in her seat and spotted a dark SUV with tinted windows riding our tail.

"Does he want to pass us? Oh god, he's close," she whispered.

We were on a narrow country road in the middle of nowhere, miles still from Spruce Hill. My heart leapt into my throat as the driver of the SUV closed the already dangerously short distance between the cars.

Though I briefly considered trying to pull off to let the car pass, a yawning pit of dread opened up inside my gut. Asshole drivers were nothing I hadn't dealt with before, but being tailed by one in a shiny new vehicle with dark-tinted windows felt altogether different.

Especially surrounded by endless stretches of farmland, forest, and little else.

At my side, Kat fumbled for a minute trying to unlock her phone, then she turned around in her seat.

"Jesus, be careful. Don't take off your seatbelt under any circumstances," I ordered.

She raised the phone, snapped a photo of the SUV's license plate since we could barely see the driver through the windshield, then turned back around. I glanced over and saw her dialing 911, but when the other vehicle struck our bumper, she cried out and dropped the phone. I struggled to control the car as it lurched drunkenly forward.

"Hang on," I said grimly, pressing my foot down on the gas pedal.

My thoughts raced faster than the vehicle, which was hovering just above seventy at the moment. If we pulled over—or if we were forced off the road—there was no telling who or what we'd be facing if our tail followed us instead of speeding past. In my mind, images flashed in quick succession: volleys of gunfire, bullets riddling Kat's beautiful body, blood coursing down her skin.

"He's going to hit us again," Kat said, a mixture of horror and panic in her voice. "Nico, he's revving up to hit us again!"

# Chapter Twenty-Three

## KAT

Dimly, I heard the emergency operator speaking from the floorboards, but I was too paralyzed by fear to even try to reach the phone. Nico pressed his foot hard on the gas, grasping the steering wheel so tightly his knuckles went white as he tried to keep the car on the pavement.

"Kitten, listen to me. There's a stretch of trees coming up on the right. We're going to pull off and as soon as the car stops, you're going to run like hell into the woods, do you hear me?"

"What about you?" I asked. My pulse roared in my ears, but his words sliced into my panic like a blade. "Nico, what about you?"

"I'll be right behind you, I swear I will be. We don't know what kind of weapons might be inside that car or how many people are in there, so I need you to take off like a bat out of hell.

Promise me. Don't stop for any reason until you get somewhere safe. I won't be able to do a damn thing if I don't know you're safe, Kat."

I opened my mouth to agree just as we were struck again, harder this time. The impact caused me to bite the inside of my lip hard enough to taste blood.

"Nico!" I gasped, but it was too late.

The black SUV rammed into the left side of our bumper a third time, sending us into a gut-wrenching spin. The other vehicle blew past us, speeding away as Nico's little sedan took a nosedive into the ditch along side of the road. In the span of an instant, I went from listening to his muttered curses to hearing nothing more than a high pitched whistle as steam wafted from the engine. The airbags erupted into a blinding white cloud in front of us.

My own hoarse whisper sounded miles away when I said, "Nico?"

Something damp dripped down my cheek, but I couldn't tell if it was blood or tears. The world still twirled outside the stillness of the vehicle, spinning for several minutes until the waves of dizziness dissipated. At that point, I realized my head was pressed against the window and tried to sit back against the seat—it took every remaining ounce of strength just to lift my head.

When I wiped the back of my hand against my cheekbone, the streak of blood on my skin cut through the fog.

"Nico!"

I managed to blink him into focus only to see the airbag deflating in front of him. His eyes were closed, his body still as death, just as it had been that day in the forest. My seatbelt locked when I tried to reach over to check for a pulse, then I saw his chest lift and fall with a breath and went limp with relief.

Harsh gasps burst from my lips until I slapped a hand over my mouth to quiet them. Eventually, my panic waned a little, enough for me to realize we couldn't just sit here and wait for the SUV to return.

"Phone. Phone," I muttered, wrestling with the belt buckle.

I needed to call for help. That goal filled my mind and blocked out everything else, even the throbbing pain in my cheekbone.

My fingers were sluggish, but once I managed to free myself from the seatbelt, I bent down to find the phone that had fallen by my feet. The screen was blessedly intact, though it took me several shaky attempts to unlock the device. I hit redial on the previous 911 call and almost cried when the same operator spoke.

"We need help," I gasped around the tears that clogged my throat. "Please, I think he's hurt. Someone just ran us off the road. We need help."

The calm voice on the other end assured me they had officers on their way already and encouraged me to stay on the line. When I was ready to break down completely upon seeing the ashen tint to Nico's normally golden skin, the operator walked me through checking the pulse in his throat. It was strong and steady under my fingertips, soothing me until the sound of sirens grew close.

"They're coming," I whispered. "I'm going to hang up now. Thank you. Thank you."

Nico shifted in his seat with a groan. "Kat?"

"Oh, thank god. We're okay, Nico."

"We're okay," he repeated.

He winced when he lifted his head, but his fingers laced with mine and gave a squeeze. Though I had no idea how bad I looked, the blood on my face caught his attention. In the glow of the flashing lights coming up behind us, he reached over and cupped my chin in his hand. After a moment of searching, he located the tiny cut on my cheekbone, rubbing his thumb gently below the wound.

"You're bleeding. Why do you always end up bleeding when you're with me?"

I gave a shaky laugh. "I'll survive. You're the one who was unconscious."

"I'm okay," Nico said softly. As he watched, my eyes fluttered closed and a single tear rolled down my uninjured cheek. "We're both okay."

Two police cars and an ambulance pulled up alongside the wrecked vehicle. With my phone still clutched in one blood-smeared hand and Nico gripping the other, I gave in to the waves of relief that stole through my veins.

The darkness tugged me down, down, and the last thing I saw was a female EMT with bright red hair peering through the web of cracks in the passenger window.

---

WITH NO IDEA HOW much time had passed, I reluctantly opened my eyes, only to squeeze them shut again under the bright lights of a hospital room. For a brief second, I wondered if I could slip away into the peaceful darkness again, then my lids flew wide and I sat up so quickly the room spun.

"Easy there, easy," a man in navy scrubs said gently.

"How long was I out? Where's Nico?" I demanded.

I waited only until my vision steadied before trying to swing my legs over the side of the bed. It wasn't a hospital room after all, just a curtained section of a larger area.

"Is this the emergency room?"

"Yes, at Eastman Memorial."

I grimaced. There was no hospital in Spruce Hill, so the ambulance had brought us into the city. "And Nico?"

"Your friend will be just fine, Ms. Willoughby. I believe they're getting his discharge paperwork ready. I'm Dr. Thorne, and you've only been out for a few minutes. The ambulance just brought you both in. You were only unconscious for the duration of the ride."

The doctor eased me back onto the bed and checked my pupils with a tiny flashlight. I squinted against the brightness, but he smiled reassuringly.

"No signs of a concussion, which is a good thing. How are you feeling? Do you remember what happened?"

"I'm fine," I snapped, then I saw the gentle amusement in the doctor's eyes and sighed heavily. "Sorry. I'm not a fan of hospitals. My head doesn't hurt, but my cheek aches a little where it hit the window. Yes, I remember every terrifying second, at least until the paramedics got there. It's a little hazy after that."

Dr. Thorne smiled at me. "Follow the light with your eyes, please. Good. The cut on your cheek is small and shallow, so you won't need any stitches, but the bruising will probably get worse before it gets better. I suggest icing it for your comfort, though there won't be much you can do about the discoloration. You have some abrasions across your collarbone from the seatbelt, but otherwise you emerged fairly unscathed. The police have been waiting to speak with you. Think you're up for it?"

I nodded silently. Even with my surroundings staying obligingly steady, my mind was still awhirl. More than anything, I wanted to lay eyes on Nico, to verify that he was really okay.

When the doctor left to fetch the police, I leaned back on the pillows and stared up at the fluorescent light overhead. As much as I wanted to get up and pace, I had no interest in being found in a heap on the floor.

"Ms. Willoughby? I'm Detective Rose Hanson and this is Officer Huxley Ford, Spruce Hill PD. Would you mind answering a few questions for us?"

I blinked at them for a moment before nodding. "Yes, of course," I replied, sitting up straighter in the bed.

Ford, a short man with a cap of tight auburn curls and a wide, friendly smile, looked vaguely familiar, though probably a few years younger than I was. The detective was a gorgeous Black woman several inches taller than Ford, her dark hair pulled into a no-nonsense bun that matched her expression.

"It was quick thinking on your part, placing that first call. We had already traced it and set out toward you before the second call came through," Ford said kindly.

I wondered if this would turn into some sort of good cop, bad cop routine, but his sympathy soothed my nerves a bit.

"It would've been quicker thinking if I hadn't dropped it on the floor," I replied, then frowned until my eyes landed on a clear plastic bag that held my phone and purse.

I eased to my feet, wavering just enough for Ford to catch my elbow, but made it to the bag so I could draw out the phone.

"I got a photo of their plates. Hopefully it's clear, I didn't have time for retakes."

"Well now," he said, sounding impressed, "I'd say that was the quickest thinking of all. Mind if I get a copy of this?"

I handed the phone to him and sat back down on the bed as he and the detective studied the photo. "How long do we have to stay here?"

Ford looked up. "That's up to the doctors. We just have a few questions for you first, Ms. Willoughby."

Hanson asked a slew of what I considered easy questions—where had we been, had I noticed anything suspicious in the last week, how did I know Nico—then watched my face closely when she asked, "Did you recognize the driver of the other vehicle?"

"I couldn't even see him, not with the tinted windows. I didn't recognize the car. That's why I tried to get a photo of the plates."

"Can you think of any reason why someone would want to hurt either you or Mr. Beaumont?"

I rubbed my eyes, wincing when I accidentally brushed across the tiny bandage over my cheekbone. "My father has made a number of enemies during his career, I'm sure, and it's likely he may be . . . unhappy with recent news reports."

"About the Clément painting, you mean? We caught wind of that this weekend. There's been some public outcry," Hanson said evenly, but I was well aware of her assessing gaze on my face.

I wished Nico were there to talk through the situation—I knew he would tell me to stick to the truth, but how much should I reveal?

"That's to be expected when you lie about your possession of a family heirloom that happens to belong to someone else's family," I bit off.

Ford's brows rose. "I don't suppose you or Mr. Beaumont would know who leaked those photos to the press, would you?" When I remained stubbornly silent, the policeman grinned. "Well, can't blame a guy for trying."

"Do you believe your father is behind what happened this afternoon?" Hanson asked.

I gave a long, heavy sigh, shoulders drooping as the air left my lungs. "I don't know. My father isn't my biggest fan, but I wouldn't have thought he'd do anything that might kill me. We got lucky, pure and simple. That crash could've ended very differently."

*Lifestyles of the rich and famous,* I thought ironically as the two of them glanced at one another. There was a curious but slightly disgusted look on Hanson's face as she studied me, which had me convinced she was thinking the same thing.

It was another moment before she asked, "But in your opinion, this was an intentional act, not just a careless driver causing an accident?"

I snorted. "Given the number of times the other car rammed us, I can't imagine it was accidental."

She nodded and handed me her card. "Give us a call if you think of anything else. We can have someone take you two home after the doctors give the okay, if you need a ride. I'm afraid Mr. Beaumont's car will be a total loss. If you see anything else suspicious, I want you to call us, Ms. Willoughby. If someone is targeting you two, we need to know."

I took the card and nodded numbly as a sudden trickle of fear slid through my stomach. Did my father have any sway over the police in town? My brain was too fuzzy to recall.

"I will. Thank you."

"And Ms. Willoughby?" Ford added, rising to his feet. When I looked up, he smiled gently. "I hope everything works out for Mr. Beaumont and the painting."

I dropped my head into my hands as they left, drawing the curtain closed behind them. Was this the reality we were stepping into? Unfortunate incidents on deserted roadways, police investigations, constantly glancing over our shoulders?

How much more could we risk in this game of chicken?

# Chapter Twenty-Four

## NICO

WHEN I SLIPPED PAST the curtain half an hour later, having finished my own chat with both the police officers and the doctors, Kat stared blindly toward the window, looking pale and terribly lonesome.

My heart seized when I saw the shadow of bruising on her cheek, but I forced myself to relax as I moved to her side and said in a soft voice, "Hey, Kitten."

Her face lit at the sight of me, then crumpled just as quickly. My arms were around her before the first tears even fell. Though my left wrist was wrapped in gauze, covering a spray of tiny cuts from the broken windshield, I ran both hands soothingly up and down her back as sobs wracked her body.

"Shh, we're okay. We're going to be just fine, I promise."

As the tremors subsided, Kat uncurled her fingers from my shirt. "Do you think he found it?"

I knew she meant my father's leverage over hers—it had been the first thing to cross my mind, too, once the terror of being run off the road faded.

"Maybe, but if it was him, maybe he's just pissed about the leaked photos."

"Are you allowed to be in here?" she asked, wiping at her eyes.

Laughter bubbled up in my throat when she peeked at me like I was sneaking around in her father's house. Clearly, I needed to get her used to being close to me in public.

"Yeah, I've been discharged. Some cuts on my arm, but the airbag took most of the impact on my side." I eyed her cheek, frowning. "You, on the other hand, managed to bash your beautiful face against the window."

"I'll live," she said, then squeezed her eyes shut against another onslaught of tears at the simple statement.

I took her chin in my hand and waited until she looked at me again before I spoke. "We both will. The nurse said you already spoke to the police?" At her nod, I kissed the tip of her nose. "Then as soon as you're discharged, we'll get the hell out of here. I wish you'd reconsider some time at the cabin."

"I already have, as a matter of fact. I'll call Erin, tell her to take the week off. She was planning to go visit her sister's new baby soon, maybe she can bump up the trip. I do have one condition, though," she said, shooting a sideways glance at me.

"Oh?"

"We're going to need some better grocery supplies this time around. Now that I know you can actually cook like a pro, frozen pizzas are definitely not going to cut it." Her smile wobbled, but it was better than tears.

I laughed and kissed her temple. "I think that can be arranged."

As we listened to the buzz of activity outside of our curtained little haven, we were content just to hold each other quietly. Every concern I'd had for her safety had been cast into stark, sober reality. It hadn't happened how I'd imagined, but I would never forget her frantic cries as the cars collided.

Even amidst the squeal of tires and crunch of metal, I couldn't stop hearing the echo of her scream when we finally went off the road, nor the terrifying thud of her head hitting the window. The smear of blood on her cheek when the police arrived was nothing compared to what I'd expected to see. I was still thanking our lucky stars for that.

Dr. Thorne returned after a short time, but Kat made no move to shift away from me. The doctor simply lifted a brow at finding us snuggled up together against the raised head of the bed, checked Kat's vitals, and finally stepped back with a resigned sigh.

"Well, my preference would be for you to stay the night for observation, but I'm going to guess from the look on your face that you're eager to get out of here."

"You'd be right about that," Kat replied.

The doctor smiled at her. "As long as you two promise to take care of each other, got it?" he asked, pointing a stern finger at us. "I'll go finish up the paperwork and send the nurse in to walk you out."

We both thanked him, then I bounced my eyebrows as soon as the curtain fell shut again. "While we're waiting, wanna make out?"

Kat choked on a laugh. "Because I'm feeling so sexy right now. How about we cuddle until we're allowed to blow this popsicle stand?"

With my arm wrapped around her waist and her head resting against my shoulder, I pressed a kiss to her temple. I couldn't think of a single thing I wanted more than to just hold her, and if the way her fingers curled tightly in the fabric of my shirt was any indication, Kat felt the same.

We didn't move from that spot until a smiling pair of nurses came to usher us out of the hospital.

Twilight was just falling by the time we set out toward the cabin. I'd gotten us a rideshare over to the airport's twenty-four hour car rental desk, so we were now equipped with an adorably tiny hatchback that made me groan and Kat coo like it was some kind of baby animal.

We stopped at a grocery store outside of the city, loaded the minuscule trunk with shopping bags, and took a long, roundabout path out to my cabin.

If I could erase the tension radiating from Kat's frame every time headlights appeared behind us, I would've given anything in my power to do so. The radio stayed off, our phones were kept close at hand, and both of us remained vigilant even as I guided the little car onto the forest lane leading to the cabin.

It seemed like a lifetime had passed since the last time we'd been there. Along that final half mile of the drive, Kat finally allowed herself to relax enough to drop her head back against the seat.

"We'll be safe here," I said quietly. I needed to hear the words aloud as much as she did.

"You're always so steady," Kat said, apparently content to let my soft reassurance seep into her. "That night we hid under the desk, if I wasn't already in love with you before that, I sure as hell was after."

I slanted a smiling glance her way. "Oh really?"

Kat hummed and let her eyes fall shut. "I didn't know what they were doing, not exactly, but you covered my ears and pressed your head to mine to shut it all out. You were my knight in shining armor. Later on, when I figured it out, I was glad I hadn't understood at the time. I used to think back on it—if I'd known what was happening, with the crush I had on you, Christ. I probably would've started giggling like a maniac."

"You might not have understood, but I definitely did. For months, I worried you'd ask me to explain what was going on. I couldn't look your father in the face for a long time." I grinned at the memory.

"Oh, I found out soon enough. I hid from my father for an entire weekend after my mother left, tucked away in a closet in one of the guest rooms with a loaf of bread and a jar of peanut butter. I slipped out to use the bathroom but kept myself shut in there the rest of the time. I heard the maids talking about it while they cleaned the room. Hell of a way to learn about the birds and the bees," she said lightly.

As I parked behind the cabin, I captured her hand in mine and brought her knuckles to my lips. "I never told you how sorry I was."

Her eyes widened. "It was my idea to hide there, wasn't it?"

"I mean about your mother leaving you alone with him. I never understood how she could do that to you."

Kat sucked in a breath. "That makes two of us."

I squeezed her hand and we got out of the car. It took a few trips to bring in the groceries, but I teasingly told Kat I was capable of carrying twice as much with my uninjured arm, so we had everything unpacked and put away in short order.

After closing the freezer door, Kat stared blankly at the refrigerator for a minute until I wrapped my arm around her waist.

"Hey, you okay?"

She leaned back against me, like she was too weary to stay upright, then spun around with a scowl dark enough to unsettle me. "We didn't bring any clothes. I'm going to be back in my kidnap wardrobe, dammit."

I let out a booming laugh and tightened my good arm around her waist to twirl her across the small kitchen.

"Dare I suggest you spend the week naked in bed with me?" I teased. The blush in her cheeks made up for those narrowed blue eyes, so I kissed her and added, "Gumby is going to pick up some stuff from my place in the morning. If there's anything you need, I can have him get it for you."

"Pokey snooping around my underwear drawer? No thanks. When is he coming out here? Since Erin has a key to my apartment, I'll ask her to pack up some clothes and my laptop. She said she'd go over to the Keeper tomorrow to make sure everything is situated for the week, so she'll be in the area."

"Tomorrow is his day off, so why don't you set it up with Erin and I'll ask him to stop by your place to meet her when she's ready?"

Having something to occupy her mind, even for the five minutes it took for her to text Erin back and forth a few times, seemed to settle her nerves. Though she said she didn't give Erin much detail about what was going on, her assistant seemed extremely bright, so I was sure she'd put some of the pieces together.

Given that I'd been right in my predictions so far, including the fact that her father was apparently willing to put her in danger before admitting he lied, my assurance that I didn't believe Erin was at risk eased some of the tension from Kat's shoulders.

We slipped into bed early and Kat fell asleep almost as soon as her head hit the pillow. I held her, careful to keep from brushing against any of her bruises. After the events of the evening, my brain simply wouldn't shut off enough to follow her into slumber.

I'd need to make a counter move, and soon.

Willoughby had to know, in no uncertain terms, that I wouldn't tolerate another attack that threatened Kat's safety. I'd resigned myself to playing nice for her sake, but since that clearly wasn't going to work, I'd have to make the point that I had plenty of other weapons at my disposal.

I grinned a little in the darkness, remembering when Kat asked if I'd been doing "computer stuff" all these years. At the time, it had seemed prudent to let her make her own assumptions about my skills. It was difficult to explain all the things I'd learned in the last decade, but those things had served me well over the years.

They would serve me even better now.

Soon, very soon, I'd enjoy showing her exactly what "computer stuff" I was really capable of.

# Chapter Twenty-Five

## Kat

ACROSS TOWN, STILL HIDDEN away in the woods two days later, Nico tapped away at his laptop keyboard while I flipped through channels on the small TV in the living room. I wasn't sure exactly what he was planning, but it was clear he was preparing himself for some kind of action.

With a sigh, I draped my head back over the arm of the couch to send him an upside-down glance. As if he felt my eyes on him, he lifted his head and smiled, his expression softening.

"Not much longer, Kitten."

I opened my mouth to respond, but the deep voice of a newscaster caught my attention. Nico's gaze followed mine back to the TV.

"Next up, we have a last minute addition—another exclusive interview with Aidan Willoughby by our own Evelyn Masters.

We're News Seven at Seven, your only source for up to the minute news."

Nico rose to join me on the couch, so I curled up in a ball to give him space at the other end. Once he was seated, he wrapped a hand around my ankles and tugged my feet, clad in fleecy socks with lambs dancing across them, into his lap.

I frowned as a brief report on a robbery gone wrong played across the screen. Some art historian had walked in on an intruder at his apartment in the rougher outskirts of town and had been killed in the resulting altercation. Apparently the victim had an arrest record for forgery back in the early nineties. Both of us stiffened upon hearing the word "art," then relaxed again when there was no mention of my father or the Clément painting.

"I'm surprised Evelyn didn't text me that she was meeting with him again," I murmured.

"Last minute addition, they said. Maybe she didn't have time to give you a head's up? It would be just like your father to call her on short notice. Anything to make a splash, you know?"

I puffed my cheeks as I blew out a breath. "I guess you're right."

While the introductory music for the news program played, Nico lifted my foot into his hand and pressed his thumb into my arch, biting back a smile at my quiet moan. Between the stress, the uncertainty, and the lingering nightmares plaguing me after the crash, I was nearing my breaking point and he knew it.

CANVAS OF LIES 257

I just hoped we'd have some good news soon and that whatever came out of my father's mouth during this interview didn't make things worse.

As before, the interview took place in my father's home office, but the Clément painting was now propped on an easel between the two chairs. My father had a charming smile on his face as he returned Evelyn's greeting.

"Mr. Willoughby, when we spoke earlier today, you said you wished to address the very public claims circulating this week, both from your ex-wife and from unknown parties, questioning the true origins of this beautiful piece of artwork. What would you like to tell our viewers tonight?"

"Thank you, Evelyn. It's not widely known, you see, but I happen to be hopelessly colorblind. Impressionist art is particularly hard for me to process, as lovely as others tell me it is. After all this attention, I'm afraid I must admit that there's been a grave mistake on my part. This painting right here was moved into the house by my staff after the death of my very good friend and personal chef, Pierre Beaumont, a number of years back. In our earlier interview, I mistook this painting for the one you see now above the fireplace."

The camera panned upward to a remarkably similar painting in a slightly different color palette. I sputtered in disbelief, but Nico squeezed my foot as the interview continued. Evelyn and my father discussed the origin of what he kept calling his true family treasure, and with a self-deprecating smile, he explained how easily he'd confused the two after so many years without coming across them side by side.

Though I was sure my eyes were about to roll right out of my skull, Nico stared intently at the screen, waiting.

"I cannot apologize enough to the entire Beaumont family for this terrible mistake. As a gesture of good will, I intend to see to the legal procedures necessary to establish ownership for the family—pro bono, of course. I hope they'll view this as an equitable solution on all sides," my father finished, smiling apologetically into the camera.

"What a lovely gesture," Evelyn replied. "I'm sure it will be much appreciated."

This time, I didn't bother to hide my disgust. "What the actual fuck?"

With another rueful smile, my father went on. "Unfortunately, the painting that's been in the Willoughby family all these years has been assessed as having little monetary value, though it holds a great deal of sentimentality for myself and my family. If my ex-wife wishes to pursue her half of a few hundred dollars, I suppose that's her right."

As the interview finished up and the channel went back to their standard news report, I turned stunned eyes toward Nico.

"What is he trying to pull here?" I asked, baffled. "He's not colorblind at all."

Nico rubbed his forehead. "Fuck if I know. Either your father has suddenly grown a sense of honor, which I highly doubt, or there's something we're missing."

"What do we do now? Stay here, go home? Could this be a trap?"

It didn't *feel* quite like a trap—my father definitely wasn't stupid enough to set one on public television—but Nico didn't seem eager to throw us both back into the fray, either.

He blew out a breath. "I don't imagine he'd try to lure me in just to kill me. The car accident proved it's easy enough to get to me without getting his hands dirty. I planned on heading home this weekend sometime, but I'd like to know what he's up to before we leave here. Tomorrow is Friday anyway, so let's see what happens between now and then."

I nodded. "Sounds like a plan."

We didn't have to wait long. An email from my father came through to Nico the next morning, one filled with plenty of legalese and the very clear implication that if Nico accepted this course of action, he was also agreeing not to sue my father in a court of law. We decided to eat breakfast before making any attempt to reply, and in that brief interlude, a sudden series of pinging chimes alerted him to one of his monitoring programs.

I finished my cereal while he grabbed the laptop. I'd gotten used to those alerts throughout the week, most of which seemed to be nothing of interest. This time, though, he cursed under his breath as soon as he pulled up the screen.

"What is it?" I asked.

Nico shook his head in disbelief. "The son of a bitch is selling the painting. Deep underground. This is some seriously shady shit."

"How can he sell it? He just made a very public move to hand it over to you. I know he's a dick, but it hasn't even been twenty-four hours since he announced it on television. How can he go back on that without facing even more ridicule than before?"

"He can't. Not unless there are two of them." Nico absently rubbed his jaw as he tipped his head in thought. "Have you ever seen that other painting from the interview, the one he said he mistook for mine?"

I frowned. "No. It looked pretty damn similar, though. Almost too similar."

"So maybe," he began, tapping his fingers as he considered the possibilities, "maybe he had it made, something enough like the original that his little colorblind speech would fool the general public. And if he has a connection to someone who can create a piece like that, who's to say he couldn't create an actual forgery of the original?"

"He's going to sell a forgery?"

Nico smiled gently and said, "No, Kitten, I'm guessing he intends to sell the real thing and foist the forgery off on me."

I flushed with embarrassment. "Right. I knew that."

"It'd be pretty dangerous for him to try to sell a forgery, especially if the buyer becomes aware there are two copies out there. Whoever buys it is going to verify that it's legit before they pay him."

"Isn't it dangerous for him to sell it after making a public announcement that he's giving it to you?"

"Your dad knows a lot of criminals. I'd bet it will be invitation only, so maybe he'll limit it to people he has dirt on, people who won't worry about whether he's screwing me over in the process." He tipped his head back in thought. "But maybe . . ."

I gave him a second to finish the thought, then another, before finally prompting, "Maybe what, Nico?"

"Maybe we can pull a little shady shit of our own," he said, a slow grin tilting the corners of his mouth. "Let me see what I can manage."

"You're much more than just tech support, aren't you?" I asked.

With my chin propped on one hand, I studied him in the same way I might consider a broken toy—like a puzzle to be solved, like I could see the inner workings of his mind, if only I looked hard enough.

Sadly, Nico's insides were far more complicated than the mechanics I usually repaired.

His grin widened. "I think that's an accurate statement, yes. I mostly work in network security, which does occasionally require me to know how to get *around* that kind of security. Fortunately, I won't be working from scratch, either—from the minute I first realized there was chatter happening behind closed doors, so to speak, about the painting coming up for sale, I started brainstorming ways to manipulate things in my direction if that happened."

Of course, that original burst of chatter had been what revealed his ransom ploy to me in the first place. I frown at him and he clearly understood what I wasn't saying, because he leaned over and pressed a conciliatory kiss to my lips.

"Well, then," I said, accepting the silent apology. "Do you need to work your magic from home, or would you rather work it from here?"

He rose, took my hands, and pulled me to my feet. "I love you," he said solemnly, before kissing me again, more thoroughly this time. "I think it would be best for us to go home for this part, but we're going to have to play it cool. We need to act like we trust that he's going to be true to his word, especially if he hasn't found what's inside the backing. Can you do that?"

I cocked an indignant brow. "Can I treat my father with casual disdain and not let on you're a genius hacker trying to screw him over in return? Of course I can. I'm surprised you had to ask."

Nico laughed and said, "Hopefully, we won't even need to see him face to face, but I have faith in you."

"Ditto, for what it's worth. He's the one I have no faith in. I mean . . . why the sudden about-face? He's got his minions forcing us off the road one minute, and then a few days later, he's playing nice? Or, at least, pretending to play nice. It doesn't make sense."

"Maybe the accident was just a show of power, maybe it was a delay tactic while he had the forgery finished? If he wanted to scare us away from making any demands before he was ready to act, it obviously worked."

"Do you think he knows about the SD card?"

"I really don't think so," he said slowly. "If he did, and he wanted me dead, whoever was in that SUV had the perfect opportunity. Once we crashed, we were sitting ducks."

Something about the situation didn't feel quite right, but I nodded. "Okay. It just seems off to me, but I'm sure you're right. I'll pack up my stuff. When do you want to leave?"

"Soon enough. I had something else in mind, first," he murmured, kissing me again and steering me toward the bedroom.

I laughed against his mouth and shoved away my uneasiness over puzzles and forgeries, hackers and scammers. Those things would return front and center soon enough, I knew, so I'd happily give him this last opportunity to sweep it all far, far into the background.

# Chapter Twenty-Six

## NICO

Before we left the cabin to return to the real world, I replied to Willoughby's email in a similarly polite, distant tone. Whatever the man was up to, I refused to draw any suspicion down on our heads, even if it meant playing dumb for the time being. With the potential for a doublecross in the offing, we needed to proceed with caution.

Once we were all packed up, we loaded our bags into the little hatchback and tried to enjoy the scenic drive home, each of us pretending not to check the mirrors far more frequently than necessary.

Despite our usual preference for Kat's apartment when it came to atmosphere and comfort, we decided to take up residence at my place—the building had better security, for starters, as well as housing everything I would need to keep a close eye on Willoughby's attempt to sell the real painting. Even if Kat's stubbornness had edged the residual fear from the crash to the back of her mind, she still seemed off balance.

Keeping her close was not only preferable but necessary, in my opinion, since she wouldn't consider distancing herself for her own safety.

And if I'd enlisted Gumby to help watch out for her when she went back to work, well, that was something I'd just keep to myself for now. She might be willing to accept some degree of deviation from her routine, namely being chauffeured back and forth to work by me, but I was fairly certain she'd object to having a casual bodyguard posted outside Kat's Keepers when I wasn't around.

If the car accident was a sign of things to come instead of a warning shot, I wouldn't risk leaving her unprotected.

In between monitoring Willoughby's underhanded sale effort, which was scheduled to take place in the form of a private online auction toward the end of the week, I dealt with my insurance company, fielded questions from Detective Hanson, who was still investigating the crash, and bought myself a new car to replace my mangled sedan. I picked out a small SUV with an impressive array of safety features.

This time, I wasn't taking any chances.

When I picked Kat up after work, her smile widened as we walked out into the parking lot.

"Well now, Mr. Beaumont, this is certainly a shiny new upgrade," she teased, running her hand along the side of the car. It was a deep sapphire blue that shimmered in the afternoon sun.

"Great gas mileage, side-impact airbags, on-board navigation and emergency alert system," I recited. Her smile dropped just a touch, so I leaned down and whispered in her ear, "And the color reminds me of your eyes. It's the exact shade they turn just as I sink into you."

The smile returned full force, just as I'd hoped, though there was a sultry hint to it now. "Oh, is it? I suppose I can't complain then, since that's one of my favorite moments."

I dropped a soft kiss to her lips, opened the passenger door for her, and gave a flourishing bow. "Your chariot, my lady."

Her snort of laughter made me grin like a fool, but I was just . . . happy. Through the window, I watched Kat grin excitedly as she buckled in and ran her hands over the smooth dash. How was it possible for such an innocent move to nearly knock me flat with desire?

Since she hadn't noticed my swift intake of breath, I forced myself to turn away and stroll around the hood to slip into my own seat.

"You're in a good mood today," she observed, moving on from caressing the dashboard to fiddling with the fancy stereo system.

"I am, as a matter of fact. Beautiful day, beautiful vehicle, beautiful woman. I picked up what was left in the other car from the impound lot. We can sleep tonight under the watchful eye of The King," I joked.

At that, she burst out laughing. "I almost forgot about that. I guess I can start looking through the other stuff, see if anything is worth listing or fixing up. I can't even remember what else we bought, aside from that Elvis painting."

While we drove toward my apartment, I relayed what I'd learned about the auction and, clearly sensing my tension rising, Kat distracted me by recounting the tale of a particularly tricky toy repair she'd managed to finish just before the clock struck five. It was all so blissfully normal, assuming one could ignore the bizarre twist of discussing the underground sale of a stolen Hugo Clément painting.

I was unsettled to realize such things were quickly becoming commonplace in our lives.

Working together on dinner nudged me further toward recognizing my desire to hold on tight to even this basic level of domestic happiness. I liked having Kat close at hand, enjoyed our conversations and our comfortable silences. It was growing harder to regret those lost years now that our lives fit together so seamlessly, though I wondered sometimes if we had always fit this way and just hadn't acknowledged it.

Kat waited until we sat down to dinner before saying, "I assume you have a plan for what happens after this auction?"

"I have the beginning of a plan," I said slowly.

My gaze landed to the left of Kat, where the velvet Elvis painting was propped against the wall. When she turned to see what I was looking at, a startled giggle burst past her lips. We both stared at it for a long moment, then Kat turned back in my direction.

"A plan involving that monstrosity?" she asked, incredulous.

"Maybe." I flashed her a grin. "I'll need to see how everything plays out before making any final decisions, but I've got some ideas. No offense, but your father really is one underhanded son of a bitch."

"You're telling me," she muttered.

Kat's knowledge of my exact skill set when it came to computers was still murky, at best, but it was all going to come down to some serious hacking. As much as I hated to admit it, I was actually looking forward to the challenge of beating her father at his own game.

It wasn't my fault he'd brought the playing field out of his comfort zone and into mine.

I reached over to cup her cheek, carefully avoiding the faded remnants of her bruise. "It'll be over soon. Just think how peaceful our lives will be—no kidnapper vans, no cars trying to run us off the road. We'll be able to escape to the cabin for pleasure instead of in fear for our lives."

She nuzzled her face into my palm. "So you're planning to keep me around, huh?"

"Are you kidding me? If you think I'm going to watch you hop on some dude's motorcycle to ride off into the sunset again, you're severely mistaken. I should've stopped you back then, but you know damn well that I would absolutely throw myself under the wheels to stop you now."

"That particular relationship lasted three whole days, I'll have you know," she deadpanned.

I laughed. "Why am I not surprised? I have to say, that little pixie cut was pretty cute, but I prefer these wild curls." I reached out to twist one around my finger. "They suit you perfectly."

Kat batted my hand away. "You're trying to distract me and it's not working, so give it up. I want to know what you're planning to do. You've obviously got some idea of how this is going to play out. Spill. Now."

I grinned, both at her indignant expression and the bossy tone. "Okay, okay. Here's what I'm thinking . . ."

# Chapter Twenty-Seven

## Kat

Late Thursday night, surrounded by caffeinated beverages and a variety of snack bags, we sat huddled together in front of Nico's desk, staring at the computer monitor. He'd managed to hack into the auction undetected, a silent observer to dollar amounts that had my eyes rounding in shock. Even though there was no one to hear us in the quiet apartment, we spoke infrequently and in hushed tones.

It reminded me of that night beneath the desk, just the two of us against the world.

As the clock ticked steadily toward midnight, I wondered if Nico could hear my heart thudding against my ribs. The price was currently at fourteen million, with only two minutes to go. It felt like some kind of alternate reality, a freaky, twisted version of my everyday life. Though I made a living reselling my finds through online auctions and was very familiar with the pulsating thrill of watching a bidder snipe an item at the last minute, those things sold at a tiny, tiny fraction of this price.

I felt like I was going to throw up just from the nerves. All the junk food probably wasn't helping, either.

Beside me, Nico was busy typing at lightning speed on the laptop before him, glancing up at the larger monitor every few seconds. He'd given me a rough outline of how the evening would go, including who the major players were and where they were located, but in this final stretch, it took all of my willpower to keep from distracting him by asking for an update.

With thirty seconds left on the clock, he reached over and squeezed my knee before returning his hands to the keyboard.

"Breathe, Kitten," he said quietly. "It'll be over soon."

"Easier said than done," I muttered, struggling to draw a breath at all.

My lungs felt tight, frozen in anticipation. I trusted Nico implicitly, but if this went wrong, I was afraid he'd never be able to forgive himself—or possibly me, simply for being related to the man profiting astronomically from what he'd stolen from Nico's family.

Then, suddenly, it was over. The screen flashed with the winning bid, a startling fourteen-point-three million, and briefly went black.

In the next second, Nico had shifted into the private messages between my father and the buyer, a man named Lucien Lavigne. Though I'd never heard of him, Nico recognized the name. When the auction first started, he told me Lavigne was a European dealer of rare and purportedly stolen gemstones, currently based in Portugal. The man had been investigated at least a dozen times but never actually charged with a crime.

A perfect match for my father, really.

"Here we go," Nico whispered, continuing to type on the laptop while the details appeared in the private messages on the monitor. "Christ, this is even better than I hoped for."

I said nothing, simply watched the conversation between my treacherous father and a known criminal mastermind. What would've happened, I wondered, if I'd been there when Pierre died? Could I have prevented all this heartache and intrigue simply by bearing witness to it?

An icy claw tightened around my heart when I realized that maybe the painting was why my father hadn't told me about Pierre's death, why I hadn't been informed about the funeral. He knew I wouldn't stand for something like this if I'd been there.

Since the day I found out about Pierre's death, I'd been angry at my father for failing to tell me about it. Now, the depth of the betrayal threatened to overwhelm me.

It felt like hours passed, but it was barely ten minutes after the auction ended that Nico finally cracked his knuckles, rolled some of the tension from his shoulders, and pushed back from the desk.

He kept his gaze on the screens to be sure he didn't miss anything, but to me he said, "Your father will have the painting shipped tomorrow through a private courier, after its authenticity is verified by Lavigne's designated party. Once it's handed over to the courier, that's where the real work starts."

When he glanced over at me, I managed a weak smile, unable to drum up any true excitement. Nico frowned at my expression and reached over to pull me into his lap. Part of me wished he could turn off the computers to just talk to me right now, but if my father suspected any kind of monitoring, Nico said he might very well transfer over to a new conversation to pass along different details. It was important that we keep watching until the bitter end.

"What's wrong? What can I do?"

I dropped my head against the side of his neck and sighed, my breath whispering over his skin. "It's okay. I'm fine. I just want this all to be behind us, you know?"

He had nothing more to type for the moment, so he ran his hand up and down my arm. "We'll get through this. It's almost over, I promise."

"Is there anything I can help with?"

"Do you know anything about Perkins-Hallihan, the private shipping service?"

He must have recognized how much I hated having nothing to do during this process. His hand shifted to my hair, moving in long, soothing strokes through the loose strands. A soft sound of pleasure slipped from my throat before I answered him.

"Yes, actually. They're a little sketchy, but we've used them in the past."

"Sketchy how?"

I wrinkled my nose. "They were accused of looking the other way while shipping stolen goods in the past, historical artifacts, that kind of thing. There was a bit of controversy around it a few years ago, but that died down. Nothing ever came of the accusation, as far as I could tell."

"What did you ship through them?"

"I had a Smokey the Bear doll from the fifties for sale late last fall that was bought by someone overseas. His mother had Alzheimer's and she talked about that particular toy frequently. I guess it was something she'd bought for him when he was a baby, but the buyer had no idea where his own ended up after all those years. He was desperate to find one before it was too late. The regular shipping services leading up to Christmas were backlogged, so we settled on Perkins-Hallihan."

"Can you tell me about the shipping process?"

I nodded against his throat. "You can bring in your own authenticator, like Lavigne is doing, or they have someone on staff who will do a pre-shipping check to the buyer's specifications. They'll take photos from all different angles, check that an item works properly, document a stamp of authenticity or a serial number. Then it gets packed up in front of all parties and a barcode label goes on the package. It's harder for someone to steal a package meant for a specific party that way."

"Harder, yes, but not impossible," he said.

"What if they find whatever your dad put in the frame during authentication? Isn't the note on the back the proof it was done by Clément?"

Nico shook his head. "If your father didn't find it yet, they have no reason to look at the frame itself that closely, and my father was very careful about hiding it in there. I couldn't even see where he'd hidden it in the wood—he told me to remove the painting and break the frame if I had to. If it went through an X-ray, they might spot it, but I don't think there's anything we can do about it now."

"Yeah." I sighed. "Okay, so what happens next?"

"Your father will send someone else to bring the package for shipment. After that interview, he can't risk being seen doing it himself. Whether the person he sends over to Perkins-Hallihan would recognize me or you, though, I'm not sure. I can do everything remotely if I have to, but I was thinking that a decoy might be helpful."

I frowned. "What kind of decoy?"

"If your father had given me the forgery already, I'd use that. It would've been perfect, really. Since he didn't, I think it will have to be the Elvis painting. It's the right size and shape. If we were to ship that out around the same time, then instead of diverting the original package, I can just swap the tracking numbers. Lavigne will still be able to track the progress of a package heading to him, it just won't be the package he expects."

"You can do all that? From here?" I asked, leaning back to look up at him.

"I can." Nico grinned. "But we'll need to get the decoy to the shipping office without one of us being seen there. I can ask Gumby to drop it off."

"No, let me see if Erin can do it. After that first package last year, which I took myself, we've sent a couple other items through Perkins-Hallihan and Erin took those over for me. They won't think twice about her sending something as weird as that Elvis painting, believe me."

I pulled my phone from my pocket, checked to verify that Erin was awake at this late hour, and fired off a quick text. Though the response included a selfie of Erin holding up a giant margarita while a beautiful redheaded woman kissed her neck, my assistant agreed to take the package over for us with no questions asked.

"All right, then. Why don't you go and get into bed? I'll just set this up to alert me if anything happens. Otherwise, our work here is done until Elvis heads off to Europe."

Nico kissed my temple before I slid off his lap. The plan was sound. He could do it, that part didn't concern me, but a thread of anxiety wormed its way through me. This mess had expanded to include serious criminals and international borders. What if it all came crashing down on us?

Even though I couldn't see a way it might come back around to implicate Nico directly—or me, which I knew would be *his* concern—this move would take the battle to a new level. This was bigger than leaking a story to an ex-wife or photos to the press. We were involving people even more dangerous than my father.

*You can't fight fair with someone who has no sense of fairness.*

Those words, spoken so long ago by the same man they applied to now, bounced around inside my head like a ping pong ball. By this time tomorrow, our part would be done, and all we'd have left to do was wait. After years of heartache and regret, the course of fate would be well and truly set.

I worried about that future as I brushed my teeth, undressed, and slipped into bed to wait for Nico. It was no fairy tale ending, but we'd never really had a fairy tale beginning, had we? As much as he'd joked about my role of princess in The Castle as children, we both knew that life in the little cottage he and his father shared had been far more idyllic than my own.

A short while later, Nico settled himself behind me, drawing my weary body back against his chest.

"I love you, Kitten," he whispered against my shoulder blade.

Though I was barely awake, I snuggled into his embrace and twined my fingers with his before drawing his hand from my hip to clasp it between my breasts.

"I love you, Nico," I murmured.

Within minutes, his comforting warmth washed away the anxiety that had blossomed inside my chest throughout the evening. Like every other hurdle we'd come across in our own separate lives, we would vault our way over this one and move forward.

Together, this time.

# Chapter Twenty-Eight

## NICO

According to my intel, Willoughby's appointment with Lavigne's appraiser was scheduled to take place just after noon the next day. Gumby had been assigned to surveillance duty on the street outside the tidy brick office of Perkins-Hallihan, while Kat and I remained at my apartment with an arc of a dozen different packaging options spread before us. All we had to do was wait for word from Gumby about how the painting was packed for shipment.

As soon as it was confirmed, we'd package the velvet Elvis in the closest option we had, deliver him to Erin, and fade back into the woodwork so I could work my magic with the tracking numbers.

I was well aware that the inaction put Kat on edge. None of her numerous skills really correlated with any part of this particular plan of attack, unfortunately, and I knew her patience with herself was wearing thin.

While we waited, I cupped the back of her neck and massaged gently. Even without her actively complaining, she'd never been one for sitting around, always buzzing with energy, ready to throw herself into the fray. These past few weeks had been tough for her, probably even more than they'd been for me.

As I checked again for a text from Gumby, I fantasized about taking Kat on an actual vacation—not a research trip or a hideaway, but a proper romantic adventure.

"Heart-shaped jacuzzi tubs, cheesy or enticing?" I asked as my thumb eased a knot of tension from her neck.

With a startled laugh, she tipped her head from side to side as she considered it. "Room for two?"

"Of course. Maybe some bubble bath, champagne. Plush robes, room service."

"Enticing," she said firmly. "Very enticing. Making some big plans, Romeo?"

I grinned. "I'm dreaming of a weekend getaway that doesn't involve kidnapping or attempted murder, that's all. Doesn't that sound nice?"

Kat leaned into my hand, but before she could do more than smile in response, my phone vibrated. All her tension returned as the time for action finally arrived. I read the message and nodded to the fireproof box at the end.

"There's our winner."

"Let's get it done, then," she said. Her tone was light, but the edges of her mouth were tight with anxiety.

The sooner this was all over, the better.

Once packaged, the box was slipped into a canvas duffle and slung over my shoulder. In my sweet new ride, as Kat had taken to calling it, we took a winding path between the apartment and Kat's Keepers. There, we'd meet up with Erin, but first we needed to make sure no one followed us.

I wondered how long that unnerving sensation would linger, how long we'd keep glancing over our shoulders, whether Kat blamed me for bringing this chaos into her life.

Then her fingers brushed the hair at the back of my neck, a simple gesture filled with tenderness and affection. I let go of those unspoken fears to embrace the here and now. Once we were parked behind the warehouse, I grabbed the duffle from the back seat, but before I opened my door, I leaned over and kissed her, hard and swift.

"What was that for?" she asked, a smile tugging at those rosy lips.

"Because I can."

Her laughter followed us as we got out of the car to meet Erin, who stood beside a purple Volkswagen. She winked at Kat and took the bag from my hand. "Hello, my lovelies. We're not going to get arrested for whatever it is we're doing, right?"

"No, you are definitely not doing anything illegal," Kat assured her. "Just ship this to the address I sent you."

"Don't think for one second that I didn't notice you said *you* instead of *we*. In any case, I don't need the details. It's going to your family in France, right?" Erin asked me.

I flashed a wide smile. I liked Kat's quirky assistant. From what I'd seen of her, of their interactions together, the two women complemented one another perfectly.

"Yes, to my uncle in Avignon. Thank you for doing this."

"No problem. You said no authentication necessary, so it's just a quick stop. You really didn't have to give me a paid day off in exchange for this, Kat."

"You're doing us a favor on short notice, and you replied to my plea for help while you were very clearly busy with a certain lovely redhead. You deserve a long weekend and I really appreciate this, Erin. Text me when it's done, okay? And thank you."

Kat gave her a quick hug and flashed a smile as Erin set the bag on her passenger seat and slid back into her car.

"See you on Tuesday, darling. Enjoy the rest of your weekend!" Erin called, bouncing her eyebrows up and down before she pulled out of the lot.

I choked on a laugh. "I have to say, your assistant seems to think she's your wingman. Wingwoman? She realizes you don't need that particular service anymore, right?"

Kat rolled her eyes as we got back into my new car. "Don't let it go to your head. Before you showed up here with Gumby that day, she was encouraging me to get it on with a history professor named Alan."

"Ouch."

"I wasn't planning to, if it makes you feel any better."

"Yes, so much better," I said dryly.

We drove straight back to my apartment, even though I wasn't entirely sure how much more Kat could take of being cooped up inside. I needed the computers to complete my work, but it was becoming stifling, this period of limbo, but I was afraid to let her out of my sight.

"Let's do something fun tomorrow," I suggested after we got inside.

Kat narrowed her eyes at me. "Are you reading my mind, Nicolas?"

I took her hands and squeezed. "No, but I don't have to be psychic to see how you're feeling. I know this has been a long few weeks for you. What should we do? Garage sale hunting? Go for a hike? Swim naked in the pond at the park?"

"I'll think about it and get back to you. Go on, work your magic. Erin should be done at Perkins-Hallihan soon." She dropped onto the couch and closed her eyes. "I'll be right here for the foreseeable future."

I leaned down to kiss her forehead before returning to my office. With the actual painting also departing for Europe, the tracking number switch would be fairly simple—by Monday evening, the Clément would be delivered safely to Uncle Philippe, while Lavigne would receive the Elvis.

No matter how hard I tried to keep myself from thinking too far beyond that, it was impossible to avoid speculating about the outcome of the swap.

Lavigne would be furious. I wasn't entirely sure Willoughby would be able to smooth things over, even if he returned the buyer's money. For a few minutes, the possible scenarios played out in my mind. Would Willoughby panic and try to cover it up by offering the forgery to Lavigne? Would he guess that Kat and I were involved in some way?

A twinge of guilt marred my concentration, but I remembered Kat's terrified cry when that car forced us off the road. The man had put his own child's life in danger. Willoughby didn't deserve my concern for his safety.

Then again, if a man like Lavigne came into possession of whatever was on that SD card, a whole host of dangerous problems could be unleashed on Aidan Willoughby.

In a roundabout way, maybe I was protecting Kat's father, after all.

Kat called to me from the other room when she received the text from Erin saying the package was officially out of her hands—or, as Erin phrased it, "The eagle has flown." With her part in the day's activities complete, Kat curled up on her side and closed her eyes again while I set myself up to swap the delivery locations for the two tracking numbers.

It didn't take long to make the adjustments, but by the time I returned to the living room, Kat was sound asleep. A faint smile lifted my lips as I spread a blanket over her and sifted my fingers through the tumble of honey blonde curls haloing her face.

With the painting finally making its way back to the Beaumont family, neither Kat nor I would lose that essential link to something bigger than ourselves—connection, belonging, acceptance. Those things might not be tangible, but the painting gave each ephemeral concept a concrete form for both of us.

We'd be safe.

Everything I'd ever wanted was finally within reach. Next order of business? Keeping it there.

---

WE SPENT SATURDAY MEANDERING through suburban yard sales, enjoying fresh cookies and apple turnovers from a purple food truck parked along Main Street, and holding hands while we watched the terrifying flock of Canada geese at the pond in Spruce Hill's Town Park as the evening sky burst into a spectacular sunset.

It was blessedly uneventful, aside from another email from Kat's father about the painting. Though Kat snorted in disgust that the man was still trying to pass a forgery off on me while making millions from the sale of the actual painting, I replied politely and an appointment was set for the following day at the Willoughby estate.

"I'm coming with you," Kat said immediately.

I had to grin at the stubborn set of her chin. "I wouldn't put my neck on the line by suggesting otherwise."

When I fell silent, Kat cocked her head and asked, "What else is worrying you?"

"I still want you to be careful. There's no reason for him to link either of us to the auction, not when he thinks I believe he's turning over the real thing to me, but after the delivery, all hell will break loose. I don't know what might happen once Lavigne gets that package." I reached over and wiped a smear of chocolate from her lower lip. "I don't want you taking any risks this week."

She nipped my thumb before I pulled away. "Same goes for you, mister. God, I can't wait until this is all over."

I slid my arm around her waist and Kat leaned into me. The sun dipped below the horizon, casting scarlet ripples across the water. When a breeze left goosebumps along Kat's skin, I tugged her to her feet.

"It's getting chilly. Let's head home," I said gently.

Quiet descended over us during the drive back to my apartment, the kind of quiet that made me wonder if Kat felt subdued or if her mind was simply racing too fast for conversation to keep up. Though neither of us had broached the subject, I was sure she, too, had at least considered the possibility of retaliation against her father once Lavigne received the package.

Even if she fully believed what we'd done was justified, would she feel the same if it got her father killed? Would she ever forgive me if that was how this played out? Would she forgive herself?

Losing the painting would be tragic, but losing Kat would destroy me.

The sudden roll of nausea in my stomach made me want to pull over and convince her that we should abandon the plan.

"Kitten . . . maybe this is a bad idea. It's not too late to change the tracking numbers back."

"After all that work? You think we should just let him sell the painting out from under you?"

Her tone was gentle, curious rather than accusing, but I took it as a good sign. She wasn't one to hide it when she was well and truly pissed.

"Lavigne isn't going to take kindly to being duped. We're throwing a pebble into the lake and once it hits the water, we'll lose control of the ripples. Your father is an asshole, but I don't want to get him killed."

"Killed," she repeated, eyes widening. "That's what you're afraid will happen?"

"Lavigne is known for his ruthlessness. I think we have to consider it as a possibility."

"I would think Lavigne's first step would be to demand his money back, not murder the man who has his payment stashed away in some offshore account. My father won't be happy, but it's not like he can't afford to give it back. Besides, if my dad knew there was something that could be used against him hidden in the painting, he never would've sold it. He wouldn't want to hand it to some criminal mastermind."

Relief swept through me that her logic matched my train of thought the night before. "You're right. I just feel like I'm in over my head here. This isn't how I expected any of this to play out. I might make a passable kidnapper," I joked, "but I'm not cut out for international intrigues."

Kat snorted at that. "This ballooned into something a lot bigger than we expected. I won't say we could've avoided it if you'd let me break into the house, but . . ."

I shot her a look. "Very funny."

"Look, you said the packages won't be delivered until Monday afternoon. Let's sleep on it, deal with my father, and if you're still worried after that, we can talk about switching the numbers back tomorrow. But I don't want you to lose that painting for my sake, Nico. Not after all this."

"I don't want to lose it either, but if it comes down to you or the painting, I know what I'd choose."

Her expression softened. "What my father did to you is inexcusable, but that painting is yours, and ultimately, it has to be your call. I'm sure Lavigne will be pissed if another swap delays the delivery, but we could still get it done in time to change it, right?"

"Right. Good thinking."

"Whatever happens, we'll deal with it together."

"What would I do without you?" I asked, lacing my fingers with hers as I stopped at a traffic light.

"Probably live in a miserable bachelor pad devoid of all personality—oh, wait," she teased.

I gave a mock growl and nipped at her knuckles, soaking in the sound of her laughter dancing around me. No matter what the circumstances, she always managed to calm me, to offer reassurance with just a quirk of her lips or a look in her eyes. I might regret involving her in all of this, but I'd never regret finally having her back in my life.

*Plenty of time,* I assured myself.

There was still plenty of time to catch that pebble before it hit the water, and plenty of time to love her with everything I had.

# Chapter Twenty-Nine

## KAT

Arriving at my father's estate after so many years away was more nerve-wracking than either of us expected. Nico pulled up to the front gate, gave his name to a literal uniformed guard, and squeezed my knee when I huffed out an exasperated breath. Spruce Hill had once been voted "Safest Town in America," but my father acted like he needed enhanced security measures to keep the riff-raff off his property. It had always been a bone of contention between the two of us.

"We're not in Kansas anymore," Nico murmured as the gate swung slowly open.

"There might be no place like home, but this hasn't been home in a long time. Let's get this charade over with."

We were greeted at the front door by Beardsley, the stiff old man who'd been our family's butler for as long as I could remember. Why we'd ever needed a butler was beyond me, but the man in question gifted me with a rare smile that chased the thought from my mind.

"Miss Katherine," he said, "what a treat it is to see you again."

Though shock still showed clearly on his wrinkled face, I stepped forward to hug the old man and his expression melted into unabashed delight.

"Beardsley, you haven't aged a day. I'm sure you remember Nicolas Beaumont."

Beardsley nodded solemnly at Nico. "Of course. I never had the chance to express my condolences about your father, Mr. Beaumont."

"Thank you, Beardsley." Nico managed a small smile, then said, "I believe Mr. Willoughby is expecting me."

"Yes, indeed," Beardsley replied, casting a quick glance in my direction.

I was quite sure his employer was *not* expecting to see his wayward daughter, but just as certain that Beardsley wasn't going to say so.

Nico took my hand in his and gave the butler a pointed look. "She's with me."

"Of course. If you'll follow me, Mr. Willoughby is in his office."

Seeing my father on television was a far cry from seeing the man up close, especially after the years that had passed. He was seated at his desk—the same heavy oak desk we'd hidden under as children on that fateful night—and he looked as sleek and polished as ever, exuding charm and charisma. All of those things had made him a star in the courtroom, but had I never noticed that streak of gray through his thick chestnut mane, the slight sagging of skin beneath his jaw? Funny, I didn't recall thinking he looked that different during those TV interviews.

*Must have had a makeup artist,* I thought absently, struggling to make sense of the feelings tumbling around in my chest. Somehow, I'd expected him to be the same as ever, the king in his castle, moving us all around like chess pieces.

Instead, he just looked old.

His eyes, a paler, icier blue than my own, widened almost imperceptibly when he saw me enter the room.

"Katherine," he said, coming to his feet. "I hadn't realized you'd be joining us."

"It didn't seem wise to send Nico alone to beard the lion in its den," I replied tartly. "I wouldn't want some unfortunate accident to befall him."

My father smiled tightly. "How nice to see that my own flesh and blood has such faith in my hospitality. I'd offer you both some coffee while we discuss business, but I'm sure you'd decline it in case I slipped poison into your cups."

Nico kept quiet, obviously remembering the sharp repartee between us, even when I was a pint-sized firebrand with skinned knees. This was not a battle he could fight for me, nor one I'd appreciate him involving himself in. I was fully capable of taking on my father in a round of verbal sparring, whereas I knew Nico could only recall the bitter taste of defeat from the last time he'd gone head to head with the man.

"No need for pleasantries, Daddy dearest. We're just here for Nico's painting."

I lifted my chin and held my father's gaze until he gave a tight nod toward one of the shelves lining the walls. I was surprised by his lack of a rebuttal, but I made sure not to let on. It was uncomfortably strange being back in this house, especially back in this particular room, and my skin itched with the need to get out of there.

Without a word, Nico went over to the crate containing the painting. He drew a deep breath before opening it to withdraw the framed canvas. Even knowing it was a forgery, he handled it with exquisite care as my father sat back down in his chair, ostensibly turning his attention to the paperwork spread across his desk. I watched as Nico studied the canvas and breathed a soft sigh at the sight of those familiar colors.

It was, after all, an amazing replica. I wondered who'd painted it, how much my father had spent on the forgery—surely a tiny fraction of the astronomical amount Lavigne had paid him for the real thing.

Seeing the hazy image of Nico's ancestor there on canvas brought a misty smile to his face. I blinked back tears myself as I thought of all the times I'd sat under the watchful presence of this beautiful piece of art, teasing Nico, listening intently to Pierre, enjoying meals filled with laughter instead of cold silence.

It seemed strange to think a fake could provide that same familiar anchor, but I saw in Nico's eyes that he felt the same.

After a long moment, he gently laid the painting back in the crate and closed it.

"I'll sign whatever you want," he said over his shoulder, "and then, no offense, I'll be perfectly happy to never see you again."

My father offered a sardonic smile as he slid a leather folio and an unnecessarily fancy pen across the desk. "The feeling is mutual, Mr. Beaumont."

I took the crate from Nico and cradled it in my lap as he sat down to read through the papers. Though I tried to avoid looking at my father, he cleared his throat after a moment and my gaze shot to his face. For the span of a breath, he simply looked at me, like he was trying to read something in my expression, then he tilted his head in question.

"And you, Katherine? Are you equally eager to be rid of me?"

With a sigh, I leaned back in my seat. "Tell me one thing. Did you orchestrate all of this bullshit just to spite my mother?"

His lips curved, but the expression was far from anything I would label a smile. "Does it matter? Mr. Beaumont is getting what he wants, after all."

Nico finished adding his signature and tossed the pen down, breaking the intense standoff going on beside him. "Yes, I am. I'd say thank you, but it seems a bit undeserved."

"I understand you two were in an accident recently," my father said quietly, his eyes still on me. "Are you all right?"

I blinked at him, wondering if this was some kind of trick. His dark brows drew down as he studied the faint remnant of the bruise on my cheek. It was obvious his concern didn't extend to Nico's wellbeing, but he looked sincerely worried about me for the first time in as long as I could remember.

Maybe he hadn't had anything to do with the accident. I wasn't sure how to process that possibility, not when being in this house again had me feeling so conflicted.

"We're fine," I replied.

The words came out less sharply than I'd intended, echoing hollowly in the space between us. I forced my eyes over to Nico, who watched the exchange with interest.

He reached over to cup my cheek. "If you're ready to leave?"

Though I widened my eyes at him for making such a chauvinistic play, I smiled sweetly and rose. "I've been ready to leave since the minute we walked in. So long, Daddio."

My father didn't bother to stand as we walked out of the room, and it didn't take a clairvoyant to know what he was thinking. If I was content to slum it with the help, then I wasn't worth another minute of his time.

For once in my life, it didn't even sting.

As we drove past the gates, Nico caught my hand in his. "Now that this little chore is complete, I think a celebratory dinner is in order."

I huffed a humorless laugh. "As long as there's carbs to be had, I'm in."

We dropped the painting off at Nico's apartment where, with a broad grin, he informed me that he'd gotten a reservation at Panache, the only restaurant in town that had earned his own father's seal of approval when they first moved here. Though my eyes widened in surprise—the place was much too rich for my budget these days—I wasn't about to turn down a delicious meal after such a trying day.

Besides, it was about time we had another proper date, complete with getting all gussied up. I banished him from the bedroom while I dressed and twisted my hair into an elegant knot. When I returned to the living room gowned in a short black sheath that hugged each and every curve, I saw Nico's throat bob as he swallowed hard.

"Holy Christ," he breathed, surveying me with an intensity that heated my cheeks even from two yards away. "Maybe we should just stay in tonight. I have a few ideas we could try out instead. There's another pizza left in the freezer and I swear I will make it worth your while."

I laughed and pointed a warning finger in his direction. "I was promised a fancy meal and I better get it before you try anything else, bucko."

"You are a demanding mistress, but very well. I'll see that your every wish is fulfilled, my lady. During *and* after dinner." With a flourishing bow, he offered me his arm.

"By the way," I whispered, leaning so close my breast brushed against his shoulder and my words tickled his jaw, "you look so hot wearing that tie, I think my panties might combust."

Clearly satisfied that I was just as desperate for him as he was for me, Nico laughed and ushered me out to the car. I was glad he didn't try too hard to change my mind, because in truth, it wouldn't have taken much persuasion on his part.

We had such a beautiful time that we lingered over the wonderful meal, then followed it with coffee and tiramisu for dessert. A near-constant smile curved Nico's lips throughout the evening. Conversation flowed easily and, for once, we left all of our worries locked away back at the apartment. There was no talk of the painting, my father, or the choices still to come.

"We should do this more often," Nico said.

He handed the server his credit card, once we finally accepted that the evening had to come to an end. It was just past ten o'clock—not terribly late to our standards, but after the whirlwind of the previous few days, we were both beginning to wilt.

I smirked at him. "Drop a huge chunk of change on dinner?"

"Go out on a real date. Our relationship hasn't exactly followed the usual progression. This is nice, spending time with you without any plots or crimes or attempted murder. Seeing you in that dress certainly doesn't hurt, either."

"It *is* nice, isn't it?" I mused, laying my napkin on the table as the server returned with Nico's card. I waited until the young man left us alone to murmur, "Earlier, you mentioned some ideas about the rest of the night. I really hope a few of those are *nice*, too."

Nico's grin split his face as he grabbed my hand. "Oh, I can do a lot better than just nice, I think. Let's get out of here."

The remainder of our evening was so far beyond *nice* that we both surrendered to our exhaustion immediately afterward, falling into a deep sleep still tangled up in each other's limbs.

# Chapter Thirty

## NICO

Sometime well before dawn, I awoke, disoriented. A cheerful, tinkling ringtone played from Kat's phone on the bedside table, but I managed to grab it before her brain kicked into gear. I looked at the unfamiliar number across the screen and shrugged as I handed it to her.

She hit the speaker button. "Hello?"

"Ms. Willoughby? This is Detective Hanson. We spoke at the hospital. I'm sorry to call at such an early hour."

"Yes, right." She rubbed her forehead.

"I'm afraid your father has been in an accident," Hanson said gently. "It would be best if you could come over to Eastman Memorial as soon as possible."

I bolted into action, throwing off the blanket and jumping out of bed. Kat watched me, but she didn't respond to the detective, who said something else I missed in my hurry to dress. Once I'd tugged on my jeans, I planted a knee on the bed next to her and squeezed her hip gently. Those sleepy blue eyes finally focused on my face as understanding swept over her features.

"I—what kind of accident?" she asked. "Is he hurt?"

Hanson let out a quiet breath. "They're working on him now, Ms. Willoughby. How quickly can you get here?"

"We'll be there as soon as we can," I answered for her. "Half an hour, maybe?"

"Good, that's good. I'll be waiting in the lobby when you come in."

I took the phone from her limp hand and tugged her to her feet. "Let's get you dressed," I murmured.

She moved like a sleepwalker as I helped her throw clothes on, blinking up at me with a confusion in her big blue eyes that broke my heart. We were out the door in under five minutes, but the numbness seemed to have seeped from her brain into her limbs as we got into the car. I buckled her seatbelt for her, closed the passenger door, and jogged around to the driver's side.

The sun was just peeking over the horizon when we pulled up in front of the hospital entrance. I spoke to the parking valet and ushered Kat into the waiting room. Detective Hanson stood when she spotted us.

"What happened?" Kat asked immediately.

Everything about her still seemed sluggish, but under the glaring hospital lights, reality was finally sinking in.

Hanson led us to a quiet corner of the lobby where Officer Ford waited, then spoke in a low voice. "As far as we can tell, he was run off the road just outside of town."

My gaze had been on Kat, ready to leap into action if she started to fall apart, but it jerked to Hanson's face at the statement.

"Outside of town," I repeated.

"Not too far from where your car landed in a ditch, actually," she added, watching us both closely.

Kat frowned. "Why would he be out driving at this time of night?"

"As far as we can tell, he was meeting with a woman who has a house out on the lake. The accident happened around nine-thirty or so last night. We just got called in on this. Witnesses described the same SUV that tailed you two. Unfortunately, Mr. Willoughby's vehicle spun into a tree instead of a ditch."

"Then it wasn't him," Kat said quietly. She looked up at me. "He wasn't behind it."

Ford opened his mouth as if to question that, but I saw Hanson give a subtle shake of her head. "Can you tell me where you both were between nine and ten last night?" she asked.

Kat's eyes flew wide as she processed the detective's implication. My veins felt like they were home to a hive full of buzzing bees, but the question wasn't unexpected.

"We had an eight o'clock reservation at Panache, on Canal Street. We were there until just after ten, then went straight back to my apartment. The keycode on the front door logs entries and there's a security camera at the entrance, if you need to verify that. I can give you the landlord's number. We were home around quarter after, maybe ten-thirty at the latest," I said quietly.

Hanson nodded, then a grim-faced doctor walked into the waiting room and made a beeline for the group of us. The man glanced at Hanson and Ford, who both nodded toward Kat. I knew what was coming before the doctor even spoke and tightened my grip on her hand.

"Miss Willoughby, I'm very sorry. Your father's injuries were just too extensive. We did everything we could, but he didn't make it through surgery."

Kat gave a tiny shake of her head, blinking rapidly. "He's dead? You're telling me he's dead. We just saw him." Her voice rose on the final word and I wrapped my arms around her.

"Thank you," I said to the doctor as Kat turned into my embrace. I cupped the back of her neck, smoothed the curls still tousled from sleep, and met Hanson's eyes over her head.

The detective's expression grew gentle. "I am sorry for your loss, Ms. Willoughby. We'll give you a few minutes."

Kat lifted her head to nod. Though her cheeks were pale, they were dry—but I felt the slight tremble working its way through her limbs.

"Thank you," she said faintly.

As the police walked away, my lips cruised along her hairline. She seemed almost unaware that I was speaking until I reached her ear and murmured, "It's okay. Everything will be okay, Kitten."

"Someone else tried to kill us, most likely the same someone who just succeeded in killing my father. This seems distinctly not okay, Nico," she replied in a low voice, closing her eyes for a second.

"Yeah," I muttered, my thoughts spinning.

When she opened them again, her gaze swept over my expression. "What is it?"

"I was worried about Lavigne's retaliation over the painting, but this couldn't have been him, not yet. Even with the authentication process, he wouldn't have acted without the painting in hand, and you were right. Why would he want your father dead? It wouldn't get his money back."

Kat nodded slowly. "So it makes no sense for us to change the tracking back now. Whatever happened to my dad, whatever happens when the packages are delivered, it won't be because of you."

Part of me felt a keen sense of relief, the other struggled with the edge of an even greater anxiety at the number of unknowns we now faced. Regardless of her relationship with the man—or lack thereof—Kat had just lost her father. The urge to comfort her swept over me like wildfire.

Whatever danger was out there, I would keep her safe. The alternative was unthinkable.

Ford and Hanson returned to us with two cups of coffee and gestured for us to sit before handing each of us a cup. For one mad moment, I wanted to tell them everything, spill every detail of the past few weeks, but self-preservation won out.

"What now?" I asked, swallowing the confession that threatened to burst free.

"Now we push on with the investigation. The plates you photographed were stolen and have been replaced by new ones that were reportedly taken off a car two days ago outside of Syracuse. We'll have unmarked vehicles outside both of your residences for the time being. If you see anything, remember anything, call me. Any time, day or night," Hanson said quietly.

We both nodded our assent, then Kat drew a steadying breath and asked, "Can I see him?"

The detective nodded. "Yes, of course. His personal effects will be returned to you once everything is processed."

I kept my arm around Kat, but the trembling had finally subsided. Instead, the steel of resolve straightened her spine and she gave one tight nod.

"It still doesn't feel real. Maybe seeing him will help."

Hanson offered a gentle smile. "Of course. Someone will let us know when they're ready for you. In the meantime, we'd like to ask just a few more questions. When I told you about your father's accident, you said, 'Then it wasn't him, he wasn't behind it.' What does that mean?"

Kat met her gaze straight on. "After our accident, you asked if I thought he was responsible. I wasn't sure, because I didn't think he would do something to hurt me, but it was a definite possibility. If the same people came after him, then it stands to reason he wasn't the one who sent them after us, doesn't it?"

When Hanson only waited silently, I tilted my head. "It could mean that, or it could mean something went wrong between your father and whoever he may have hired to come after us."

"You two are quick," Hanson said. "Did Mr. Willoughby give you back your painting yet, Mr. Beaumont?"

I nodded. "We met yesterday afternoon, privately, at his suggestion. Kat went with me. We were at the estate for less than an hour, went back to my place to change, then we left for dinner."

A nurse approached us and gave Hanson a meaningful look, but the detective held up a finger. "Just one last question, Ms. Willoughby. When's the last time you saw your mother?"

Kat jerked as if struck. "My mother? I assume you don't mean on television, Detective Hanson," she said sharply, "so that'd be about seventeen years ago, when she left me with my father after the divorce."

Hanson held up her hands in a gesture clearly meant to be soothing. "We just had to ask. They're ready for you, Ms. Willoughby, if Mr. Beaumont will excuse us?"

Though I didn't like the idea of her facing the task alone, Kat squeezed my arm and nodded.

"Let's get this over with," she said quietly.

Ford stayed behind with me, and though his questions led me to believe he suspected there was more to the situation than we were letting on, I was fairly certain they had nothing solid to connect us to any of it.

Unfortunately, that also meant he had no answers to any of the questions winging through my head.

I never expected to be grateful for our own terrifying accident, but if it kept us out of the limelight in what I expected might be a rather high-profile investigation into Aidan Willoughby's death, maybe it was for the best.

# Chapter Thirty-One

## KAT

Following the nurse down a quiet hallway, I stole a glance at Hanson and wondered why she'd asked about my mother. As far as I knew, the woman wasn't even in the same state yet as her quest for publicity continued. A horrifying thought struck me so suddenly that I stopped in my tracks.

"Oh, Christ. Do I have to notify my mother?"

Hanson valiantly smothered a smile at the expression of dread on my face. "We can take care of that, if you'd like."

"Yes, please. And then when you ask for a raise after having to deal with her, I'll write you a letter of support."

At that, Hanson laughed, but then the nurse opened the door to a silent room and all humor fled. I hesitated only for a heartbeat before walking toward the bed. My father had been larger than life, even just hours ago, but there on the bed, covered to the neck by a white sheet, he looked almost frail.

I felt Hanson's gaze on me as I studied his peaceful expression. None of it made sense, but I didn't think I had the energy to untangle the mess surrounding us right now, so I focused on the task at hand. Aside from an ugly bruise on his forehead, my father's face was surprisingly unmarred.

I'd spent a lifetime already mourning his absence, and now the finality of it left me utterly empty.

"I don't know what happens next," I said softly. "I don't even know if he wanted to be buried or cremated. How do you organize a funeral for someone you barely know?"

Hanson moved to stand beside me and looked down at my father's body. "His lawyer might know. I'm sure he had a will drawn up, being a lawyer himself. Katherine—"

"Kat," I interrupted. "No one calls me Katherine. Except him, I guess, and he's gone."

"Kat, then. You don't have to worry about all of that just yet. Give yourself some time to process."

This unexpected kindness from the stoic detective made my eyes burn. Though Hanson didn't bring up the investigation, I understood what she wasn't saying—this wasn't over yet. The end of all of these machinations over the painting had seemed so close. Now it felt like we were staring down a long tunnel, one filled with shadows and hidden enemies.

"Do you think we're in danger?" I asked, turning away from my father's body to look up at her.

Hanson considered me for a long moment before responding. I was sure she knew there were things we weren't sharing with the police, that much had been clear from our first meeting. If anything, it only seemed clearer now.

"If I knew the whole story, I could give you a better answer," she replied finally. "Tell me what's going on here, Kat, and we'll find a way to help you. Without being able to see the whole picture, you're making it very hard for us to assist in whatever way we can."

Though I considered it, I couldn't make that choice without consulting Nico. His hacking had definitely been beyond the bounds of the law, but if the packages hadn't been delivered yet, that had no bearing on my father's death. The rest of the saga was pretty much public knowledge at this point, down to the source of the leaked photos that had pressured my father into announcing the return of the painting to Nico. As far as the rest of the world knew, there was no forgery in existence.

"There's nothing more to tell," I replied wearily, pressing the heels of my hands against my eyes.

"You and I both know that's not true, but since I don't believe you or your boyfriend were involved in your father's death, I'm going to let you go home. Get some rest, talk to Mr. Beaumont. We're not the enemy here. We might be able to help you both, if you'd let us."

I looked at her for a long moment, then nodded. "I know. I appreciate everything you're doing, Detective Hanson. I have your card if I think of anything more that might be of use."

We walked back to the waiting room after one final glance at my father's unusually peaceful expression. Nico stood as soon as he spotted us, drawing me into his arms when I approached. It boggled my mind just how much that contact settled me, inside and out. He was like a piece of my heart that slotted perfectly back into place whenever he was near.

"Okay?" he asked softly.

"I'm fine. I'd like to go home now, if that's all right with them."

Hanson shook our hands, offered her condolences once more, then slipped her hands into her pockets as we left the hospital. Just as we exited, though, I heard the detective murmur, "Thick as thieves."

She didn't know the half of it.

# Chapter Thirty-Two

## NICO

THE DRIVE HOME PASSED in silence, but Kat kept my hand clutched firmly in her own, clinging to it like a lifeline. The quiet was almost as unnerving as the hollow look in her eyes.

I set one hand on the small of her back as I guided her into the apartment. She moved like all of her strength had slowly leached from her body, her gaze slightly unfocused, her steps a little unsteady.

"Kitten," I said gently, catching her chin in my hand. "Talk to me, love. Tell me what's going on in that beautiful head of yours."

A deep breath shuddered from her lungs. "I want the painting to go to your family, Nico. I don't want you to change the tracking back."

"Okay. Whatever you want. Both paintings will be delivered in a few hours." I ignored the ball of dread in my stomach when I thought about Lavigne opening the velvet Elvis.

"But his money—I think we need to return the money. I don't want any more danger hanging over us. Is there a way for you to do that?"

"Of course. I'll take care of it. It'll all be fine. You don't have to worry about anything."

It wouldn't be easy, but it would be a big weight off of us both. If Kat inherited her father's fortune, I sure as hell didn't want Lavigne coming after her to get his money back.

It took only a little coaxing to get Kat tucked back into bed so I could focus on transferring the money that had already gone into Willoughby's offshore account back to Lavigne's. I set it to return as soon as the tracking on the Elvis painting registered as delivered—a move that would hopefully ward off sending Lavigne into a complete fury. This wasn't my area of expertise, however, so the work took me the better part of the morning.

I peeked in at Kat, who was still fast asleep. Something about seeing her curled up in the middle of my bed, her golden curls splayed across my pillows, sent a surge of emotion through me. Lavigne would be pissed, certainly, but he'd have his full payment back. News of Willoughby's death would reach the man soon enough.

Instead of slipping into bed with her, I headed to the kitchen for a cup of coffee and then sat down on the sofa.

*We're missing something.*

The thought jostled around in my brain, but I felt like I was wading through jelly trying to pluck it from the air. Instead of forcing it, I closed my eyes and let my mind drift to the painting. I'd tucked the forgery into the back of a closet before we left for dinner. Once the real artwork was safely in Uncle Philippe's hands, I planned to hang the canvas Willoughby had given me—either here or at Kat's apartment, wherever we were going to spend the most time.

No matter who painted it, the subject was family.

It represented my life's journey, everything that led up to this moment, and it deserved a place of honor in my home, even if it wasn't the original. I knew Kat felt the same.

When she padded out of the bedroom several hours later, I was half-asleep on the couch with the empty mug balanced precariously on my knee. She slipped it from my lax grip and set it on the coffee table before lifting my arm so she could snuggle in beside me. A soft sigh slipped from my lips as I shifted to tuck her body closer into my side before drifting off to sleep.

Waking up on the couch that afternoon was even more disorienting than Hanson's middle of the night phone call. I lifted my free hand to rub at my bleary eyes before realizing that my phone was vibrating from the pocket of my jeans.

When I managed to wrestle it free, Kat murmured, "What is it?"

I pressed my lips to the top of her head as I blinked the notification into focus. "The paintings have been delivered and Lavigne's money has been returned. How are you holding up?"

"It still doesn't feel real. I just keep picturing him there behind his desk, smirking at us." Kat rubbed her eyes and sat up. "Are you going to have Philippe check the SD card?"

That topic had been bouncing around in my head for a while. "I don't think so. I did tell him it's in there, but without knowing what's on it, I don't want to put him at risk. If he can find it, maybe I'll have him ship it back here. It's probably best to keep the painting under wraps for a while."

She nodded, then her stomach rumbled. "I need to eat something."

"I'll make us some sandwiches," I said as I rose. When I returned with two plates and two cans of soda, Kat was listening to her voicemail, jotting information down on a napkin she'd found on the coffee table.

"My father's lawyer called, he'd like me to meet him at the house tomorrow to go over my father's will. I guess word gets around fast when one of your cronies dies. I don't even know how I would've figured out who his lawyer is, so there's one thing off my to-do list. Detective Hanson left a message too, asking to see the painting sometime. Maybe I could have them meet us at the house tomorrow when we're there with the lawyer, instead of here?"

I considered it, trying to determine if there was any hidden danger lurking in that decision, but ultimately I nodded. "Yeah, it's probably better that way."

While Kat made the phone calls, I set out our humble meal on the coffee table. Though she looked significantly less glazed than she had after receiving the news, there were still faint smudges beneath her eyes. Catching me studying her, she gave a half smile.

"I'm fine, just worn out. This wasn't how I expected the week to go. I meant to tell you before, I think Hanson knows we're hiding something."

"We're hiding a number of things," I replied with a slight shrug, "but nothing that has to do with the attack on us or the attack on your father. We're as much in the dark about that as they are. I don't know how much we could tell them without implicating me in a crime. It seems easier not to say anything than to figure out where that line is."

Since she seemed to have come to the same conclusion, she simply focused on her sandwich. Just as she popped the last bite in her mouth, I leaned back and sighed.

"If you're questioned and they ask you directly about anything, I don't want you to lie for me. You need to answer them honestly. We'll deal with the fallout if we have to."

Her gaze shot to my face, conflict warring in the depths of her eyes. "I just want it to be over."

I realized she'd sidestepped my instructions to tell the police the truth, but I recognized a losing battle when I saw one. Kat would no sooner implicate me than she would cut off her own arm. Still, I had to try.

"It'll be over soon enough." I stroked her cheek with my fingertips and smiled gently. "Why don't I run you a nice hot bath and we'll just relax for the rest of the day, okay? We can worry about everything else tomorrow."

# Chapter Thirty-Three

## KAT

MY FATHER'S ATTORNEY WAS not at all what I expected. The lawyers I'd been forced to smile at and make polite small talk with during events throughout my childhood had been very much like my father—slick and suave, with blinding smiles and perfectly tailored suits. If you'd seen one, you'd seen them all.

Wallace Compton, on the other hand, looked about as grandfatherly as I could imagine, with thin white hair and twinkling green eyes. He wore a tweed suit that looked a size too small for his robust frame and tiny gold-framed glasses that would've been perfect on Santa Claus.

"Ah, my dear," he said, rising to his feet as Beardsley led us into the library. "I'm so very sorry for your loss."

"Thank you," I replied, hoping the words didn't sound as wooden as they felt.

The sympathy in the butler's eyes when we first arrived had nearly brought me to tears, but I mustered a tight smile as I shook Compton's hand. It was easier to keep things simple. Surely my father's own estate lawyer knew that I'd been practically estranged from the man. He didn't need a rundown of the sordid details.

"If it's acceptable to you, Katherine, the police have requested to be present during the reading of the will. They should be here any minute, along with your mother."

My head snapped up in surprise. "My mother?"

Compton had the grace to look slightly abashed. "I'm afraid so. She is mentioned in the will, so I had to contact her, you see."

Nico took my hand and gave it a light, reassuring squeeze. I'd hoped to avoid any real contact with my mother, but very little had gone according to plan lately, so I tamped down the urge to stomp my foot in frustration.

"Of course," I said quietly.

Detective Hanson and Officer Ford were the next to arrive. Nico rose from his seat and spoke to them quietly, gesturing to the bookshelf where he'd placed the painting in its wooden crate. They nodded but remained standing at the side of the room when he returned to my side.

"I'll show it to them after the will is read," he murmured.

I opened my mouth to reply, but the shrill sound of my mother's voice in the hall prompted me to shut it with an audible snap. For a solid three seconds, I held Nico's gaze, summoning the strength to face the woman who'd abandoned me. When the new arrivals swept into the room, Nico and I both stood to greet them.

"Katie, my darling girl!" my mother cooed, yanking me straight into a cloud of expensive perfume. No one else had ever called me Katie, at my own request, and I tried not to grind my teeth.

Ferdinand Chesterfield stood behind her like a smarmy bodyguard, smiling in a way I was sure the man thought would appear paternal. If he so much as touched me, I was afraid I might scream. Based on the way Nico glared at the man, it seemed like screaming would be the least of our worries should Chesterfield lay a finger on me.

"Mother," I bit out. I drew stiffly away and nodded to Chesterfield before waving a hand toward Nico. "You must remember Nicolas Beaumont?"

Nico held out a hand to my mother but was pulled into a similarly dramatic embrace. I smothered a laugh as he tried not to choke on the cloying scent of her perfume, then he scowled at the way Chesterfield leered at me.

Nico met Hanson's curious gaze over my mother's head. Whatever the woman babbled into his ear, I was sure he didn't process a single word of it.

Fortunately, Compton came to the rescue. He cleared his throat and gestured to the chairs placed around the table in front of him. "If you'd all take a seat, we can get started.

This shouldn't take up much of your afternoon. Mr. and Mrs. Chesterfield, my name is Wallace Compton. We spoke on the phone. I served as Mr. Willoughby's estate lawyer. His will was updated rather recently, though the changes were only minimal."

Hanson and Ford had repositioned themselves so they could see the faces of those in attendance. Both of them studied the Chesterfields with an intensity that surprised me. When my mother angled a glance toward Nico, all of us caught her curled lip, but Nico only lifted a brow before turning his attention back to the lawyer.

I stifled a snort. Thank god he was here with me for this.

"Now, this is all fairly straightforward," Compton said, smiling kindly at me, "so I'll start with the most recent additions. Mrs. Chesterfield, as per the divorce decree, is not entitled to any part of the estate. However, Mr. Willoughby requested that she receive the painting you see on the wall here."

When he gestured to the false "family treasure" that my dad had revealed in the second interview, my mother let out an ear-splitting shriek. I almost choked, suppressing a laugh. Nico squeezed my hand and I pressed my face into his shoulder to hide my amusement.

"How dare he! That stupid son of a bitch thinks he can foist that ugly piece of shit on me and give away my millions to this French bastard?"

Humor fled as I jerked in my seat, ready to fly into a fury on his behalf, but Nico laid a restraining hand on my knee. I saw

Hanson watching with interest and forced myself to sit back. We all waited for Chesterfield to quiet my mother down again so the lawyer could continue. Once she finally descended into sullen silence, Compton cleared his throat once more.

"Right, then. Let's continue, shall we? As the Clément painting was recently proven to have belonged to the Beaumont family long before Pierre Beaumont came into Mr. Willoughby's employ, that artwork rightfully belongs to Nicolas Beaumont and is not included in the will. The rest of the estate, in its entirety, is left to Miss Katherine Willoughby as Aidan's only child. There is, however, a rather unorthodox stipulation."

This was not what I'd expected, stipulation notwithstanding. My father had barely spoken to me for the past decade. Why on earth would he leave this all to me? Was it another move made just to piss off my mother?

"His entire estate? Surely he left money to other relatives or charities or something?" I said, blinking at Compton in confusion as my mother let out another wail.

The old man smiled gently. "No, it's all spelled out here, Miss Willoughby. However, he also specified that the inheritance requires you to take up residence here at the house, effective immediately upon the reading of his last will and testament. You're to remain in residence for a period of six months from the date of his death, after which the property and all of the items within are yours to keep or sell as you please."

I stared at him as he paused and shuffled the papers in front of him. "Six months," I repeated, stunned.

"I've been instructed only to divulge the alternative upon your refusal to accept these terms. Should you agree, there's a letter that he requested you read in private. Here are the estimated values of your inheritance."

While I looked over the figures with a growing sense of utter disbelief, my mother's caterwauling suddenly ceased, cloaking the room in anticipatory silence. The quiet felt suffocating, but Nico's hand folded around mine and I blew out a breath as I met his eyes.

The question in mine must have been clear, because he said very simply, "It's up to you. Whatever you decide, we'll figure it all out."

I thought about my sweet little apartment, my morning walks to work, the life I'd built without a single cent from my father. Then I considered all the people who worked in this house, all the good I could do with those funds in exchange for half a year of my life. It would be well worth six months of commuting back and forth to work to ensure the money went to good causes and not into the greedy hands of my mother or Ferdinand Chesterfield.

There was no telling what my father's secret alternative might be, but if past experience was any indication, it would be nothing good. He'd never been the benevolent sort.

"Okay, then. I guess I accept the terms," I said, earning a broad smile from Compton even as uncertainty lingered in my gut.

"Excellent. I believe that will be all, then. Miss Willoughby, please don't hesitate to reach out if you have any questions." He handed me a business card along with a sealed envelope with my name scrawled in my father's handwriting before turning to gather up his papers.

Chesterfield jumped to his feet before the older man could leave the room.

"You can't possibly expect us to let this stand," he growled. "We'll have you in court so fast your head will spin!"

My mother fluttered at his elbow, but Nico's attention shifted to the police officers behind them, drawing my gaze as well. Hanson looked even more stone-faced than usual, while Ford's expression vacillated between fascinated and appalled.

Though the threat was clearly directed at Compton, I smiled serenely. "Would you like the painting shipped to St. Croix, Mother?"

A raucous new wave of wailing sprung up from their direction and I fought the urge to cover my ears, choosing instead to press my forehead against Nico's chest while everyone else dealt with my mother. By the time Beardsley and Compton managed to usher the furious Chesterfields from the house with the worthless painting in hand, I had a pounding headache. I dropped into an armchair by the fireplace and closed my eyes while Nico withdrew the forgery to show the police.

"You said Mr. Willoughby had you sign a contract, do you happen to have that with you?" Hanson asked.

Nico drew the folded contract from his pocket and handed it to the detective, who let out a whistle as she skimmed the agreement.

"Seems a little overboard, don't you think?"

"My father was nothing if not thorough," I muttered, "and almost certainly paranoid. That contract was probably standard practice for him."

As she handed back the papers, Hanson asked, "What will you do with it, now that you finally have it back?"

A small smile tugged at Nico's lips. "I grew up hearing stories about Céleste Bicardeau and eating meals in view of that painting. For the time being, I look forward to seeing it hung in a place of honor again, and in the future? Hopefully I'll be sharing those stories with my own children."

My heart stuttered, then warmth flooded my chest when he met my gaze from across the room. Whatever happened, we were in this together. No matter how overwhelming it would be to deal with this house, to live with every knick knack and every memory, it would be easier because I'd have Nico by my side.

To my surprise, Hanson and Ford didn't linger or ask any other questions. They shook my hand, repeated their condolences, and left. Beardsley, bless him, brought in a tray of tea and shortbread cookies as soon as we were alone. The sentiment was much appreciated by both of us, though it made me feel all of four years old again.

"So," Nico mumbled after downing his first cookie. "The Castle has a new queen. Do I need to ask if you want company here, oh esteemed Mistress of the Willoughby Estate?"

"If you leave me here in this mausoleum alone, I'll end up setting it all on fire," I replied, tossing him another cookie. "I guess we'll need to go grab some clothes before tonight. I don't think I have it in me to start packing up anything else from my apartment just yet."

"What about the letter?"

My nose wrinkled as I glanced down at the envelope on my lap. "I don't know if I'm ready for that, either."

He stroked a hand over my hair, smiling when I leaned into his touch. "No need to rush. I seem to remember an impressive whirlpool tub upstairs—why don't you go soak while I run back to my place to pack up what we need for the next few days? Everything else can wait."

Though I felt guilty sending him off alone, the prospect of a bath was too good to pass up.

"Fine," I agreed, leaning over to kiss him, "but only because that tub is probably the one thing I ever missed about this house."

# Chapter Thirty-Four

## Kat

Though the bathtub was as spacious and extravagant as I remembered, the reality of spending the night in my childhood home leaned more toward disconcerting. My body relaxed in the hot water, but my mind could not. Memories of this house pummeled against my heart like hail, images of endless summer days exploring with Nico, of hiding in the kitchen to chat with Pierre, of the rare occasions when my father had spoken to me like a human rather than an inconvenience.

I let them fall until the deluge slowed to a trickle, leaving my chest aching.

When I finally got out and dressed again, I had a text from Nico that he was back from fetching our clothes and waiting downstairs in the library. I trudged slowly down the main stairs to find him, attempting to view the house with an objective eye.

Aside from Beardsley, who steadfastly refused to even think of leaving us to our own devices, I'd asked him to inform the rest of the staff they'd be given the week off with full pay. They were all lovely people, but the thought of being fawned over in the way my father had so enjoyed made my skin crawl. How had he ever tolerated living here in this mansion by himself?

It was bad enough walking through these cavernous halls, past collectibles and other artwork that could feed a family for a month, just to get to the kitchen so we could scrounge for dinner.

As a child, I definitely hadn't understood the wealth surrounding me—now, it weighed on me like a lead apron.

Nico's smile when I poked my head around the doorway lightened the load enough for me to breathe freely, at least. He set aside a book and rose from a wingback chair, slipping his hand around mine. It was like curling up under a security blanket, comforting and familiar, and I was so thankful for his presence that I had to blink back tears.

He hesitated at the doorway of the kitchen, his eyes scanning the shining stainless steel appliances and spotless countertops. This had been his father's domain, the playground of so many of our earliest memories together. It looked different now, familiar and yet altered. I hadn't spent as much time in this part of the house in later years, but I leaned my head against his shoulder.

"The new chef made some changes, I see," I murmured.

I could hear the thickness in his throat when he said, "Yeah, it sure looks that way. Come on, let's find something to eat. I'm sure your father wasn't living on frozen pizzas."

The fridge was well-stocked and organized with care, a fact for which my empty stomach was immensely grateful. We found foil containers of leftovers from some recent event, grabbed silverware, and, by silent mutual accord, wandered out the back doors onto the patio to eat.

Side by side, we sat in lounge chairs and stared out into the autumn twilight.

The cottage where Nico and his father had lived was just visible through the trees. The current chef wouldn't have any trouble finding a new position, I knew. Oddly, it seemed more bizarre to imagine a stranger living in the cottage than to envision myself moving into this giant house. It would simply feel like a hotel to me for the duration of the six months, but the cottage had been a true home, once.

I'd need to find a good finance manager to help me provide all the staff members with generous severance packages, maybe some kind of recruiter to help them find new positions. There was certainly no need for an army of employees to flutter around me for the foreseeable future, but I wouldn't leave a single one of them hanging.

They deserved better, after dealing with my father.

When he laid his empty carton aside, Nico stretched out his long legs and rolled his head along the cushion behind him to look at me. "Your mom was pretty pissed, huh?"

I snorted. "Leaving her that piece of junk painting was a particularly snarky touch, even for my father."

"Not entirely undeserved, though," Nico replied, grinning.

"Not at all undeserved, from where I'm sitting. I could almost be impressed, if his games hadn't put me in the middle of all of it. But her husband gives me the creeps. I hope they fly home soon."

He raised a brow. "You think she'll try to guilt you into a payoff or something?"

"I wouldn't be surprised," I said grimly. "As it stands, she ignored my existence for most of my life. I figure I can ignore hers for six months. Will you be upset when I donate every last cent from the sale of this ridiculous place to charity?"

"Not even a little. Are you sorry I came hurtling back into your life?" Nico smoothed his thumb across my cheekbone.

There was a certain softness in my chest when I smiled and said, "Not even a little." I pressed my face into his hand. "I—Nico, you don't have to stay here, if you don't want to. You didn't sign up for this. I know this place holds a lot of bad memories for you."

He shook his head. "No more than it does for you. If you think I'm the kind of asshole who would leave you alone here to deal with all this by yourself, you are most definitely mistaken. You're stuck with me now."

"There's no one I'd rather be stuck with. Let's go pick a bedroom." I rose and tugged his hand until he came to his feet.

"We're not going to reclaim your childhood room? There goes every high school fantasy I ever had," Nico muttered.

"You know, your perception of that time and my own are lightyears apart, Beaumont."

He slid his arm around my waist and nuzzled my neck. "I'd say blame your father, but that seems a little callous at this particular point in time."

I laughed softly and pulled him along with me into the house. The curving staircase in the center of the foyer led to our first choice: left or right. The wing to the right included the master suite and, at the far end of the hall, my childhood bedroom. Without hesitation, I turned left.

We peeked into the rooms one by one. The first had been turned into a den of sorts, featuring a brown pullout sofa and a television that was unimpressive even by my low standards. Over the ragged sofa, an autographed baseball bat hung on the wall.

"Man cave?" Nico mused. "I would've imagined a big screen TV and surround sound."

"You and me both," I muttered.

The second and third doors led to guest suites with queen beds and tasteful but generic color schemes. I found I had no real preference—it really was like looking at hotel rooms. Though I'd teased Nico about his apartment, at least its minimalism came across as a conscious choice.

"I guess the choices are burgundy or navy," I said with a wry smile.

The navy accents belonged to the room at the far end of the hall and thus farthest from the room I'd grown up in, so Nico nodded his head toward that door. "Navy. I love you in every shade of blue. Especially naked, with your hair all spread out around you."

I scoffed a little, but the heat in my cheeks told him the comment had done its job. Knowing him as I did, his goal for the next few days would be distracting me from the fact that we were sleeping in my father's house.

It would be a tall order.

Flopping down on my back across the bed, I stared up at the ceiling and wondered why we were even here. I'd shoved the letter from my father into my pocket, content to forget about it as long as possible, but now its presence was a burning reminder that the man was still manipulating us from beyond the grave. With a huff, I pulled it out and stared at the spidery *Katherine* across the front.

"Are you ready to read it?" Nico asked, perching on the edge of the bed beside me.

"I'm not sure I'll ever be ready, so we might as well get it over with, right?"

"Do you want me to stay while you read it? If you want privacy, I can go get the bags."

I didn't *want* privacy, but I had no idea what the letter might say, so I said, "Go ahead, but you don't have to stay away while I read it. It's affecting you, too."

Nico bent down to kiss my forehead and left me to open the envelope while he fetched our bags from the downstairs hall.

*Katherine,*

*I've made a number of enemies throughout my career, so as a precaution, I've updated my will regularly over the years. This house and everything in it would always have been yours, and while I'm sure you're fuming over the stipulations of your inheritance, I have my reasons.*

*Even as a toddler, you had a mind of your own. I might not have been involved in your life, but I've kept tabs. I could not be more proud of the way you've forged your own path and succeeded in a way that is so uniquely your own.*

*I know six months is a lot to ask of you, but I hope to make it worth your sacrifice. In the attic, you will find a collection of antique toys and games I have come across since you left home, some in need of repair, others in good condition. You didn't need my help, nor do I expect you ever would have asked for it, but consider this recompense for how my choices have negatively impacted your life.*

*Should you choose to abandon the house before the six months is up, Wallace will contact an auction house and all proceeds will be donated to Path of Hope in your name, but they won't have your level of expertise in assessing the collection in the attic.*

*Love,*
*Your father*

Sometime during my reading, Nico had returned, but he sat silently on a chest at the foot of the bed. I met his curious, concerned gaze and a choked laugh burst from my lips. I rolled off the bed, handed him the letter, and moved to the window as he read it.

Not for the first time, it seemed like a trap, like a move too kind-hearted to really have come from the father I thought I knew. My feelings were tangled and conflicted—I wasn't ready to mourn him, not when he'd done so much to hurt the man I loved, but all the what-ifs, the possibilities of some kind of reconciliation, had been cut off at the root.

I let out a slow breath and stared out into the distance.

Like my old room, this one was at the back of the house, with a view of the trees and gardens where we had played hide and seek as children. In the distance, its bulk hidden by the twilight, the peak of the Spruce Hill Lighthouse rose above everything else along the shore. Silently, I counted, waiting for the flash of light to cut through the darkness as it always had.

*There.* Once it had come and gone, I leaned my forehead against the cool glass, staring into an inky black landscape behind my own reflection.

"Wow," Nico muttered when he finished reading. "How do you feel about that?"

"Have you ever known me to walk away from a treasure trove like he says is hidden up in the attic?"

Nico's laughter tickled the back of my neck as he wrapped his arms around my middle. "No, I can't say that I have. I'm sure you're already fantasizing about what you might find up there."

"You really don't mind staying here for six months?"

"Six months is the blink of an eye, especially when you're stuck here with me. We'll see it through, and then the future is up to us."

I leaned back against his steady frame and turned my head to press a kiss to the underside of his jaw. "You're absolutely right."

# Chapter Thirty-Five

## Nico

We stayed there at the window for a long time, lost in our thoughts, until I said quietly, "It feels like a hundred years have passed since I was last here."

Memories of that final visit ricocheted through me. It was probably foolish to carry so much anger for a dead man, but hopefully the passage of time would help to dispel that. When her arms folded over mine, I smiled against Kat's ear. No matter how unsettled our lives became at any given moment, holding her was like finding an anchor. Each crappy memory of life at the estate was softened by all of the good times we had together, brought bubbling to the surface by the feel of her warm, soft form leaning against my chest.

"I know it's early," Kat said, glancing over her shoulder, "but I'm exhausted."

I pressed my lips to her temple. "Let's get ready for bed. It's been a long couple of days."

We located the bare minimum of necessities from our bags and prepared for sleep. Whether it was simply being in a strange place for the night or the more specific sensation of being back at The Castle, where every move toward the Willoughby princess was watched and weighed, I kept my boxers and tee on as I stretched out on the bed. When Kat returned from brushing her teeth clad in an oversized nightshirt, I had to smile.

"What?" she asked, sliding under the covers to cuddle up against my side.

"We usually don't wear so much to bed," I teased, "but here it feels . . . I don't know."

"Like the ghost of my father is still watching you like a hawk?"

I laughed and buried my face in her hair. "Yes, and like I definitely don't want to get caught wandering the halls naked."

Exhausted as we were, we whispered together late into the night as though we were children at an illicit sleepover rather than the new—if temporary—inhabitants of the house. When Kat eventually drifted off, sprawled across my chest, I continued combing my fingers through her hair for a long time afterward. The feel of those silken curls over my skin was meditative, casting me nearly into a trance.

I lost all sense of time, all train of thought, as I listened to the soft, even sounds of her breathing.

Had I stopped stroking her hair sooner, I might have fallen asleep several moments earlier and missed the sound of glass breaking from somewhere downstairs. My hand paused mid-stroke as every one of my senses fired back into action. Beardsley's room was on the first floor, but I was pretty sure it was at the other end of the house. The old butler's hearing wasn't what it used to be, so I hoped Beardsley was safe enough in his bed.

I hesitated for a moment, debating whether I should go check it out without alerting Kat, then gently shook her shoulder. If she woke up to find me gone, she'd throw herself in the path of danger without blinking.

"Kitten, I think there might be someone downstairs. I want you to lock the door behind me and call the police," I said in a low voice.

Kat rubbed her eyes with one hand and reached for her phone with the other. I was already pulling on jeans when I saw the words filter into her sleepy brain. She bolted upright.

"Jesus, Nico, you're not going down there alone," she whispered.

I kissed her, hard and swift. "For once in your life, promise you'll stay right here, got it? Lock the door behind me."

Once she nodded in agreement, I slipped from the room and waited for the sound of the lock to click before heading toward the stairs. Though I didn't hear anything else from downstairs, I stopped at the den and grabbed the baseball bat from the wall.

*Willoughby would be rolling over in his grave,* I thought, then grimaced when I realized the man hadn't been buried yet.

My bare feet were silent against the gleaming wood stairs as I made my way into the pitch black front hall. At the bottom, I paused, listening. A faint rustle met my ears and I turned to follow the sound down the hallway that led toward Willoughby's office and the library. I was struck by the memory of creeping along this same route with Kat the night of that fateful party, both of us determined to win hide and seek by hiding somewhere no one would dare to look.

We'd won, all right, but Kat had lost too much that night for us to gloat.

I pushed aside the familiar ache that accompanied those memories of the night her life changed forever as I continued down the corridor. The house boasted a state of the art alarm system, but we'd sent Beardsley to bed early and hadn't bothered to work through the old man's illegibly scrawled directions in order to set it ourselves. I was silently cursing that decision when I heard the distinct sound of muttering from the library.

With the bat angled over my shoulder, I edged closer to the doorway. Part of me understood and accepted that confronting a thief was a terrible idea—what the hell did I care if someone stole from Aidan Willoughby's vast hoard of wealth?

The other part of me had a gut feeling it wasn't just a cat burglar searching the house for items to pawn.

Above all, I prayed Kat would actually stay put and that the police were on their way, because the baseball bat would be useless if the intruder had a weapon. After a brief internal debate, I pulled my phone from my pocket and set it to record.

I forced a deep breath into my lungs as I pocketed the phone again and stepped into the doorway. Light from the old-fashioned street lamps at the front of the house spilled through the window, casting an elongated rectangle of illumination on the floor. It was so dim that I had to squint until the intruder took an angry step toward the fireplace. The glow was just enough for me to recognize the man's face.

"Need help finding something, Mr. Chesterfield?" I asked, my voice mild despite a rush of adrenaline at my suspicions being confirmed.

The lawyer whirled around, sneering at me from across the room even as he drew a gun from his waistband. "Where's the painting?" he growled.

I lowered the bat to lean against it like a cane, hoping the move made me look like less of a threat. "I put it in the office after everyone left. Would you like me to go fetch it for you?"

Chesterfield was a relatively fit fifty-something with the kind of physique that had been honed at a health club, but the gun gave him a distinct advantage. The way he waved it made me nervous as hell, like the man had no idea how to safely handle a firearm. Even if he didn't mean to shoot, he could easily injure or kill me.

"Lead the way," Chesterfield hissed. "But first, why don't you drop that bat? You try anything stupid, I'll put a bullet in your brain. Either way, I still end up with that fucking painting."

Letting the bat fall to the floor, I turned and walked toward the office, praying he wouldn't shoot me in the back out of spite. Chesterfield sounded even more unhinged than he had earlier in the day, muttering under his breath as he followed a few paces behind me. I moved with exaggerated caution, taking slow, heavy steps down the hallway. My bare feet didn't make much noise, but I hoped the sound of Chesterfield's footsteps would alert Kat if she happened to follow me downstairs.

Christ, I hoped she was still safe up in the bedroom.

"How do you see this playing out, Chesterfield?" I asked, striving for a friendly tone despite the ball of dread in my stomach. I led the way into the office and flipped on the light.

Chesterfield squinted at the sudden brightness but didn't complain. I breathed a silent sigh of relief—if the police showed up, it'd be easier for them to find the right room this way, without having to search the entire mansion.

"Where is it?" Chesterfield demanded. "Don't screw with me, boy, or I'll have to ask my stepdaughter, won't I?"

Icy tendrils squeezed my heart. "Relax. You can take the painting. We're not going to stand in your way." I lifted a hand toward the fireplace where the wooden crate was propped against the stone surround.

The older man snatched it, an expression of pure glee crossing his features before his eyes narrowed on my face. Shoving the crate at my chest, Chesterfield ordered, "Show it to me."

I did as I was told, grateful for any delay that might give the police time to show up before he decided I was no longer of use. When I set the framed canvas on the big oak desk, a slow smile spread across Chesterfield's face. I dropped my gaze to the painting and let the familiar image calm me.

I needed all the help I could get.

We stood close together now, separated by only an arm's length. My muscles tensed as I considered my next move. The gun was no longer pointed at my chest, so this was likely the best chance I'd get at wrestling it out of Chesterfield's hands, if I decided to go that route. Silently, I wondered if there was any possibility the man might simply take the painting and walk away—murder was a serious step up from burglary, after all.

Before I could consider my next course of action, the truth hit me like a ton of bricks.

"It was you," I breathed. "You're the one who sent that car to run us off the road. You had Willoughby killed."

Chesterfield barely looked at me, focused as he was on the painting. "They'll never tie me to any of it. It was all my darling Julia's idea, after all."

"All of that for a painting?" My mind scrabbled for a foothold, some way to keep Chesterfield talking until the police arrived.

"Are you defending that rat bastard? He had no qualms about stealing it from your family, did he? Did you really want him for a father-in-law? Aidan Willoughby didn't deserve this beauty any more than he deserved Julia. He wouldn't give her what she needed, but I will. With this, I'll give her anything her heart desires."

Angled away from the window as he was, Chesterfield didn't see the motion lights flicker on along the winding driveway, but I did. I thought quickly through the options, realizing that telling Chesterfield it was a forgery seemed like a surefire way to send the man into a rage.

It wasn't worth the risk, even if, under other circumstances, I would've enjoyed seeing his expression upon learning the truth.

"So you'll sell it?" I asked, trying to keep him distracted as long as possible.

Chesterfield gestured at me with the gun. "Pack it back up. I'll do whatever I please, got it?"

Nodding absently, I took my time setting the forged canvas into the crate and replacing the cover. Where the hell were the police? I was running out of time, and if Chesterfield killed me, there was no one else in the house to protect Kat except old Beardsley. She definitely had better odds against her stepfather than the butler did.

*Don't think, don't think about it.*

The refrain echoed through my head. As I turned, I lifted the crate as though to hand it to Chesterfield, then I kept lifting and swung it in a sharp arc back down to connect with the man's wrist. Chesterfield gave an unholy scream as the weapon fell from his hand, but I decided surviving the tussle was more important than reaching the gun first, so I threw my body in the opposite direction just as the gun went off.

It looked like some kind of pantomime as I landed on the floor in front of the desk. I lay there, staring at the scene before me and wondering why the only sound I could hear was a dull whoosh, even when my new angle revealed Kat swinging the baseball bat at Chesterfield's left knee. The man's mouth opened wide in a silent scream as he collapsed onto the rug six feet away.

I blinked up at Kat, watched her lips moving as though she were speaking, but I couldn't hear the words. Had the gunshot been loud enough to damage my eardrums?

As a flurry of police officers flooded the room behind her, Kat tossed the bat aside and dropped to her knees beside me, running her hands over my shoulders and chest like she was searching for a gunshot wound.

When one of them slapped handcuffs around Chesterfield's injured wrist, I finally heard the shriek and lowered my head back down to the floor.

Kat's frantic voice broke through the haze, saying, "There's an ambulance on its way."

"Ambulance?" I repeated. I lifted a hand to the side of my head and realized I must have struck the corner of the desk on my way down. When my fingers came away bloody, I mumbled, "Oh. Right."

After a few minutes of what looked like complete pandemonium, Hanson strode into the room. In place of her usual business suits, she wore a pair of torn jeans and a leather jacket.

Stupidly, I thought back to Kat's torn sleeve on the day of our somewhat unorthodox reunion, and I almost laughed.

Hanson, however, did not look amused. The usually unreadable expression on her face hardened into something grim when her gaze landed on Chesterfield. I watched from my place on the floor as Hanson spoke with the other officers, then the detective headed in my direction.

"Mr. Beaumont," she said in a light tone that didn't fool me for a second. "Ms. Willoughby. I didn't expect to see you again so soon."

I reached into my pocket and handed her my phone. "I don't know if I caught it all on here, but he confessed to everything."

When I moved to sit up, Kat wrapped her arm around my waist and Hanson offered me a hand. "I probably don't have to tell you it was stupid and reckless to come down here instead of waiting for the police."

"No, you probably don't," I replied, rubbing a hand over my face. "So much for promising to stay upstairs behind a locked door, huh?"

"You knew that was never going to fly," she muttered as she curled into my side. A faint tremble coursed through her and I tried not to think about how else this might've turned out.

A pair of paramedics arrived and Hanson waved them over. "I want to get your statement and have that injury checked out. Ms. Willoughby, if you wouldn't mind going with Officer Ford?"

Kat squeezed my torso tightly before nodding and walking out into the hallway with the young policeman.

After Hanson seated herself at Willoughby's giant desk, I relayed the sequence of events while the paramedics dabbed antiseptic on my head, checked my vision, and left me with an instant ice pack as I finished describing my conversation with Chesterfield to Hanson. A dull ache set in behind my eyes.

She leaned back in the chair, studying my features. I made sure she saw nothing but sincerity in my expression, and if Chesterfield's confession held up, that was two cases closed. Resignation passed through her eyes as Hanson nodded, shook my hand, and rose. She looked like she needed either a strong cup of coffee or a stiff drink and wasn't feeling picky about either option.

"I think that's all for now. Let's go find your girlfriend."

Light flooded the hallway and rained down from the chandelier in the foyer, where Kat sat perched at the bottom of the stairs in yoga pants and her nightshirt. Beardsley was beside her, rubbing her hands between both of his while Ford leaned against the banister, looking like this was an everyday occurrence in his world. Kat jumped to her feet when she caught sight of me and launched herself into my arms.

I clasped her tight, murmuring over and over, "It's okay, Kitten, it's okay." Relief seeped through me as the words pierced my own brain.

Before I could wallow in it, however, she drew back and slapped her palms hard against my chest. "Of all the dangerous, idiotic things you could do! What the hell were you thinking, coming down here by yourself? Did you think for one second I would leave you to deal with that alone?"

A laugh from one of the police officers was swiftly disguised as a cough, but my gaze stayed locked on Kat. Her cheeks were flushed, eyes bright with fury, and I was certain she'd never been more beautiful.

"I love you," I said simply.

Try as she might, Kat couldn't hold onto the scowl. Her fingers twisted into my shirt. "Don't ever run into danger like that again. Promise me, Nico."

"I promise," I whispered. I kissed her forehead and pulled her back into my arms. Over the top of her head, I nodded to the officers. "I promise, Kat. It's all over now."

# Epilogue

## NICO: SIX MONTHS LATER

*IF ONLY HER FATHER could see this,* I thought, grinning at the view from the front door of The Castle.

My silly nickname for Kat's childhood home had become ingrained in our minds, even though she didn't quite agree that she'd always been the princess, nor that she was now its queen. She liked to envision herself more as the rebellious witch who dismantled the wicked king's domain piece by piece to return that wealth to the people of the kingdom.

I wasn't sure what role that gave me, but if it meant being at Kat's side through it all, I was one hundred percent committed.

Early spring sunlight glinted through the trees, giving the entire property a golden hue that suited my cheery mood. Today, the gates stood wide open, folding tables lined the driveway, and furniture dotted the expansive yard. Classic rock floated from a portable speaker near the house, mingling with the soft sounds of conversation and the occasional exclamation over an exciting find. I couldn't bite back a broad smile when I watched a small group of kids go running from one side of the yard to the other, ducking behind trees and under tables.

If hide and seek had set the course of our lives, it seemed fitting that it should be part of this momentous day, as well.

Thanks to Kat, the staff had been taken care of with extremely generous severance packages, the house had been listed for sale right at market value, and several charities had been earmarked to receive hefty donations from the estate. The proceeds of today's yard sale, along with any items remaining at the end of the day, would go to Kat's favorite charity organization, Path of Hope.

In the end, neither of us resented the final manipulations her father had thrown our way. We were able to do a world of good with her inheritance, as well as my own. I blew out a slow, happy sigh as I set off down the stairs and headed into the fray.

After finally convincing Kat to take a much-needed vacation—for pleasure, this time—we'd returned to Avignon and spent two glorious weeks relaxing and playing tourist. I'd even managed to smooth Uncle Philippe's ruffled feathers after we decided to book a hotel suite instead of staying with the family. It had been well worth the effort, and we were already planning to return again later that summer for Jérôme's wedding.

While we were there, we managed to remove the SD card without breaking the frame of the painting. We'd discussed the options—destroy it, see what was on it, leave it hidden in the painting forever.

Kat's unrelenting curiosity won out.

Using a secure laptop, we opened the enclosed file and found an audio recording of a conversation between Aidan Willoughby and none other than Lucien Lavigne.

Eyes wide, we stared at one another as the two men spoke, discussing an arrangement they'd made for Willoughby to ensure the disappearance of certain key witnesses in a case brought against Lavigne in exchange for a hundred million dollars in blood diamonds.

"If Lavigne had found this, we would be dead," Kat whispered. "What do we do with it?"

In the end, it had traveled back home with us—then been anonymously delivered to Detective Hanson to pass along to law enforcement who might be able to use it to bring Lavigne down. After that, we pretended Lucien Lavigne didn't exist.

Out of sight, out of mind.

It was Uncle Philippe who had talked me into taking the original painting back home with us, encouraging me to donate it to the museum's permanent collection, where Kat and I could see it whenever we wished. And, he'd added with a wink, where our children would be able to visit their ancestor someday.

With the entire family backing the suggestion, I'd finally agreed.

The forgery, in turn, had been sent to Philippe, for its sentimental value. Now Céleste Bicardeau could keep watch over both the French and American branches of the family. The original painting had been authenticated by the museum and displayed there for the past two months, alongside a pair of other exquisite landscapes by Hugo Clément.

When I looked over toward Kat several minutes later, I found her crouched down next to a dark-haired little girl who'd taken a liking to one of her old porcelain dolls. She nodded solemnly as she listened to the child, then reached back onto the table to hand over a small box of clothes for the doll. The little girl's expression brightened into blinding luminescence as she clutched the box in one hand and the doll in the other to run toward her mother with her treasures.

Our gazes locked across a stretch of lawn and I offered a jaunty salute. Kat blew me a kiss before turning to talk to another family who'd approached the table of toys. I watched for several minutes longer, enjoying the animated way she conversed with complete strangers, until a familiar figure came strolling toward me from the direction of the driveway.

"Detective Hanson. To what do I owe the pleasure?" I asked. I shook the hand she offered before sticking my own back in my pocket.

A wide grin split her face. "Oh, just stopped by to see what trouble you two were getting up to these days. Seems you're just full of good works lately, huh?"

I offered a benign smile. "Seems we are," I agreed. "It's the least we could do."

While Hanson stood beside me, we watched Katherine Willoughby charm a young couple into buying a hand-carved wooden cradle. "I heard the damnedest story through the grapevine the other day," the detective mused, rocking on her heels.

"Oh?"

"An old friend of mine works for Interpol. Guess they made a pretty high profile arrest based on an anonymous tip, but she told me there was a tale going around about this guy raving about getting screwed on the purchase of a Clément about six months ago. Seems the money was returned to his account just after he opened the package to find one of those velvet Elvis Presley paintings inside. Imagine that, huh?"

Through no small amount of effort, I managed to keep my features carefully blank. "Truly bizarre, when you think about it. You don't strike me as one for gossip, Detective."

After a long moment, she laughed quietly and clapped me on the shoulder. "No, I suppose I'm not. You take care of yourself, Mr. Beaumont, and take care of her, too. No offense, but I'd be happy *not* to get called in on anything else involving the pair of you."

I flashed a grin. "Believe me, we're in agreement over that. But Detective? Thank you. For everything."

She gave a swift nod and I stood there for a long moment, watching as the detective wandered off into the crowd and peered down at a few items as she went. Once she was a good distance away, I let out a tight breath before shaking my head and making my way over to Kat.

She glanced over her shoulder at me, raised a brow, and directed an elderly man toward the table where Beardsley manned an ancient cash register Kat insisted on buying from an antique store a few weeks back. How she managed to get it working again was beyond me, but she'd enjoyed every second of the challenge. Seated behind it, the old butler looked like something out of a vintage photograph.

"What did Hanson want?" Kat asked in a low voice, looping her arm through mine.

I kissed the side of her forehead. "Just checking up on us, I gather. Looks like we're going to be making another hefty donation after this weekend. You've done an amazing job with all of this. I'm so fucking proud of you."

"I didn't do it alone," she replied with a grin. "Now, come with me, there's a couple of newlyweds admiring my father's desk. It would be my crowning glory to see that particular piece sold."

Leaning close to her ear, I whispered, "Ah, but I have such good memories of that desk, spanning so many decades of my life. Memories under it . . . memories on top of it. I'll be sad to see it go."

"Even after you cracked your stubborn head open on it?"

"Even then," I said, grinning.

Kat's eyes gleamed up at me. "Well, I suppose we'll just have to make some new memories, Nicolas Beaumont. Are you game?"

"Always," I agreed, and together we headed off to seal the deal.

# Also by

Looking for more of Kat and Nico? Sign up for my newsletter at https://rachelfitzjames.com/ to get a free bonus epilogue!

### **Spruce Hill Series**

**Unpacking Secrets**

**A Lonely Road**

**Canvas of Lies**

**Crumbling Truth**
Coming November 2025

# Acknowledgements

My greatest thanks regarding this book go to those who told me to ignore the advice that you should avoid prologues at all cost. I'm sorry if you hate them, but after trying 375 different ways to get Kat and Nico's adorable childhood friendship into the story without a prologue, I gave up.

Unlike every other book in this series, this one did not start out in Spruce Hill (mostly because I didn't expect to turn my favorite small town into a 10-book series when I began writing it). After deciding to stick with a town that swiftly evolved from just the locations in the first couple books, turning Kat into Spruce Hill's defiant princess really made this story take off. I adore Kat and Nico with every ounce of my heart and I hope you do, too.

Eternal gratitude for my family, who fielded such questions as "what should I name this fictional Impressionist oil painter?"

to "what toy do you think is dissected on Kat's desk?" The little details in this book were truly a team effort.

To Melissa Rotert for being by my side through every second of this journey, I love you everything.

Christie Curry, Christina Brennan, and Briana Newstead, this book would not be what it is today without you constantly rereading all 8,000 versions of the opening, the twists and turns, the changes and improvements. From the bottom of my heart, thank you for sticking by me (and Kat and Nico!) for all of it.

Heather Frances, as usual, thank you for discovering the tiny tidbits that needed tweaking in this book and pointing them out! Your insights are invaluable and I hope you know how much I appreciate it.

To readers, both new and repeat, who've taken a chance on me and found something to love in Spruce Hill—you have my eternal gratitude. I wouldn't be here without you, and sharing these stories with the world is the scariest but most fulfilling experience I could imagine as an author, so thank you!

# About the author

Rachel Fitzjames is the author of a contemporary romantic suspense series set in the fictional town of Spruce Hill, NY. She started writing on her brother's ancient computer back in the early 90s and never looked back, though her first short story about an underground cat thievery ring was sadly lost. With a degree in geography inspired by wanderlust, Rachel has a keen appreciation for the escape that the romance genre allows. She is a lifelong resident of Western NY and created Spruce Hill in order to give a little bit of home to all of her characters.

Connect with Rachel at her website, https://rachelfitzjames.com/, or on Instagram and Threads at @rachelfitzjames.

Made in the USA
Middletown, DE
01 September 2025